BOOT HILL

BOOT HILL

AN ANTHOLOGY
OF THE WEST

EDITED BY

ROBERT J. RANDISI

A TOM DOHERTY ASSOCIATES BOOK
New York

BOOT HILL: AN ANTHOLOGY OF THE WEST

Copyright © 2002 by Robert J Randisi

"The Naked Gun" copyright © 1967, 1994 by John Jakes

Book design by Heidi Eriksen

A Forge Book
Published by Tom Doherty Associates, LLC
175 Fifth Avenue
New York, NY 10010

www.tor.com

Forge® is a registered trademark of Tom Doherty Associates, LLC.

Library of Congress Cataloging-in-Publication Data

Boot Hill / edited by Robert J Randisi.
p. cm.
ISBN 0-765-30081-8 (hc)
ISBN 0-765-30082-6 (pbk)
1. Western stories. I. Randisi, Robert J.

PS648.W4B66 2002
813'.087408—dc21   2001058280

First Hardcover Edition: May 2002

First Trade Paperback Edition: May 2003

Printed in the United States of America

0 9 8 7 6 5 4 3 2 1

Weep not for us who early made our beds
Wrapped in our blankets, saddles for our heads,
For we are happy here, secure and still,
Locked in this rock-strewn, silent, sun-baked Hill.
— JOSEPHINE McINTIRE

CONTENTS

Contents

INTRODUCTION

FOOTPRINTS
ON THE HILL

"They died with their boots on," hence the naming of the first Boot Hill, widely believed to be the one started just outside of Dodge City in 1872. Others hold that Tombstone gave birth—odd choice of words—to the first Boot Hill. And there is still another opinion that it first appeared in Fort Hayes—or Hayes City, as it was later called—as early as 1870. For our purposes with this anthology, we'll go with Dodge City.

Since the Gravedigger will be your guide through this collection of stories, my introduction will not touch on the history involved. Instead, I'd simply like to introduce you to the people I invited—and who accepted—to put their own footprints on Dodge City's Boot Hill.

All of the stories in this collection are original, written especially for this book, except for John Jakes' "The Naked Gun." I consider it an honor to be able to reprint the story here, and I want to thank Mr. Jakes for supplying an original epitaph to a story he wrote thirty-five years ago. I think it was extraordinarily generous of him. The story is here because—well, it fits. Mr. Jakes' most recent novel is the Civil War spy novel *On Secret Service* (Dutton, 2000).

Elmer Kelton routinely tops any list of the Greatest Living Western Writers—such as one compiled by his colleagues in the Western Writers of America. A busy man, I am flattered that he usually responds with a "yes" when I invite him into an anthology, and usually with a story of the quality of "The Ghost of Abel Hawthorne." This is the only western ghost story in the book. *Badger Boy* (Tor, 2000) was his most recent novel at this writing, but Tor has brought many of Elmer's books back into print in paperback recently, and deservedly so. His *The Good Old Boys* (TCU Press, 1989) was made into a marvelous TNT western with Tommy Lee Jones.

Wendi Lee is the author of many novels in both the mystery and western genres, and has successfully combined the two genres in her Jefferson Birch series. She has appeared in many of my anthologies, the reasons being twofold. They have to do with efficiency, and quality. To put it succinctly, she delivers and . . . she delivers. In "Sinners" she tells the story of two women and how one baby connects them. While her most recent novels feature her lady P.I. Angella Matelli, this story illustrates she has not lost her touch with westerns. Her most recent novel of the west was *The Overland Trail* (Tor, 1996).

James Reasoner is an amazingly prolific author of every kind of genre fiction you can think of, having written literally hundreds of books under many pseudonyms over the years. He is presently penning an extensive series of Civil War books, but took time out to write "The Guns of Dusty Logan," possibly the most unusual story in this collection, about a very special pair of pistols. *Vicksburg* (Cumberland House, 2000) is the most recent entry in his series.

L. J. Washburn is an award-winning writer of mysteries and westerns whose "Hard Ground" features possibly the youngest tenant of Boot Hill. It is also one of only two stories in this book that might be called a love story. She has written many of her novels and short stories from the point of view of her tough gunman-turned-stuntman Lucas Hallum (*Wild Night,* Shamus winner for Best Paperback of 1991), so it is the child's point of view that makes this story so special. Her western novels include *Bandera Pass* and *Riders of the Monte.*

Tom Piccirilli has made his bones in the horror genre, where he has been nominated for several awards, the most recent being the Bram Stoker for Best Horror Novel with his book *The Deceased.* "The Comfortable Coffin of Miz Utopia Jones Clay" is his first western story, but certainly not his last. His first western novel is scheduled to be published shortly, featuring the same characters. An accomplished short-story writer, his collection *Deep into that Darkness Peering* contains forty of his stories.

Randy Lee Eickhoff has written several acclaimed novels featuring historical characters of the Old West, as with his novels *Bowie* (Tor, 1998) and *The Fourth Horseman* (Tor, 1999), his Doc Holliday book. In "Anonymous" he demonstrates how difficult it is, sometimes, to tell who the sinners really are. But of course, Dodge City and Sin went together quite well, didn't they?

John Helfers and Kerrie Hughes collaborate for the

first time here, with what is also their first western short story, "The Last Ride of the Colton Gang." John has edited several anthologies in different genres, and has appeared as a writer in over twenty. He is at work on his first novel.

Troy D. Smith is the most recent winner of the Spur Award for Best Paperback Western Novel with *Bound for the Promised-Land*. "The Sellers" is very interesting as it seems to start out as one thing and almost ends up as a love triangle story. A talented and versatile writer, he tells me he has completed a Civil War novel and is presently at work on a fifties detective novel.

I believe Robert Vaughan was the last person I invited into this book, which means he had the least time to work with. But when you're the author of over three hundred novels, as he is, you don't need a lot of time to do a short story. After I read "The Piano Man," he told me that this was his first short story in over thirty years. You couldn't tell by reading it. Editors don't usually do this, but if I had to pick a story that was my favorite in the book . . . oh, never mind. I don't want to get anybody all riled up. He has recently published *Clarion's Call* (NAL, 2001), a novel he finished for his friend, the late Ralph Compton.

Richard S. Wheeler won his third Spur award, for Best Western Novel, a couple of years ago with his *Masterson* (Tor, 1999.) It won't be his last. He is one of the most respected western authors of our time, staggeringly prolific as well as versatile. His output over the past few years has included both historical and contemporary (*The Buffalo Commons,* Tor, 1999) novels of the west. He also demonstrated his abilities as an editor when he put together the anthology *Tales of the American West* (Penguin, 2000). Here he gives us

"Dead Weight," a story that could only have appeared in an anthology called *Boot Hill*.

Ed Gorman has won awards in virtually every genre in which he has written, including a Spur award for his short story "The Face." Oddly, many of his western stories are marginally western, as many take place in his native Iowa. Here, however, with "A Disgrace to the Badge," he steps firmly into the Old West with his customary sure hand. His most recent western novel is *Ghost Town* (Berkley, 2001).

Marthayn Pelegrimas originally started her career in the horror genre and has since branched out into westerns and, under a pseudonym, mysteries. Her first western story, "The Tailor of Yuma," appeared in the anthology *Tin Star*. She will also be appearing in the upcoming anthology *Guns of the West*, edited by Martin H. Greenberg and Ed Gorman. With "Planting Lizzie Palmer," she becomes even more firmly entrenched in her new genre. This is the only story in the book to feature the name of a person actually buried on Boot Hill. Her first historical novel, *On the Strength of Wings*, was published in August of 2001.

Marcus Galloway is new to the business, but under two different names he has already launched a promising career with half a dozen short stories in several different genres, including a western tale called "Medicine Man," which appeared in the original audio anthology *How the West Was Read II*. "A Damned Nuisance" is his first print western short story.

Dodge City is Legend. The list of famous names connected with its growth—and demise—is endless. Some of them—

Ben Thompson, Wild Bill Hickok, Bat Masterson—appear within these pages. What appear in every story, however, are the spirit and ironies of Dodge City, and Boot Hill.

The talents of established veterans and fresh, new voices have joined here to produce a one-of-a-kind collection of short stories about one of the better known conventions of the Old West. Whether Boot Hill originated in Dodge City of Tombstone or Hayes, soon after most graveyards in most western towns bore the name. To most of us, though, whether we write westerns, or simply enjoy reading them and watching them in the movies and on TV, the words Boot Hill will always conjure up the Queen of the Cow-towns—Dodge City.

ROBERT J. RANDISI
St. Louis, Missouri
December 2001

BOOT HILL

THE GRAVEDIGGER

Robert J. Randisi

Don't never sneak up on a feller when he's diggin' a grave!

Sorry, but ya gave me a fright, there. They call me the
Gravedigger. Welcome to Boot Hill. Reckon you're a-
wonderin' what all the fuss is about, all these holes an' such.
Lemme lean on my shovel here, a minute. Backbreakin'
work, diggin' graves, but honest. That's what I was lookin'
for when I come here in 'seventy-four. By that time Boot
Hill already been here two years. Don't know 'zackly why
they stuck it up here on this hill. Some say it was ta keep
water from gettin' ta them, others so's ever'body could see it
from miles around. Mebbe it's even so's the dead could have
a good view. All I know is this is the highest point
hereabouts. Coulda called it High Point Hill, I guess, but
they called it Boot Hill 'cause so many of them that's buried
here died with their boots on—usually from violence.
'Course, just 'cause they was shot, or stabbed, or killed some
other violent way don't mean they was bad. No, sir. All these

19

dead folks got their own stories to tell—if'n they could tell 'em, that is.

'Course, I reckon I could tell ya some stories, couldn't I? I need me a rest, anyways. Been expectin' some help along now, cain't be diggin' up all these graves by my lonesome. But seein' as how this here is the highest point around and I cain't see nobody comin' up ta help me yet, guess I could take a break for a spell and spin ya a yarn or two. I mean, tell ya what happened to some of these poor folks that's buried up here.

Lemme jest leave my shovel here . . . I'll wipe off some of my sweat with my bandana . . . least there's a breeze up here, most times, 'cept in like July or August . . . now follow me and I'll show ya some of these headstones. None of them is anythin' fancy, ya understand, mostly just some words carved onto some wood we got from breakin up packin' cases an' such. When somebody's gettin' buried up here ain't usually nobody to pay for no fancy stone. 'Sides, we ain't got no stone or marble or nothin' like that ta use, an' bringin' it in from Back East would cost too much. As for the writin' on 'em, sometimes folks jes' put somethin' simple like a feller's name . . . don't always know when they was born, but you kin usually tell when they died, that's for sure. Other times there's folks who get downright poetical. Lesse . . . not that one, jes' a date and weren't nothin' interestin' about the way he died . . . no, not that one, neither. Don't wanna waste yer time with borin' stories, I know you got other things ta do, and I gotta get back ta work sometime . . . mebbe over here . . .

Ah! Here's one. Come on, move in around this here marker. Ya see what I mean about the marker, jes' some ol' piece a wood with some writin' on it, but it's kinda pretty writin' and the story behind it's kinda, well, entertainin', I guess you'd say. As you kin see wasn't nobody sure when he was born, but he was planted here even afore I got here and I heard the story from the undertaker himself.

Jes' get on close enough ta read the words yore own self and I'll tell ya what happened . . .

THE NAKED GUN

JOHN JAKES

G. BODIE
183?–1873
"DO NOT SIN
AGAINST THE CHILD"
GEN. 42:22

George Bodie sat smoking a cigar in the parlor of Chinese Annie's house on Nebraska Street when the message came.

Bodie had his dusty boots propped on a stool and his heavy woolen coat open to reveal the single holster with the Navy Colt on his hip. He might have been thirty or forty.

His cheeks in the lamplight were shadowy with pox scars. He was ugly, but hard and capable looking. His smile had a crooked, sarcastic quality as the cigar smoke drifted past his face.

Maebelle Tait, owner of the establishment—Chinese Annie had died; her name was kept for reasons of goodwill—hitched up the bodice of her faded ball gown and poured a drink.

"Lu ought to be down before too long," she said. From somewhere above came a man's laugh.

"Good. I've only been in this town an hour, but I've seen everything there is worth seeing, except Lu. Things don't change much."

Maebelle sat with her drink and lit a black cheroot. "Where you been, George?"

Bodie shrugged. "Hays City, mostly." His smile widened and his hand touched his holster.

"How many is it now?" Maebelle asked with a kind of disgusted curiosity.

"Eleven." Bodie walked over and poured a hooker for himself. "One more and I got me a dozen." He glanced irritably at the ceiling. "What's she doin'? Customer?"

Maebelle shook her head. "Straightening up the second-floor parlor. We got a group of railroad men stopping over around two in the morning." Maebelle's tone lingered halfway between cynicism and satisfaction.

The front door opened and a blast of chill air from the early winter night swept across the floor. Bodie craned his neck as Tad, Maebelle's seven-year-old boy, came in, wiping his nose with his muffler. Maebelle's other child, three, sat quietly in a chair in the corner, fingering a page in an Eastern ladies' magazine, her eyes round and silently curious.

"Where you been, Tad?" Maebelle demanded.

He glanced at Bodie. "Over at Simms' livery stable. I . . . I saw Mr. Wyman there."

Bodie caught the frowning glance Maebelle directed at him. "New law in town?" he asked.

Maebelle nodded. "Lasted six months, so far. Quiet gent. He carries a shotgun."

Bodie touched the oiled Colt's hammer. "This can beat it, anytime."

Maebelle's frown deepened. "George, I don't want you to go hunting for your dozenth while you're on my property. I'm glad for you to come, but I don't want any shooting in this house. I got a reputation to protect."

Bodie poured another drink. The boy Tad drew a square of paper from his pocket and looked at his mother.

"Mr. Wyman gave me this."

He held it out to Bodie, with hesitation.

"He said for me to give it to you right away."

Bodie's brows knotted together. He unfolded the paper, and with effort read the carefully blocked letters. The words formed a delicate bond between two men who nearly did not know how to read. Bodie's mouth thinned as he digested the message:

WE DO NOT WANT A MAN LIKE YOU IN THIS TOWN. YOU HAVE TILL MIDNIGHT TO RIDE OUT.
     (SIGNED) DALE WYMAN, TOWN MARSHAL.

Bodie laughed and crumpled the note and threw it into the crackling fire in the grate.

"I guess the word travels," he said with a trace of pride. "Maybe I will collect my dozenth." He raised one hand. "But not on your property, Maebelle. I'll do it in the street, when this marshal comes to run me out. So's everybody can see." His hand went toward the liquor bottle.

Maebelle pushed Tad in the direction of the hall. "Go to the kitchen and get something to eat. And take sister Emma with you."

Grumbling, the boy took the tiny girl's hand and dragged her toward the darkened, musty-smelling hallway.

The girl disengaged her hand, and stopped. Curious, she lifted Bodie's hat from where it rested on a chair.

Maebelle slapped her hand smartly. "Go along, Tad. You follow him, Emma. Honest to heaven, that child is the picking-up-est thing I ever knew. Born bank robber, I guess, if she was a boy."

"Where the hell's Lu?" Bodie wanted to know.

"Don't get your dander up, George," Maebelle said quickly. "I'll go see."

She went to the bottom of the staircase and bawled the girl's name several times. A girlish "Coming!" echoed from somewhere above. A knock sounded at the door and Maebelle opened it. She talked with the man for a moment, and then his heavy boots clomped up the stairway. As she returned to the parlor Bodie looked at the clock.

"Quarter to eleven, Maebelle. An hour and fifteen minutes before I get me number twelve." He chuckled.

Maebelle busied herself straightening a doily on the sofa, not looking at him.

Bodie helped himself to still another drink, and swallowed it hastily. "Don't worry about the whiskey," he said over his shoulder. "I'm even faster when I got an edge on."

Light footsteps sounded on the stair. Bodie turned as the girl Lu came into the room. She ran to Bodie and kissed him, throwing her arms around his neck. She was young beneath the shiny hardness of her face. Her lips were heavily painted, and her white breast above the gown smelled of dusting powder.

"Oh, George, I'm glad you got here."

"I came just to see you, honey. Two hundred miles." His arm crept around her waist, his hand touched her breast. He kissed her lightly.

"Well, I'm not running this for charity, you know," Maebelle said.

"I'll settle up," Bodie replied. "Don't worry. Right now though . . ."

He and Lu began to walk toward the stairway.

Another knock came at the door. Maebelle went to open it, and Bodie heard a voice say out of the frosty dark, "Evening, Miz Tait. Lu here?"

Bodie dropped his arm.

Maebelle started to protest, but the man came on into the lighted parlor. The cowboy was thin. His cheeks were red from wind and liquor, and he blinked at Bodie, with suspicion. Lu gaped at the floor, flustered.

"Hello, Lu. Did you forgit I was comin' tonight?"

"Maybe she did forget," Bodie said. "She's busy."

"Come on, Fred," Maebelle said urgently. She pulled the cowboy's arm. "I know Bertha'd be glad to see you."

"Bertha, hell," the cowboy complained. "I rode in sixty miles, like I do every month, just to see Lu. It's all set up." He stepped forward and grabbed Lu's wrist. Bodie's fingers touched leather, like a caress.

"You're out of luck, friend," Bodie said. "I told you Lu's busy tonight."

"Like hell," the cowboy insisted, pulling Lu. "Come on, sweetie. I come sixty miles, and it's mighty cold. . . ."

"Get your hands off her," Bodie said.

Lu jerked away, retreated and stared, round-eyed, like a worn doll, pretty but empty.

"Don't you prod me," the cowboy said, weaving a little. His blue eyes snapped in the lamplight. "Who are you, anyway, acting so big? The governor or somebody?"

"I'm George Bodie. Didn't you hear about me tonight?"

"George Bo . . ."

The cowboy's eyes whipped frantically to the side. He licked his lips and his hand crawled down toward the hem of his jacket.

"Not in here, George, for God's sakes," Maebelle protested.

"Keep out of it," Bodie said softly. His eyes had a hard, predatory shine. "Now, mister cowboy, you got anything more to say about not bein' satisfied with Bertha?"

The cowboy looked at Lu. Bodie and Maebelle could read his face easily: fear clawed, and fought with the idea of what would happen if he backed down before Lu.

His sharp, scrawny-red Adam's apple bobbed.

His hand dropped.

Bodie's eyes glistened as the Navy cleared and roared.

The cowboy's gun slipped out of his fingers unfired. He dropped to his knees, cursed, shut his eyes, bleeding from the chest. Then he pitched forward and lay coughing. In a few seconds the coughing had stopped.

Bodie smiled easily and put the Navy away.

"One dozen," he said, like a man uttering a benediction.

"You damned fool," Maebelle raged. "Abraham! Abraham!" she shouted. "Get yourself in here."

In a moment an old arthritic black man hobbled into the room from the back of the house.

"Get that body out of here. Take the rig and dump him on the edge of town. Jump to it."

Abraham began laboriously dragging the corpse out of the parlor by the rear door. Boots, then feminine titters, sounded on the stairs.

Maebelle held down her rage, whirled and stalked into the hall.

"It's all right, folks," she said, vainly trying to block the view. People craned forward on the steps. Abraham didn't move fast enough. "Nothing's happened," Maebelle insisted. "The man's just hurt a little. Just a friendly argument."

"He's dead," a reedy male voice said. "Any fool kin see that."

Bodie stood in the doorway, his arm around Lu once more, complacently smirking at the confusion of male and female bodies at the bottom of the stairs. He heard his name whispered.

The thin voice popped up, "I'm getting out of here, Maebelle. This is too much for my blood." A spindly shape darted toward the door.

"Now wait a minute, Hiram," Maebelle protested.

The door slammed on the breath of chill air from the street.

Maebelle walked back toward Bodie, her eyes angry. "Now you've done it for fair. That yellow pipsqueak will spread it all over town that George Bodie just killed a man in my house."

"Let him," Bodie said. He glanced back at the clock. "In an hour I got an engagement with the marshal anyway. But that's in an hour."

Lu snuggled against him as he started up the stairs. The crowd parted respectfully. Maebelle scratched her head desperately, then spoke up in a voice that had a false boom to it:

"Come on into the parlor, folks. I'll pour a drink for those with bad nerves."

Abraham had removed the body, but she still noticed a greasy black stain on the carpet. Her eyes flew to the clock, which ticked steadily.

Bodie awoke suddenly, chilly in the dark room. His hand shot out for the Navy, but drew back when he recognized the boy Tad in the thin line of lamplight falling through the open door. He yawned and rolled over. Lu had gone, and he had dozed.

"What is it, boy?" he asked.

"Mr. Wyman's in the street, asking for you."

Bodie swung his legs off the bed, laughed, and lit the lamp. The holster hung on the bedpost, with the Colt in it.

"What time is it?" Bodie wanted to know.

"Quarter of twelve. Mr. Wyman hasn't got his shotgun. Said he wanted to talk to you about something."

Bodie frowned. "What sort of an hombre is this Mr. Wyman? Would he be hiding a gun on him?"

The boy shook his head. "He belongs to the Methodist

Church. Everybody says he's real honest," the boy answered, pronouncing the last word with faint suspicion.

Bodie's eyes slitted down in the lamplight. Then he stood, scratched his belly and laughed. "I imagine it wouldn't do no harm to talk to the marshal. And let him know what's going to happen to him."

Bodie drew on his shirt, pants, and boots. He pointed to the holster on the bedpost. "I'll come back for that, if this marshal still wants to hold me to the midnight deadline. Thanks for telling me, boy."

He went out of the room and down the stairs, a smile of anticipation on his face.

The house was strangely quiet. No one was in the parlor. But Bodie had a good idea that Maebelle, and others, would be watching from half a dozen darkened windows. Bodie put his hand on the doorknob, pulled, and stepped out into the biting air.

Wyman stood three feet from the hitch rack.

He had both hands raised to his face, one holding a flaring match, the other shielding it from the wind as he lit his pipe. Bodie recognized the gesture for what it was: a means of showing that the town marshal kept his word. Wyman flicked the match away and the bowl of the pipe glowed.

Bodie walked forward and leaned on the hitch rack, grinning. The cold air stung his cheeks. Across the way, at Aunt Gert's, a girl in a spangled green dress drank from a whiskey bottle behind a window.

"You Wyman?"

"That's right."

"Well, I'm Bodie. Speak your piece."

Bodie saw a slender man, thirty, with a high-crowned hat, fur-collared coat, and drooping mustache. His face was pale in the starlight.

"I started out to see if I could talk you into leaving town," Wyman said slowly. "I figure I don't want to kill anybody in my job if I don't have to."

"I'll say you got a nerve, Marshal," Bodie said, laughter in his words. "Ain't you scared? I got me my dozenth man tonight."

"I know."

"You still want to talk me into riding without a fight?"

Wyman shook his head. "I said that's why I came, why I started out. On the way I heard about the killing. Hiram Riggs ran through the streets yelling his head off about it. I can't let you go now. But I can ask you to come along without a fight. Otherwise you might wind up dead, Bodie."

"I doubt it, Marshal. I just purely doubt that."

Bodie scratched the growth of whiskers along the line of his jaw. He lounged easily, but he saw Wyman shift his feet as the rasp-rasp of the scratching sounded loudly in the night street.

"You know, you didn't answer my question about being scared."

"Of course I am, if that makes you feel better," Wyman said, without malice.

"Nobody ever told me that before, Marshal. Of course most didn't have time."

"Why should I lie? I'm not a professional."

"Then why are you in the job, Marshal? I'm sort of curious."

"I don't know. People figured I'd try, I imagine."

Sharply he raised his heel and knocked glimmering sparks from his pipe. "Hell, I'm not here to explain to you why I don't want to fight. I'm telling you I will, if you won't come with me."

Bodie hesitated, tasting the moment like good liquor. "Now, Marshal, did you honestly think when you walked over here that you'd get me to give up?"

Starlight shone in Wyman's bleak eyes for a moment. "No."

"Then why don't you go on home to bed? You haven't got a chance."

In a way Bodie admired the marshal's cheek, fool though he was.

Wyman turned his head slightly, indicating the opposite side of the street. For the first time Bodie noticed a shadowy rider on one of the horses at Aunt Gert's rack.

"When I come, Bodie, I'll have my deputy. He carries a shotgun too."

Bodie scowled into the night, then stepped down off the sidewalk, trembling with anger.

"That's not a very square shake, Marshal."

"Don't talk to me about square shakes. I knew that cowboy you shot. He couldn't have matched you with a gun. And there've been others. If you're trying to tell me two against one isn't fair, all I've got to say is, if I had a big cat killing my beef, I wouldn't worry whether I had two or twenty men after him." Hardness edged Wyman's words now. "I don't worry about how I kill an animal, Bodie. If you'd given that cowboy a chance, maybe I'd feel different. But I've got to take you one way or another. You wrecked the square shake, not me."

Bodie's fingers crawled along the hip of his jeans.

"Can't do it by yourself?" he said contemptuously.

"I won't do it by myself."

"Why not? You can't trust your own gun?"

"Maybe that's where you made your mistake, Bodie. I'd rather trust another man than a gun."

"I don't need nobody or nothing but my gun. I never have," Bodie said softly. "Where's your shotgun, Marshal?"

Wyman nodded toward the silent deputy on the horse. "He's got it."

"I'll put my gun up against you two," Bodie said with seething savagery. "You just wait."

Bodie started back for the entrance, and from the shadows before Aunt Gert's came a sharp voice calling:

"He might run out the back, Dale."

And Wyman's answer, "No, he won't . . ." was cut off by Bodie's vicious slam of the door.

Maebelle stuck her head out of the parlor as he bounded up the stairs, his teeth tight together and a thick angry knot in his belly. He had murder on his face.

He stomped into the bedroom, was halfway across, when the sight of the bedpost in the lamplight registered on his mind.

His holster—and the Navy—were gone.

Bodie crashed back against the wall, a strangled cry choking up out of his throat, his eyes frantically searching the room.

He lunged forward and ripped away the bedclothes. He pulled the scarred chest from the wall, threw the empty drawers on the floor, then overturned the chest with a curse and a crash. He raised the window, and the glass whined faintly.

He stood staring out for a moment at the collection of star-washed shanties stretching down the hill behind the house. Then he sat down on the edge of the bed, laced his fingers together. His shoulders began to tremble.

He let out a string of obscenities like whimpers, his eyes wide. He jumped to his feet and began to tear at the mattress cover. Then he stopped again, shaking.

He felt Wyman laughing at him, and he heard Wyman's words once more. Black unreason boiled up through him, making him tremble all the harder. With an animal growl he ran out of the room, stopped in the hall, and looked frantically up and down.

He kicked in the door across the room. The girl shrieked softly, her hand darting for the coverlet.

"What the hell, amigo...," began the man, half-timidly.

Like an animal in a trap, Bodie scanned the room, turned and went racing down the staircase. He breathed hard. His chest hurt. He felt a sick cold in his stomach like he'd never known before. Hearing his heavy tread, Maebelle came out of the parlor. Before she could speak, he threw her against the wall and held her. Words caught in her throat when she saw his face.

"Where is it?" he yelled. "Where's my Navy?" His voice went keening up on a shrill note. "Tell me where it is, Maebelle, or I'll kill you!"

"George, George . . . Lord, I don't know," she protested, frightened, writhing under his hands.

He hit her, slamming her head against the wall, turning

her face toward the top of the stairs. She choked. The fingers of one hand twitched feebly against the wall, the nails pecking a signal on the wallpaper.

"Emma . . . ," she said.

She sagged as he released her. He cleared the stairs in threes to where the round-eyed, curious little girl stood at the landing in her nightdress, shuffling slowly forward as if to find the commotion, and holding the Navy in one hand, upside-down, by the grip, while her other finger ran along the barrel, feeling the metal. Bodie tore it away from her and struck her across the face with the barrel.

Then he turned, lunging down the stairs again, muttering and cursing and smiling, past Maebelle. She watched him with a look of madness creeping across her face.

At the top of the staircase, the girl Emma, as if accustomed to such treatment, picked herself up and started down, dragging the leather holster she had picked up near the baseboard. She came down a step at a time, the welt on her cheek angry red but her eyes still childish and round. . . .

Bodie peered through the curtains.

He could see Wyman and his deputy in the center of the street, waiting, their shotguns shiny in the starlight. He had never wanted to kill any men so badly before.

He snatched the door open, slipped through, and flattened his back against the wall, the Navy rising with its old, smooth feel, and a hot red laugh on his lips as he squeezed.

Wyman stepped forward, feet planted wide, and the shotgun flowered red in the night.

Then the deputy fired. Bodie felt a murderous weight against his chest.

The Navy clattered on the plank sidewalk, unfired.

36

Bodie fell across the hitch rack, his stomach warm and bleeding, the shape of Wyman coming toward him but growing dimmer each second. Bodie felt for the Navy as he slipped to a prone position, and one short shriek of betrayal came tearing off his lips.

Wyman pushed back his hat and cradled the shotgun in the crook of his arm.

Across the street window blinds flew up, and then the windows themselves, clattering.

Maebelle stuck her head out the front door.

Lu came down the stairs, crying and hugging a shabby dressing gown to her breasts, bumping the girl Emma.

With round, curious eyes, Emma righted herself, drawn by the sound of the shots.

She started down more rapidly, one step at a time, toward the voices there on the wintry porch, and as she hurried, first the holster slipped from her fingers and then the bright shells from the other tiny, white, curious hand. They fell, and Emma worked her way purposefully down to the next step, leaving the playthings forgotten on the garish, somewhat faded carpet.

. . . GRAVEDIGGER . . .

Pretty desperate, right? Anyway, that's the way I heard it. Mebbe somebody else'll tell ya different, but they ain't here right now, is they?

Follow me, there's another one right near here, feller was also buried afore I got here. I'll tell ya a little bit about

Dodge while we're walkin'. There weren't no law here back
then, when Dodge City was new. Started out as Fort Dodge,
but then by 1872 it got built up pretty much and folks started
callin' it Dodge City. Like I said, there was no law, folks
pretty much took the law into their own hands when they
thought they was wronged. An' any ol' hand with a shovel
would bury 'em until I come along right around 'seventy-
three and then when I showed up in 'seventy-four lookin'
for some work and the undertaker hired me on. We been
plantin' 'em together ever since.

Now this one here . . . gather round now, so's you kin
read every word . . . this one here was kinda weird. At first
I thought folks was jest funnin' me, tryin' ta tell me scary
stories. Wasn't much was really knowed about this here feller
'cept his name was Abel Hawthorne and, like it says on the
marker, he kinda wasn't right in the head, if ya know what
I mean. I don't even know how much of what I heard is
true, and how much was made up, but somebody claimed
ta know what happened, and this here's the way it was tol'
ta me . . .

THE GHOST OF
ABEL HAWTHORNE

ELMER KELTON

HERE LIES
BUFFALO SKINNER
NAME UNKNOWN
DIED FEBRUARY 23, 1873
MENTALLY DERANGED

The last thing Morgan Poe could remember was sitting in a low dive south of the Dodge City railroad tracks, drinking the rawest of rotgut whiskey until he was barely able to lift the bottle. Now someone was kicking him hard, trying to jar him out of his stupor.

"Get up, you drunken whelp! Raise up before I decide to shoot you and put you out of my misery."

The angry voice reverberated in Poe's head, provoking excruciating pain. "Leave me alone," he cried. He tried to protect himself by drawing his body into a tight ball. The kicking and the cursing continued. Poe tried to lash out, flailing his arms in futility.

The voice commanded, "Get up and climb in the wagon. You still owe me money, and you'll work it out whether you like it or not."

Poe growled but made no move to comply. It seemed as if he had suffered abuse like this from everybody he had ever worked for. He was damned sick and tired of it. Someday . . .

The voice said, "We'll have to lift him into the wagon, Billy. He's too drunk to stand up."

Poe struggled against the strong hands that took hold of him, but he lacked strength for a fight. Through blurry eyes he saw the contemptuous face of his black-bearded boss, Abel Hawthorne, and the blank expression of the young buffalo skinner Billy Sprout. They seemed to dance in aimless circles, as did the hide wagon toward which they half carried, half dragged him.

Poe protested, "I had a bottle back there."

Hawthorne said, "It was empty, like your head. It's a wonder the cold didn't kill you, lying out in the open. I guess you had too much whiskey in you to freeze."

Poe could not remember how he came to be sprawled outside, against the log wall of the whiskey mill. His last half-clear recollection was of being slumped at a table, trying single-handedly to drink up all of the saloon keeper's stock. He guessed that he had passed out, and they had robbed him before dragging him outdoors and leaving him at the mercy of the winter night. Feeling inside his pockets, he found nothing except confirmation of his suspicions.

The two boosted him up over the tailgate and unceremoniously dropped him onto the wagon bed. His stomach turned over, and he felt deathly ill. "I'm dyin'," he said. "I need a doctor."

"All you need is a good sobering up," Hawthorne declared. "You'll get it by the time we reach the buffalo range."

He felt the wagon jolt across a rut, and he doubled up in pain. He cried out, but no one responded. Intending to climb out of the wagon, he tried to lift himself up, but he could barely move. He felt himself falling into a bottomless pit. He lapsed into a darkness black as midnight.

When he awakened he tried to open his eyes but found the winter sun blinding in its brilliance, and he squeezed them shut. His head pounded as if a blacksmith were hammering it against an anvil. Though the wagon bed was empty except for supplies, the stench of past trips' buffalo hides had penetrated deeply into the wood. He was already sick enough; he didn't need that.

As his vision gradually cleared, he made out Hawthorne's bulky form on the wagon seat. Looking back, he saw Billy following with a second wagon and more hunting and camp supplies.

Hawthorne turned to give him a cold appraisal. "Comin' alive, are you? Thought for a while we might have to dig a hole and throw you in. It'd be good riddance if I didn't need you."

"You got no right to Shanghai me this way," Poe protested. "Let me down from here."

"It's too long a walk back to Dodge. Good chance the Indians might get you. Anyhow, you're going to skin buffalo 'til you work off what you owe me. You're not worth much for anything else, but you're a fair hand with a skinning knife."

"I ought to cut your throat with it for draggin' me out here."

"You haven't got the guts."

Poe had hated Hawthorne ever since their first hide-hunting trip together. He hated him now more than ever, but he seemed helplessly tied to the hunter. The crafty Hawthorne was always advancing him money, which Poe drank up at the first opportunity. Constant debt had doomed him to indefinite servitude, just as it had back home. It seemed to him that he had been in arrears to one boss or another as far back as he could remember. When the debt became hopelessly large, he had always contrived to run away from it. That was how he came to be working out of Dodge, skinning buffalo. The eastern money panic had forced him west in search of employment.

Poe begged, "I'm sick enough to die. I know you keep whiskey for yourself. Let me have a drink. Just one."

"One, and then another, and then another after that. No, you'll sober up now if it kills you."

The old wagon's springs had long since collapsed. The rough ground jarred Poe's innards so that he almost wished he *could* die. It was a mercy when Hawthorne finally drew the horses to a stop and declared it was time to quit for the night. "You and Billy make camp," he ordered. He jumped down and walked around to his horse, tied behind the wagon. "I'll make a circle before dark. Been seeing buffalo signs the last couple of miles."

Poe waited until Hawthorne rode off before he tried

to climb out of the wagon. He almost made it, but his foot slipped from a wooden spoke in the rear wheel. He fell to the ground and could not rise to his feet. Billy stopped his wagon and shouted cheerfully, "I'll help you."

"Don't need your help," Poe retorted. He gripped the wheel and slowly pulled himself up. He held on until the ground stopped moving. He resented Billy for seeming always happy with whatever life chose to hand him. The youngster was pliable as new leather. Poe saw him as nothing more than a lackey for Hawthorne. He suspected the boy was slow in the head, or he would realize that Hawthorne was shorting him on his pay the same way he was doing Poe.

He lifted a shovel from its place on the side of the wagon. "Here, Billy, go dig a fire pit. I'll unload the camp supplies."

"Sure," Billy said, as if he loved to work. "And I'll gather up enough buffalo chips to cook supper with."

While Billy's back was turned, Poe rummaged through a canvas bag that belonged to Hawthorne. He found what he was looking for, several bottles of whiskey. Uncorking one, he took two generous swallows that warmed his stomach and seemed to ease his pain. He thought Hawthorne might notice that the bottle was not as full as it had been. For a moment he was tempted to urinate in it to bring it back up. That would serve Hawthorne right. But he reconsidered, for he might want to sample the bottle again himself. He put the cork back in and placed the bottle in the bag with the others.

His hand fell upon something else that aroused his curiosity. Unable to identify it by feel, he brought it out and found it to be a sock. Inside was a roll of paper tied with string. Poe pulled it out of the sock and felt his breath go short.

Money!

He had heard Hawthorne express his distrust of banks ever since one had gone busted with his money in it. But Poe had always assumed Hawthorne kept his money in somebody's safe in Dodge, or perhaps buried it in some secret place. He had no idea that Hawthorne brought it with him out on the buffalo range. It seemed a foolish thing to do. Somebody could easily rob him.

Another thought staggered him. *Somebody like me.*

He briefly considered appropriating one of the draft horses and escaping back to Dodge with the money. But Hawthorne's horse was faster than any of these. He was almost certain to overtake Poe before he could reach town. At best he might take him to jail. At worst he might simply shoot him. Many a man had disappeared out on those open plains, never to be heard from again. Usually the authorities did not bother much about it. Dodge's society was mostly transient. One hunter or skinner would hardly be missed.

Poe decided to bide his time. If they made a good haul of hides on this trip, Hawthorne's roll of bills would grow even larger. There would be time enough after they returned to Dodge to relieve Hawthorne of all that excess weight and hop a freight train east.

Hawthorne brought a satisfied expression back into camp. "I found a pretty good herd a couple of miles to the southeast. They won't drift much between now and morning. I ought to get a nice stand."

Billy asked, "Why didn't you go ahead and shoot as many as you could?"

It was a foolish question, but Billy was a foolish boy. Hawthorne replied with disdain. "Wolves might damage the hides overnight. Besides, the carcasses would be stiff and cold by morning, tougher for you and this drunk to skin."

Billy seemed not to notice Hawthorne's condescending attitude. About the only thing that ever seemed to trouble the boy was the threat of Indians. He asked, "You see any sign of Cheyennes?"

"No. They're probably holed up somewhere for the winter."

"They sure don't like us killin' the buffalo. If they was to come, there ain't but the three of us to fight them off."

"They won't come, not in this cold weather. And by the time we start the next trip we'll have a larger outfit. My brother Joseph is coming out from St. Louis to join us. When he gets here we'll have two or three more wagons, and more men."

Billy seemed pacified, more or less. He rubbed his head. "I sure don't fancy the notion of them Cheyennes liftin' my scalp."

Poe thought, *They wouldn't find anything under it.*

Hawthorne had brought Poe's bedroll along. Poe crawled into the blankets soon after forcing down a poor supper of sowbelly and hardtack. At least tomorrow there should be fresh meat, if his stomach had recovered enough to receive and hold it.

Hawthorne's Sharps Big Fifty rifle kept Poe and Billy busy the next three weeks, skinning, staking down fresh hides to cure. The work was bloody and smelly, and Poe hated it. But he contented himself by conjuring up mental images of the good life he would have Back East after he relieved the boss of his ill-gotten wealth. Champagne and beautiful women. Just what he needed to make him forget the dulling drudgery which hard times had forced upon him.

Winter blizzards could be savage on the plains. He had sensed one coming by the look of the northern sky, gray as lead along the horizon. The north wind came howling with the fury of a thousand starving wolves, bringing sleet that stung like buckshot. That was followed by blinding snow, the wind driving it almost horizontally. Hawthorne led the skinners, the wagons and teams down into a stream bed where timber afforded a modicum of protection, though not nearly enough.

Billy unhooked his team and removed the harness. The horses promptly drifted southward, disappearing into the blizzard. Billy ran after them, shouting for them to stop.

Damn fool kid, Poe thought. *He'll get lost and die out there.* But he made no move to follow him, to bring him back. He would probably die out there too if he went.

Poe and Hawthorne, working together, rigged a windbreak of sorts by lashing a tarp across the north side of one wagon and weighting the bottom of it against the ground with camp equipment. The tarp slowed the wind and allowed them to build a fire just far enough out that they would not burn the wagon.

Hawthorne said, "You'd better go find that fool Billy."

"And die out there? Hell no! Go yourself if you think that much of him."

Hawthorne knotted his gloved fists and for a moment

46

seemed to contemplate striking Poe. He said, "All right, damn you, I'll go. But when we get back off of this trip, I'm cutting you loose. I'll never hire you again."

You don't know how true that is, Poe thought with satisfaction, watching the boss trudge off with the wind at his back. In less than a minute the snow obscured any trace of him. Poe entertained a fantasy that neither Hawthorne nor Billy would ever return. All the boss's money and all the hides they had collected would then be Poe's. In Dodge people would ask a few questions, then accept what he told them.

He wrapped up in his blankets and tried to get warm, but the cold had gone to the bone. His whole body shook. The wind kept trying to blow out the fire, and he had to continue feeding wood into it to keep it alive. His fingers were so stiff he could barely bend them. His teeth chattered.

Whiskey, that was what he needed. Surely Hawthorne had not drunk up all of his private supply. Whatever remained must be in the canvas bag beneath the wagon seat. He climbed up on the wheel and rummaged around until his stiffened hands found the bag beneath the cover of snow. He opened it, feeling for a bottle. He came first upon the sock with the money in it. That would become his in due time, but right now money was of no value out here on the prairie, where the cold threatened to kill rich man or poor. Whiskey was worth more than all the money in the world, whiskey and the inner warmth it would bring him. He dropped the cork and took two long swallows.

He heard a vicious snarl from behind him. Rough hands tugged at him, pulling him down from the wheel and throwing him back against it with savage force. Abel Hawthorne's eyes blazed with fury, the lashes and his beard coated with white snow. "You thief! You damnable thief! After my money, are you? I ought to kill you!"

Poe heard himself protest that he was only after a drink of whiskey, but the wind seemed to tear the words away from him. Hawthorne gave no sign that he heard. He smacked a gloved fist into Poe's face, then another. He grabbed Poe around the neck and began to choke him, slamming the back of his head against the wheel's iron rim.

Frightened, Poe saw that rage had robbed the boss of reason. He wouldn't stop until Poe was dead.

Hawthorne's heavy buffalo coat covered a pistol holstered on his hip. Poe managed to jerk a button loose and shove one hand into the opening. His fingers closed on the revolver. He jerked it from the holster, cocked the hammer back and jammed the muzzle against Hawthorne's belly. He pulled the trigger.

Hawthorne's hands loosened their hold on Poe's neck. His eyes widened, fury giving way to surprise, then dismay. He squalled out a curse as blood spilled over his lips and down into his black beard. He stared at Poe with hatred, the most intense Poe had ever seen. Then, slowly, he sank to his knees, coughing, clutching at his stomach.

"Murderer," he wheezed. "Murderer."

His accusing eyes seemed to burn through Poe, but Poe could not look away.

He did not understand what was holding Hawthorne up. After what seemed an eternity, the boss slumped backward. He lay with legs buckled, the accusing eyes still staring at Poe, damning him even as their light flickered and died.

Poe could not pull his own eyes away from Hawthorne.

He stood oblivious to the cold as he watched snow covering the body. Finally he realized the fire was in danger of going out. He threw more wood on it, then dragged Hawthorne away from the wagon so he would not have to look at him.

He huddled before the fire, the blankets wrapped around his shoulders. Perfect, he tried to tell himself. Billy was gone, hopelessly lost out there in the blizzard, and Hawthorne was dead. The wagons and the hides and the money were his. He should be celebrating. But instead he felt as if a cold lump of lead lay in his stomach. It was as if he were freezing from the inside.

A voice kept whispering in his ear, audible over the howling of the wind. *Murderer. Murderer.* And those malevolent eyes seemed to keep staring at him from the embers of the fire.

Poe spent a sleepless, open-eyed night, watching the place where Hawthorne lay buried in snow, half afraid the man might yet rise up to damn him some more. By morning the storm had blown itself out. Poe feared he would find the horses frozen to death, but they had weathered the cold and were only hungry. The two Billy had gone after were still missing, as was Billy himself. Poe had just two draft horses and the one Hawthorne rode. That meant he could not take both wagons. He chose the one stacked high with hides. At two or three dollars apiece, there were not enough in the other wagon to worry about, especially against the roll of bills that had belonged to Hawthorne.

The temperature must still have been well below zero. The snow had blown into drifts several feet deep, but the flat ground, frozen hard, was scoured almost bare or at most had an inch or two of covering. He could maneuver the

49

wagon around the drifts, he thought. If he waited for the snow to melt, mud might make travel virtually impossible. He should go now, while he could.

He hitched the team and tied Hawthorne's horse behind the wagon. He could not see the body, but he knew where it was. He had no intention of trying to dig a grave in the frozen ground. Wolves would find Hawthorne when the thaw came. Chances were that nobody would ever discover him. Even if they did, they would assume that here lay another victim of the Cheyennes.

The Cheyennes. That would be his story when anybody in Dodge questioned him. The Cheyennes had gotten Hawthorne and Billy. At first he had thought he would simply say the two had become lost in the storm, but people would ask him why he had abandoned the search for them so soon. This story was better. No one would question whether they were dead or not. People would take Poe's word that they were, and that he had buried them.

He drove away and left Hawthorne's body lying in the snow. But somehow, Hawthorne went with him. Poe had a gnawing sense of the man's presence as the wagon rocked and jolted along on the hard ground. The wind was relatively quiet compared to last night's, but it still whispered in his ear: *Murderer. Murderer.*

There was no trail. Even if there had been he could not have followed it. Though his general direction was north, he had to turn east or west at times to avoid deep drifts. Now and then he came upon one that lay diagonally across his path as far as he could see and he had no choice but to challenge it. Occasionally the horses floundered, and he had to fight to get them up and out.

Once, that first day, he thought he might have to abandon the wagon. He considered cutting the team loose to manage on their own. He would take Hawthorne's horse and the money and ride on to Dodge. But he finally brought the wagon clear and saved the load of hides.

He was exhausted by the time he made camp in a dry creek bed where wood was plentiful. He built a fire of wasteful size, hoping to thaw his frozen bones. Though it threatened to blister his skin, he never got over the feeling of being cold deep inside. He dozed off once, awakening with a start as he imagined he saw Hawthorne standing on the other side of the fire, staring at him. Instinctively he drew Hawthorne's pistol from his belt and aimed it, but the figure disappeared.

He realized he had been about to shoot a hole in a nightmare. He felt foolish, but he remained shaken. After that, he lay sleepless for a second night, his eyes open, fearful he might see something more, yet fearful it might come and he *not* see it. He drank up all but one bottle of Hawthorne's whiskey.

The sky cleared during the night. At sunrise Poe threw off the blankets and prepared a poor breakfast from frozen buffalo hump, augmented by black coffee. His stomach was so roiled that some of it came back up. With leaden feet he went about harnessing the team and setting out in the direction of Dodge.

After two bone-cold nights without sleep, he began experiencing intervals of hallucination. Two buffalo bulls pawing for grass beneath the snow became a massive herd, and he feared they would stampede over him. A half dozen antelope raced across in front of him, but they appeared to be

Cheyennes. He trembled in fear until the specter passed and he recognized the animals for what they were.

Then Hawthorne was sitting beside him on the wagon seat. Poe wanted to jump but could not bring himself to move. Hawthorne turned to face him with those terrible burning eyes.

"Get away from me!" Poe screamed. He drew the pistol and fired, startling the team. They surged forward, forcing Poe to grab the wagon seat to keep from being pitched to the ground. When he brought the team back under control Hawthorne was gone, evaporated in the frigid winter air. Poe shook uncontrollably. After a time he managed to get hold of himself, or thought he had. Then he heard Hawthorne's voice in the wind again.

Thief, he kept saying. *Murderer.*

By the time Poe camped that night, he was dead on his feet. He forced himself to eat a little and drink coffee laced with some of the whiskey from Hawthorne's last bottle. He soon fell into a deep sleep, or perhaps it was a stupor. Whatever it was, he awakened at the first sign of daylight, feeling somewhat better.

He looked around, half expecting to see Hawthorne. The man did not appear. Poe's spirits lifted.

Perhaps he had finally left the ghost behind. He reasoned that the whiskey and the cold and the lack of sleep had been the cause of his imagination running wild. Hawthorne was probably halfway to hell by now. He was never coming back. Poe fed the horses and fixed himself a good breakfast. By tonight, he judged, he ought to make Dodge. Tomorrow he would sell the hides and the horses and the wagon. He would take Hawthorne's roll, and this time he would not ride a freight train. He would buy a seat on a passenger car, like real people.

He emptied Hawthorne's final bottle and cast it aside as the low outline of Dodge City came into view to the north. Tonight he would celebrate. A good supper, plenty of good whiskey, and maybe the companionship of a good-looking woman.

It was too late in the evening for business when he pulled into the south edge of town. He camped, staking the team. By habit he found himself walking toward the dive where he usually went to drink, but he stopped. He did not have to patronize places like that anymore. He could afford the Long Branch or some of the other classier places on the north side of the tracks. Anyway, those people had robbed him and cast him out into the freezing night. He didn't owe them anything, except possibly a little vengeance. Maybe just before his train left he would come down and set their place afire. That would teach them how to treat a customer.

No sir, tonight he would do his celebrating on the other side of the tracks.

And celebrate he did. He lost account of the whiskey he drank and the girls he danced with. He was dimly conscious that Hawthorne's roll of bills was steadily shrinking, but he could not stop himself. Sometime past midnight he was slumped in a corner barely touched by light from a lamp at the end of the bar. The lamp seemed to swing to and fro, like an outdoor lantern in the wind, except that there was no wind in the saloon.

He sat alone. The girls who had danced with him earlier avoided him now. That irritated him. He shouted for one to come and sit with him, but none responded. He tried to push to his feet, but his legs betrayed him. He cursed the girls until the bartender came and warned him to shut up or leave.

He gave up on the girls and decided to continue drinking alone. But he did not remain alone. He became aware of a dim figure sitting across the table from him. He had not seen the man arrive and sit down. One moment the chair was empty, and the next he was there.

"Who are you?" Poe demanded. He leaned across the table, trying to peer into the face.

He reeled back in horror, for he was looking at Abel Hawthorne, at those furious, accusing eyes. Hawthorne seemed to be saying *Murderer. Thief.*

Poe tried to arise but could not stand. He braced his hands on the edge of the table and shouted, "You're dead. Get away from me!"

Hawthorne did not move. He continued to accuse Poe of murder, of stealing his money.

Poe dug from his pocket what remained of the bills and threw them at the ghostly figure. "Take it. For God's sake take it and leave me alone."

The figure did not move. Poe managed to grasp a chair and swing it. The apparition vanished. Poe kept swinging the chair, shouting at the top of his voice.

The bartender and a helper grabbed Poe by the arms and dragged him to the door. The bartender kicked him out into the cold.

"We run a class joint here," he shouted. "Don't you be comin' back."

Poe lay on the wooden sidewalk for a time, unable to move. Eventually he grasped a post and pulled himself up.

He lurched along the street, stumbling, going to his knees, arising and staggering farther before the next fall. He found his camp, rolled up in his blankets and fell into a fitful half-sleep. Hawthorne's angry voice kept pounding in his head until he fell into a deep darkness.

Morning found him still disoriented. He tried to eat a little breakfast but promptly lost it. He looked around with bleary eyes, half expecting the ghost of Abel Hawthorne to appear again. He reasoned that what he had seen in the saloon last night had come up out of a bottle like an evil genie. He felt in his pocket but found no money. He vaguely remembered throwing it at the apparition. The bartender and his helper had not offered to pick it up and give it back to him. They had probably split it between them.

Well, he still had the hides and the wagon and the horses. They ought to fetch him a decent price. Then he would buy just enough whiskey to settle his stomach and lay the ghost of Abel Hawthorne. After that he would catch a train. He would put Dodge and the buffalo range behind him for once and all.

He hitched the team but could not climb up on the wagon. He tried once, slipped and smacked his chin hard against the sideboard.

As if I didn't already hurt enough, he thought bitterly.

He walked beside the wagon, working the lines to guide the team to the hide-buying yard. Long ricks of dried hides were stacked house-high beside the railroad tracks. A man and a boy stood in front of a wooden shack, watching his approach. Poe could not bring up the man's name from his foggy memory, but he recalled that Hawthorne had sold hides to him.

Poe said, "I got a load here. What you payin'?"

"Two-fifty for a grown hide, two for kips. How many you got?"

Poe had no idea. As hard as he and Billy had worked skinning them, there ought to have been a thousand. "You'll have to count them for yourself. I want to sell it all. Horses too."

The man frowned as he studied the horses and the wagon. "Say, ain't this Abel Hawthorne's outfit?"

"Was," Poe said. "He's dead. Indians." His voice was a little shaky. He was not sure the man believed him. He went on, "They come upon us in a blizzard. Killed Hawthorne and the boy Billy that was with us. Run off with one team. I had to leave a wagon behind."

The man leaned down and quietly said something to the boy, who went trotting away. Then he said, "I'll have to wait 'til I get a crew here to unload and count the hides."

"Could I have a little somthin' in advance? I'm in powerful need of a drink."

"I've got a bottle in the shack here. Come on in."

Poe followed him inside. The man opened a desk drawer and handed him a bottle. "Hair of the dog that bit you, if I'm any judge."

Poe did not stop at one swallow. He took two, and then another. The whiskey burned, but the feeling was welcome on his troubled stomach. "I'm obliged," he said. "Now, about that advance . . ."

"No need goin' anywhere 'til we count the hides. You're welcome to sit here and drink the whole bottle if you're of a mind to."

"You're a kind Christian gentleman." Poe tipped the

bottle again. By the time that drink settled, he was feeling good.

He heard a voice from outside. The hide buyer stepped out the door and conversed a moment with someone Poe could not see. Then the two men came in. Poe immediately saw that the second man wore a badge on his coat. The officer said brusquely, "I understand you brought in Abel Hawthorne's outfit."

"It's mine now. Hawthorne's dead."

"So I am told." The lawman frowned deeply. "How come the Indians didn't kill you too?"

Poe tried to think fast despite his muddled brain. "I was out draggin' up wood for the fire. They hit and was gone in a wink."

"So you figure this outfit belongs to you now?"

"Ain't nobody else to claim it. Anyway, Hawthorne owed me wages."

The lawman said, "That'll be up to a judge to say. Let's go talk to him."

Poe followed the lawman outside. The morning sun hit him in the eyes and half blinded him for a moment. Blinking, he saw another man standing beside the deputy. He took a step forward, then saw the black beard, the familiar face. He felt his stomach drop out from under him.

He screamed, "Hawthorne! For God's sake, why won't you stay dead?"

Hawthorne just stared at him. In a blind panic Poe drew his pistol and fired. He saw the man duck and step away.

The deputy shouted, "Drop that gun."

Poe fired again, wildly, blinded by whiskey and fear.

He saw the lawman's hand move quickly, coming up with a pistol. He saw the flash and felt the stunning impact against his breastbone. It burned like the fires of hell. He tried to steady the pistol, but a second bullet thudded into his chest. He felt himself falling face first into the cold snow. The last thing he saw as his vision faded was Hawthorne's boots, inches away.

The lawman knelt and turned Poe over. "Deader than a skinned buffalo. I never would've expected him to go wild thataway."

Joseph Hawthorne asked, "What do you suppose possessed him?"

"I expect he stole that wagonload of hides and thought I'd caught up with him. But I don't see why he would shoot at you instead of at me."

Hawthorne shrugged. "I was supposed to join my brother Abel here in Dodge. You say the wagon belongs to him?"

The hide buyer answered, "I recognized the team, and his initials painted on the wagon. I'm afraid this man was right about your brother bein' dead, but I'd bet it wasn't Indians that killed him." He gave Hawthorne a moment's intense study. "I swear, you look just like him."

"I should," Joseph Hawthorne said. "We're twins."

...GRAVEDIGGER...

Ain't that the damndest story you ever heard? Ya gotta forgive me for laughin', but it is kinda funny, a fella thinkin' he's seein' a ghost and all...

Well, strange as that story was there's one over here ...
see here, where there's two markers? Ain't only men buried
up here on Boot Hill, no sir, here we got a man and a
woman. Fact is, they was husband and wife, and what happened to them was not only pretty strange, but pretty durn
sad, too, when you consider they had a new baby to think
about.

Wait a minute, I just wanna take a look ... no, ain't
nobody comin' up here ta help me, yet. You know, I dug a
bunch of these graves myself, 'cause that's my job, but today's
a little different. See, for what I gotta do today I need some
help ... well, they'll be along directly, I guess. T'aint no need
for me ta get all worked up about it. I mean, if the town
council wants this job done right they'll be sendin' me some
help directly ...

Meantime, I guess I kin tell ya this story about Lon
and Henrietta Beatty, only it ain't jest a story about them.
There's the baby, then there's the Reverend Grieves and then
there's Emma Mills, as good a woman as ... well, jes' listen
whilst I tell it ...

SINNERS

WENDI LEE

LON BEATTY — WHO NEVER KNEW LITTLE WINIFRED

HENRIETTA BEATTY — WHO LEFT POOR LITTLE WINIFRED
AN ORPHAN TO REST BESIDE HER HUSBAND

Sunday was not considered a good day for a woman to go into labor due to the blue laws, but sometimes it wasn't up to the expectant mother. Henrietta Beatty started her labor pains right after church just after the Reverend Grieves shook her hand and blessed her. Well, suddenly Henrietta had a look like she'd just swallowed a lemon whole, and a puddle formed beneath her skirts and she didn't even have a chance to blush. She just started a-screamin' and a-hollerin', this being her first child, and none of the other midwives wanted to do for Henrietta because it was the Lord's Day and He had said a body shouldn't work on His day. But the baby didn't know that and poor Henrietta wasn't about to keep her knees shut—something she apparently hadn't been able to do nine months earlier—until Monday morning.

So Emma rolled up the sleeves of her best Sunday dress and went to work on Henrietta. Reverend Grieves had enough presence of mind—and enough respect for the laws of nature—to make a bed for Henrietta in a corner of the church, being as how she couldn't move more than a few feet without screamin' and cryin'.

Several members of the church were not above breaking the blue law in order to preserve the church floor—Frank Boland and Arnold Latrask set to work with rags and old blankets, making a nest for poor Henrietta to lay on while she pushed and sweated and cried and moaned and made an awful racket.

Little Winifred Beatty entered the world five hours later with a lusty cry and a shiny squinched-up red face. She was not a pretty sight, but Emma was certain that with a little cleaning up, little Winifred would look almost human, which was the point. Emma had never been one to hold with the notion that all babies were adorable from birth.

It was several days later when Reverend Grieves stopped his buggy in front of Emma's house. Henrietta sat beside him with little Winifred in her arms, and neither adult looked too happy.

Emma had spent the early morning at the river, scrubbing her clothes on the flat rock, trying once again to wash out the blood of childbirth from her Sunday dress.

"Mrs. Mills, it's a fine day!" the reverend greeted her.

Henrietta wasn't quite as gracious. Maybe it was the

jolting ride out to Emma's place, maybe it was because some women became sorrowful after giving birth. In any case, Henrietta acknowledged Emma with a short nod before clambering out of the buggy, reaching back inside—as if she were an afterthought—to get little Winifred.

"Good day, Reverend. Henrietta, you're looking well, and so is little Winifred," she replied, and this time she was being honest. Little Winifred was beginning to look almost human. One might even say she was cute as a bug. "Would you both like a glass of lemonade on this hot day?"

"Why, thank you, Miss Emma," the reverend replied as he took off his black flat-brimmed hat and wiped his brow with a grimy white handkerchief. Even Henrietta's expression brightened a bit at the mention of lemonade on a hot day.

The reverend, who was about Emma's age of twenty-five and unmarried, had moved to Harmony a few months ago to inspire the congregation at the Harmony Church of the Holy Ghost. When Emma looked at him in the right light, he didn't look all that awkward and young. She even thought he might be good-looking if he took off that black flat-brimmed hat and shaved off the scraggly goatee. She suspected that he thought it made him look older. Of course, she tried not to think of Reverend Grieves as anything more than a man of God since she had been widowed within the year. A little over nine months ago, to her recollection.

Emma turned to Henrietta, recollecting that she was currently without a husband as well. Only *her* husband was still alive—just not around. Henrietta Sothern had been no older than sixteen when she had met and married Lon Beatty—too young to know Lon was no good. Or maybe it was that Henrietta had been too young to *care* that Lon ran with the Oak Hill gang and was already reputed to have killed at least one man. There was a wanted poster on him for the murder. And Emma wasn't sure if Henrietta knew of Lon's reputation with women. Even while he was married to her, all of Harmony knew that Lon had women in Dodge and other towns, and even other territories. He wasn't around much after the first three months of their marriage, but apparently had stopped by long enough to provide Henrietta with company in the form of little Winifred. Of course, it was common knowledge that Henrietta took jaunts into Dodge occasionally, and everyone in Harmony suspected that she met Lon there, considering that he was a wanted man. It would be no good for him to come home to Harmony and be thrown in the hoosegow. But how long could a marriage last when the husband had to be constantly on the lookout for the law?

Emma led her guests to a bench in the shade of the cottonwood tree that sheltered her one-room house, then excused herself to go inside to pour three mugs.

"Is this an official visit," Emma asked as she handed out the mugs, "or were you just passing by?"

Henrietta had put little Winifred, who was asleep by now, on the ground, a quilt folded up beneath the baby to keep her comfortable. Henrietta looked a lot better than the last time Emma had seen her. Her figure was back and her chestnut hair was shiny and curled. She had large green eyes and a dimpled smile that she turned on Emma as she accepted a mug.

The reverend took a sip of lemonade. "I'm not sure how to answer that. I just came from the marshal's office. Lon Beatty has been spotted in Dodge."

As if on cue, Henrietta frowned, put the mug down on the bench beside her, covered her face with her hands and proceeded to sob.

Emma blinked. Henrietta's husband, little Winifred's father. "Oh, my. Did Marshal Lamont send a message to the law in Dodge to pick him up?"

The reverend looked down. "He did. The sheriff in Dodge City hasn't been able to lay his hands on Lon."

More likely, Emma thought, he was *afraid* to lay hands on Lon and was letting Lon strut about town like a rooster in charge of the henhouse. "Seems to me someone from Harmony ought to go there," the reverend was saying, "and get the message to him that he has a baby daughter."

The intent look with which he fixed his eyes on Emma made her distinctly uncomfortable. "You're not suggesting that I go—"

Henrietta cut in. "I suggested to the reverend that I leave Winifred with you for a few days, Mrs. Mills, while I go in there myself, but the reverend seems to think—"

"That it wouldn't be appropriate for a mother to leave her newborn," the reverend finished for Henrietta, who scowled behind his back. Emma didn't like to think unkind thoughts, but she did get the impression that Henrietta did not take her duties as a new mother seriously.

"Normally I wouldn't suggest that you do this, Mrs. Mills," the reverend continued, "but if the sheriff of Dodge is too afraid to approach Lon, it would be uncalled for to ask a man to do this job. Any man who approaches him is fair game for a bullet."

Henrietta dabbed at her eyes with a lace handkerchief. "But a woman might stand a chance."

Timothy, Emma's late husband, would not have approved. He had always left Emma at home when he entered Dodge City. Emma feared for her husband each time he left until he returned safely. The last time, he had been found in his hotel room, his money gone and a hole in his head. The killer was never found, which was not unusual. Emma got the impression that the Dodge City law didn't try very hard. Men died in Dodge all the time. A neighbor went to Dodge to bring Timothy's body back home in a pine box.

Emma turned her attention back to the present, to the reverend and Henrietta and sleepy little Winifred.

Reverend Grieves looked troubled. "I don't hold with sending a woman into a situation where a man might stand a chance. But," he glanced at Henrietta, who had turned her attention to her baby, then leaned over to whisper to Emma, "I have it on good authority that Lon likes pretty women." He straightened up and said in a normal voice, "All we want to do is get the message to him about Henrietta and little Winifred."

"I've only met Lon once about two years ago at their wedding," Emma mused. "Perhaps Henrietta should go into Dodge—she knows him by sight, even if he's wearing a disguise. I can stay here and watch the baby."

But Henrietta started a-cryin' and a-sobbin'. Reverend Grieves looked disconcerted and uncomfortable—he kept looking over at Henrietta, then down at his lemonade. Henrietta's fussing finally abated, but not before little Winifred awoke with a vigorous cry.

Henrietta finally sniffed, reached over for Emma's hand and said, "Winifred's got the colic and I can't leave her now. *Please* do this for me. For little Winifred." It was hard to disregard the fact that Henrietta seemed to be ignoring little Winifred, who was red in the face and hiccoughing by now. It was also hard not to pay attention to the fact that a moment ago, Henrietta hadn't been all that thrilled with the idea of Emma going after Lon. Still, Emma looked at the helpless baby and knew that she would do it.

"I'll do it," Emma said, withdrawing her hand to reach down and pick up the baby. She stood and put little Winifred over her shoulder, gently jiggling her and patting her back until the baby let out a great big burp, along with some drool on the shoulder of her only clean dress.

Henrietta stood, grabbed her daughter and smiled at Emma. "Thank you, Mrs. Mills. You are a true friend."

The reverend finished his lemonade and put the mug on the bench as he stood to go. He placed his hat on his head and adjusted his wire rims. "Thank you, Mrs. Mills." As they headed for his buggy Henrietta suddenly thrust little Winifred into the startled preacher's arms and headed back to Emma. She pulled a sealed paper from a pocket in her apron. "Oh, yes, please give this to Lon when you find him."

She turned around and walked to the buggy, the burdened reverend attempting to help her up to her seat, then handing her the baby. He turned back to Emma, took out some money from his coat pocket and handed it to her. "I took up a collection last Sunday from our parishioners. You'll need it for a hotel room and meals. I don't know how long you'll be looking for him, but wire me if you need more money."

She took the money reluctantly. "What if Lon's gone by the time I get to Dodge?"

He frowned. "Don't go after him. If you can find someone who knows him, hand over the missive. I don't want to hear that you were hurt in the process of finding Lon." He took her hand and held it a moment longer than necessary.

Emma felt her cheeks getting hot. She withdrew her hand and smiled. "I won't get hurt. Thank you for trusting me."

Reverend Grieves seemed about to speak again, but thought better of it. He climbed into the buggy seat, took up the reins and, with a nod, took his leave.

Emma stood and watched his buggy disappear into the distance. Then she turned back to her cabin to pack a few things for her journey.

Timothy had often described Dodge City as a dangerous, lawless place. As Emma guided her wagon down the center of town, she heard gunshots at least three separate times, two men were thrown out of saloons, and one fistfight started outside the assay office. Her late husband had often told her that he didn't want to take her to Dodge because there was liable to be a gunfight in the middle of the main street at any time of day or night. But what he had forgotten to mention was the number of buffalo hides that lined the street, manned by buffalo hunters trying to sell them. The stink was enough to drive most sane people out of Dodge. But Emma realized that most of the people in Dodge couldn't be sane—Timothy had often mentioned the lawlessness of the town, that Dodge almost welcomed the outlaws and that the outlaws outnumbered the lawmen a hundred to one.

She had passed Boot Hill on her way into town—the

cemetery where outlaws and penniless luckless bystanders were buried. Boot Hill had been created out of necessity— so many people died in Dodge from bullets or knifings that a makeshift cemetery had been created—a plot of land where the sinners and the martyrs were planted. Nothing grew there but misery.

Emma shuddered, remembering that when her neighbor had returned with the coffin loaded in his wagon, he told her that he'd had to pay someone to dig up the body— Timothy had been buried in Boot Hill without ceremony. She was glad he was home now, resting in a grove of sycamores on a hill overlooking the river that passed their homestead.

After paying the stable boy for a stall for her horse and wagon, Emma went next door to the Diamond Hill Hotel, paid for two nights and, after freshening up, left her warbag in her room. She was hungry, so she stepped into a nearby eating place called May's and ordered a meal.

It was quiet in May's, and since the woman who served her was also the cook, Emma assumed that she was May.

"You must have just come to Dodge," the woman said as she cleared used mugs off a large plank table. She was stocky, with graying hair pulled up in a messy bun as if it had been an afterthought. Wisps of hair floated around her face.

"Yes, just a little while ago," Emma agreed. "How did you know?"

"Women don't often come in alone." May said, eyeing her. "May I ask what your business is?"

"Do you know of a man called Lon Beatty?"

May's eyes narrowed in thought. "Don't believe so. You

his wife?" It was clear that May had come across many abandoned wives searching for a wayward husband.

Emma shook her head and explained her reason for
being in Dodge.

"Well, it sounds as if this Lon is outside the law, and
Dodge is a lawless place. What does he like to do, may I
ask?" It was clear that May was talking to herself, so Emma
did not answer the question. "I imagine church is out of the
question. But I bet he worships women. Am I right?"

This time, Emma did answer. "I have heard gossip that
Lon enjoys more than one woman. But I—"

"And he probably gambles and drinks," May added
decisively. "If I were searching for a wayward husband, or
friend's husband," she added for Emma's benefit, "I'd try the
Golden Buffalo down the street. Gambling, drinking and
women, Big Al's establishment has it all."

Emma thanked her.

"Of course," May added, "Dodge isn't a place for a lone
woman. And Big Al isn't a man I would send a person of
your caliber to without a warning."

"What sort of warning?" Emma asked.

May looked everywhere but at her. "Just be careful. Big
Al has a way with women. If you want to go into that place,
you really should have a deputy escort you."

Emma thanked her again, paid for her meal and left.

She decided against asking the law to escort her into
the Golden Buffalo, recalling the reverend's warning that
"any man was fair game for a bullet." She didn't want to be
responsible for someone getting hurt, in case Lon was there
when she went inside. When she walked into the saloon and

asked for Al, a fat, balding, unshaven man with a wet, smelly cigar plugged into one side of his mouth appeared.

"I'm Big Al, darlin'." His eyes raked her up and down. "What can I do for you?"

Emma choked on her immediate response—"You can stop looking me up and down and talk to me from across the room"—but she managed to say, "I'm looking for a man named Lon Beatty."

"Don't know 'im."

"What time do most of your customers come in here?" she asked.

"At night. But we don't allow ladies in here then. Too much trouble."

She raised her eyebrows. "Since I have been in here, I have seen at least two ladies."

Big Al took the cigar out of his mouth with stubby grime-encrusted fingers and laughed. "Those weren't no ladies, those were saloon girls."

She sighed, frustrated. "Do you have any jobs open then?"

Now it was Big Al's turn to be surprised. "For you? You look like a schoolmarm. We don't run a school here."

Emma managed a smile. "I can assure you I am not a schoolteacher, Mr.—Big Al. Do you have a job for me?"

Big Al amazingly took the cigar out of his mouth again, stepped back and walked around her. "Yeah, you got a job here—*if* you fit the costume."

Big Al worked with her all afternoon on dealing Monte, and by the time the customers began arriving in the early evening, she was fairly proficient at it. She also found herself dressed in a gaudy red, black and yellow dress, matching feathers in her upswept hair and black lace fingerless gloves.

It took three nights of dealing Monte before Emma spotted Lon. She had promised herself that this was the last night she would work at the Golden Buffalo. Since the first night, Emma had been asking around if anyone knew Lon Beatty. She often got the feeling that plenty of people could pick him out, but no one would admit that to her.

The feathers in her hair drooped forward, getting in the way of her vision, and she blew them aside for the fourteenth time. She almost missed Lon when he came in. His hat was pulled low to conceal his identity, but it served to draw attention to him instead. He went straight for the poker tables, settling in at one particular table as if the chair had his name engraved on it.

All she had to do was hand the note to him, but she couldn't leave her post. She kept an eye on him throughout the night. To amuse herself, Emma kept track of how he was doing, but he didn't appear to be winning. He didn't look all that happy about it, either.

Finally, her shift ended. Her feet ached in too-tight boots as she hobbled across the room. She slipped the sealed note from her yellow sash and walked up to Lon.

"Lon Beatty?" she asked, just to be sure she wasn't getting the wrong man.

He looked up at her, his eyes narrowing with suspicion. "I ain't innerested in Monte, sweetheart. That's a pussy's game." He put his cards down—Emma glanced at his pasteboards and it was a hand worth folding. He stood up. "But I might be innerested in something else." He reached for her and she quickly held out the note.

"You might be interested in this message." He took it from her.

She started to walk off.

"Hey! Wait a minnit. You look familiar," he called.

Emma paused, flushing. Then she smiled and said, "Coincidence."

She went back to the hotel, thinking about Henrietta and Lon and little Winifred. It wasn't a perfect marriage— Lon wasn't a great husband, but maybe the birth of his daughter would bring him back home. Emma thought back to her marriage to Timothy. They had only been married three years, but they had known each other all their lives. She missed him so much that her soul ached.

No one was manning the hotel desk when she entered the lobby. The guest register lay on the surface, beckoning to her. Timothy had been staying here when he was killed. In fact, he had been shot in one of the rooms. It had been bothering her for the last few days that she was staying in the same hotel, but it was the only decent hotel in Dodge.

She hesitated, wanting to satisfy her curiosity—which room had he stayed in? She wasn't sure if she'd be relieved or uncomfortable if she discovered she was staying in the room he'd died in. She had spent the last few nights searching the walls for bullet holes, but this was Dodge, and bullet holes were a dime a dozen.

She paged back through the book, finally coming to the date he died: August 12, 1875. Running her finger over the names, she spied his familiar autograph and she lovingly caressed his name with her fingertip.

"Can I help you?" The burly bewhiskered clerk had come out of the back room.

Emma looked up, trying to blink back the tears. "Oh!" She was flustered.

He softened his suspicious look. "Are you feeling all right?"

The ache in her subsided as she took a deep breath to calm herself. Emma managed a weak smile. "I'm sorry. I just had an urge to look up the date of the last time my late husband stayed here. He stayed here back in August. He was shot in his room. Maybe you were here . . . ?"

The clerk came over and looked at the registry. Emma pointed to Timothy Mills' signature.

"Ah, yes. He stayed in room three." He looked up quickly. "We didn't, by any chance, put you in the same room?"

She shook her head. "No. I'm in eleven."

He nodded, a look of relief crossing his face. "I do remember that day." Another look flitted across his face, staying long enough for Emma to catch before he turned away from her.

She reached out and caught his sleeve. "Please, tell me. What do you remember about that night?" She had a wild notion that she might find his killer, solve the mystery of how he died.

The clerk turned back to her, his eyes troubled. "I think I've said too much. I don't think you want to hear any more."

She reached into her small purse and placed a coin on the counter between them. "Please. I'm strong enough." She wasn't sure if this was true, but she knew she could never rest until she knew the truth.

He hesitated, then said, "There was a girl. This was not the first time they met here."

Emma felt her stomach drop to the floor. Even so, she managed to keep her composure. In fact, she felt a little relieved. She'd always known deep down inside that Timothy had been unfaithful to her when he went on his trips to Dodge. Maybe that was why he never took her with him—the danger had not been that his wife might get hurt, but that his wife might run into his mistress. "Please tell me about her. Did she sign in as well?" She reached for the register.

"No. She came from out of town too, I'm pretty sure of that. When she checked in after him, she had the dust of travel on her."

"Tell me what she looked like."

He described her. Emma expected a surge of anger to come, but nothing happened. In fact, she felt quite numb. She took out another coin and shoved the money toward the clerk. "Thank you for your kindness," she said.

He pushed the coins back toward her. "I can't."

She managed a smile. "Yes, you can. You've freed me." She went to her room, which was at the end of the hall. A fresh breeze blew in from an open window at the end of the corridor. When she opened the door to her hotel room, she knew she wasn't alone. She could soon make out a large form in the corner chair, watching her enter.

"Excuse me, sir, but you have the wrong room . . ." She turned up the kerosene lamp, throwing light on Lon Beatty's features.

"I remember you," he said, getting up and crossing the

75

room to her. "You were married to Timothy Mills." His scowl told her all she needed to know—that he knew about his wife and her husband.

"Why are you here?" she asked, too drained to summon up any fear of him.

He held out the note. "You invited me."

She blinked and reached out for the note. "You're mistaken. That note announces the birth of your daughter, Winifred. Henrietta gave it to me to give to you."

He blinked. "My—"

Suddenly, the door opened again and Henrietta stepped inside. It took Emma a moment to register that Henrietta must have traveled to Dodge to surprise them. "Not *your* daughter, Lon. Timothy's. That's why you left me, isn't it? After killing him." Henrietta had a revolver pointed at her husband. "You figured out that my baby may not be yours."

He backed up, his hands patting the air. "Now, Henri—"

Henrietta didn't wait for his explanation or pleas. She fired once, twice, three times—every bullet hitting Lon as he danced backwards and finally crumpled to the floor.

Emma opened her mouth to scream. Nothing came out—no scream, no cry, no moan—nothing. She listened, hoping to hear the sound of men running this way after the gunshots, but no one came to her aid. For a moment, Henrietta seemed to have forgotten that Emma was in the room. She appeared to be studying her own handiwork. Until Emma removed her hands from her mouth.

Henrietta turned her gaze on Emma the way a mother tiger eyes new prey for her young. "I'm sorry you had to witness this, Emma. I was hoping you'd have been sidetracked, or that you'd come back after I killed him." She shrugged. "But now you know. Timothy loved *me* and Winifred is proof of that."

Emma glanced at Lon's still, bleeding form. "No one need know about this, Henrietta. I have no desire to hurt your child." Emma remembered the open window at the end of the hall—that was how Henrietta planned to escape. She would kill Emma first. Probably she would leave the gun near Emma's body to make it look as if she'd had a lover's quarrel with Lon, killed him and then herself. All these thoughts flitted through Emma's mind in less than a second.

Henrietta aimed the gun at Emma's chest. "I'm sorry, but I have to do this. I have to protect little Winifred from the truth of her birth. This works out so much better—now that Timothy is gone, his death avenged—" She looked at Lon's lifeless body, a scornful expression on her face. "Lon was unfaithful to me every chance he got. I was unfaithful to him a few times and branded a whore—"

"How do you know little Winifred is Timothy's and not Lon's?" Emma's voice came out in no more than a whisper.

"Why, a woman knows these things," Henrietta replied in a sweet voice. "You wouldn't know because you've never been with child. Timothy said you were as barren as the Dead Sea. No, Winifred is Timothy's baby, all right. He talked about leaving you but Lon caught up to us first."

"Why didn't he kill you then?"

"I told him I was pregnant. Lon may be a stone-cold killer of men, and he might have murdered me for being an unfaithful wife, but he couldn't be sure whose child I was carrying. He didn't want to kill his own blood."

Emma suddenly wondered about Winifred—had Henrietta killed her baby? "Where's little Winifred?" Emma asked with alarm.

"Staying with the good reverend," Henrietta replied with a cold smile, cocking her head slightly. "I think I would make a good preacher's wife—once the mourning period is over. Don't you?"

The brief thought that Henrietta was crazy as a rabid raccoon came to Emma's mind. Then she squeezed her eyes shut, and heard the shot. But she didn't feel it. She opened her eyes, briefly felt her front for bullet holes, then noticed Henrietta lying at her feet, the gun still in her hand.

Turning around, she saw Lon's smoking gun in his limp hand—he'd rallied long enough to take Henrietta with him.

The clerk arrived just in time to steer a weak-kneed Emma to the bed before she passed out.

Emma woke up with the help of smelling salts and a doctor hovering over her. The sheriff stood beside him. She looked around, but the bodies of Lon and Henrietta Beatty had been removed.

"How are you feeling?" the doctor asked.

"I've felt better."

"Can you tell us what went on here?" the sheriff asked.

When she was finished giving him an account of everything that had happened, the lawman nodded as if that was that.

"Why didn't anyone come to my aid after the first shot?" she asked.

The clerk was standing just inside the door. "I'm sorry, gunshots are common in Dodge City. I ran to get the sheriff. I'm afraid I'm not brave enough to investigate gunshots on my own. The last clerk who did so got killed for his trouble."

She nodded, understanding his caution.

"What do you want done with the bodies?" the sheriff asked, clearly wanting Emma to take them back to Harmony with her.

She shook her head. "What do you normally do with the dead here in town?"

He pushed his hat back slightly. "We have a place here, just on the edge of town. The locals call it Boot Hill 'cuz a lot of men die with their boots on. For a charge, we put a marker on the grave."

Emma pulled out the money she had made from dealing Monte that night. She wrote the epitaphs on a scrap of paper, and handed the money and the paper to the sheriff.

"Will you be staying for a funeral, ma'am?"

Emma was tired of Dodge. Suddenly it sounded good to just check out of the hotel today and start the drive back to Harmony. It was a full moon tonight. She had a little girl, an orphan, who needed her. She wanted to wake up tomorrow morning with Winifred in her arms. Whether the father was Timothy or Lon, she was an innocent in all this death and deception.

"No, Sheriff. I would like to leave as soon as I pack my things."

He studied her for a moment. "I won't stand in your way." But the unspoken question that hung between them was why she would want to leave town without "sending off" the man who had saved her. Emma would never know whether Lon Beatty had deliberately saved her life or was just doing a job that had been left unfinished nine months earlier. Either way, she would forever be grateful for his intervention. She felt a fool for not seeing that Timothy and Henrietta's visits to Dodge almost always corresponded.

"They left an orphan behind, a baby," Emma explained, "in Harmony. Someone needs to take care of the baby. I think they'd understand if I didn't stay for the funeral."

The sheriff nodded. "Doesn't seem like there's much here for you but sorrow."

Emma agreed. "I want to leave that sorrow behind. There's nothing here for me at all."

An hour later, she had packed and started the drive out of town. But she couldn't help noticing that there were men on Boot Hill already digging two fresh graves. She looked away until she rounded the bend where Dodge City and Boot Hill vanished from her sight.

. . . GRAVEDIGGER . . .

Don't that just tear at yore heartstrings just a little? Just goes ta show ya people ain't always what they seem—'cept mebbe folks like Emma. She was exactly what she seemed ta be, which made her kinda special. She took that baby and went Back East somewheres, which was probably a real smart thing for her ta do.

And speakin' of special there's a grave right around here that's got a story behind it that's one of my favorites. Ya see, it happened just about the time I got here. Hell if I'd ever heard of Dusty Logan before that, or a fella by the name of Cobb.

Come on over here with me. I know 'zackly where this grave is because—well, ta tell ya the truth, I got a soft spot in my heart for ol' Dusty, 'cause his was the first grave I ever dug here on Boot Hill.

Here 'tis. Even got a stone, and an epitaph—learned that word when I first started this here job—that tells what happened without tellin' what really happened.

See, sometimes there's more to diggin' a grave than jest buryin' a fella—but if I say too much now I'll give away the end, and I don't wanna do that. Tell ya the truth this here is a story I purely love ta tell, and you'll see why . . .

THE GUNS OF
DUSTY LOGAN

JAMES REASONER

HERE LIES DUSTY LOGAN
1848?–1874
A FAST MAN WITH A GUN
JUST NOT FAST ENOUGH

Cobb didn't like Dodge City. For that matter, he didn't like any of Kansas. He was of the firm belief that the prettiest little stream in the world was the Red River, the border between Texas and Indian Territory—as long as a fella was riding south. Riding north, which meant leaving Texas, the Red was ugly as sin.

But he was here to do a job, not to enjoy the trip. He reined the big paint horse toward the hitch rack in front of a sturdily constructed frame building. A sign hanging from the awning over the boardwalk proclaimed this to be the Dodge City Marshal's Office and Jail. Just the place Cobb was looking for.

He swung down from the saddle, looped the paint's reins around the rail, and stepped up onto the boardwalk. Passersby gave him nervous looks. A woman even stopped at the sight of him, turned around, and went back the way she had come rather than walk past him. Cobb suppressed a grin. He was a fearsome-looking creature, he supposed. At least here in Kansas, where life wasn't as rugged as it was in Texas.

Almost anywhere, Cobb would have been an impressive specimen of humanity. He topped six feet by a couple of inches, making him half a foot taller than most men, and his broad shoulders were evidence of the strength and power in his body. His weathered, rough-hewn face sported a week's worth of dark stubble. His thick dark hair was cropped off square in the back. He wore a faded red bib-front shirt, buckskin trousers, and high-topped black boots. A battered, broad-brimmed Stetson hung on the back of his neck by its chin strap. A cartridge belt was buckled around his hips, and an old, heavy Colt rode in the holster. The walnut grips on its butt were almost black from being handled so much over the years.

Cobb gave one of the skittish townies a nod and stepped over to the door of the marshal's office. He opened it and stepped inside. A man in a leather vest stood in a corner of the room beside a pot-bellied stove, pouring a cup of coffee from a dented black pot. He looked at Cobb and said, "Help you, mister?"

"You'd be the marshal of Dodge City?"

"That's right," the man said with a nod. He put the pot back on the stove and sipped from the cup in his hand. He was stocky, in late middle age, and had white hair.

"I know I look more like a desperado than a lawman," Cobb said as he reached into a pocket cunningly fashioned into the leather of the broad cartridge belt, "but you and me are fellow star packers, Marshal."

Cobb brought out a silver star set into a silver circle— the emblem of the Texas Rangers. He let the badge lay on his big palm for a moment as the marshal looked at it in surprise. Then he tucked it back into the pocket on the belt.

"Name's Cobb. I come for Dusty Logan."

"Dusty Logan?" The marshal's eyes narrowed. "You're too late. He's dead."

Now it was Cobb's turn to look surprised. "We got word in Austin that you were holding him here. My cap'n even sent in the papers so's we could extradite him all legal and proper-like."

The marshal shrugged and walked over to his paper-littered desk. "That's all well and good, Ranger Cobb." He pushed some papers aside and set down his coffee cup. "I'm sure I've got the extradition papers here somewhere. But no documents in the world can bring a man back to life once he's dead and in his grave."

"Damn," Cobb bit out. "What happened? I thought he was locked up here, safe and sound."

"He was." The marshal sat in a leather chair behind the desk and motioned Cobb toward a ladderback chair with a wicker bottom. Cobb reversed it and straddled it, not much liking the way it creaked under his weight. "I had to ride over to Hays a couple of weeks ago. Left my deputy in charge here. He was a good man, but not as good as I thought."

Cobb caught that ominous *was*.

"Logan tricked poor ol' Barstow, made him think he was real sick. When Barstow went into the cell, Logan got his hand on his gun and killed him. Then he stepped out here into the office, got his own guns, and went down the street to one of the saloons for a drink."

Cobb frowned. "He busted out of jail and then stopped for a drink?"

The marshal shrugged. "He knew I was out of town, knew that Barstow was the only other law in Dodge right then. I guess he figured it was safe enough. Nobody else around here was going to have the nerve to say boo to him, let alone try to stop him."

Cobb grunted and said, "Yeah, I noticed your citizens ain't the saltiest bunch in the world."

"Don't let them fool you," the marshal snapped. "Dodge City can be a mighty rough place most of the time. But everybody knew Logan. He cut a pretty wide swath since he rode in here six months ago. Killed eight men in that time, all of 'em in fair fights. I never had any charges to lock him up on until he got greedy and tried to rob a couple of cattle buyers. One of the gents tried to put up a fight. He wound up getting killed for his trouble, but he kept Logan occupied long enough for the other fella to bend a chair over his head and knock him out. What was Logan wanted for down in Texas, anyway?"

"Murder," Cobb said. "He shot a homesteader, pistol-whipped the man's wife, then burned their cabin down around them and their kids. Logan killed seven people that day, all because he thought the homesteader tried to get the better of him in a horse trade."

The marshal shook his head. "He was a mad dog, all

right. I figure it would have been only a matter of time until he did something like that up here. I never saw a fella with so much killing rage lurking right under the surface. We'd have hanged him here if the folks at the capital hadn't decided that Texas had a prior claim on him."

"Hydrophobia skunk's more like it," Cobb muttered. "You were sayin' about how Logan escaped and then stopped for a drink . . . ?"

"Yeah, he went into the Prairie Queen Saloon. People must've heard the shot when he gunned down Barstow, and when Logan walked into the saloon, everybody in there guessed what had happened. Art Brenham, the gent who owns the Prairie Queen, told Logan that nobody wanted any trouble with him." The marshal scratched his jaw. "Art was wrong."

Cobb tried not to sigh in frustration. Getting any useful information out of this local lawman was proving to be a lengthy, difficult chore. "What happened?"

"Logan started bullying people around, shoving them out of his way, insulting them. I figure he was trying to pick a fight. I think he wanted to kill somebody else before he left Dodge. Sort of a farewell gesture, you understand?"

Cobb understood, though such thinking really would make sense only to a cold-blooded killer like Dusty Logan.

"He knocked down a young fella name of Bardwell," the marshal continued. "Has a farm north of here. None of us knew much about him. He was wearing a gun that night, an old army pistol. He got up after Logan shoved him down and reached for his iron. Logan laughed and let Bardwell get his gun all the way out before he slapped leather. You ever seen Logan's guns?"

Cobb shook his head.

"Fancy, pearl-handled revolvers. Real shootist's guns. But they let Logan down that night. Both of 'em hung in their holsters for some reason. Slowed Logan down just enough for Bardwell to plug him. One shot, right in the heart. That was all it took." The marshal picked up his coffee, took a sip, and made a face. "Would you look at that? You got me talking so long my coffee went and got cold."

"Sorry," Cobb said. "I reckon you buried Logan?"

"Well, not me personal-like. But the town undertaker did. County paid for it. Planted him up there north of town on Boot Hill, along with all the other folks who've died of violence around here."

Cobb put his hands on the back of the chair he was straddling and pushed himself to his feet. "Reckon there's no reason for me to stay around here, then. Without a prisoner, I might as well start back to Texas."

"I'm sorry, Ranger. When I got those extradition papers, I sent a wire to your headquarters in Austin, letting them know that Logan was dead, but I reckon you'd already left and it was too late to call you back." The marshal stood up as well. "It's a long ride to Texas. You don't want to start back today. Let your horse rest overnight. And you can come to my house for supper. My missus is a mighty good cook, if I do say so myself."

Cobb thought about it for a second, then nodded. The paint was a good strong horse with plenty of sand, but Cobb had pushed the animal pretty hard on the ride up here to Kansas. The paint could use a good feed and a night of rest in a comfortable stable. And a home-cooked meal didn't sound too bad to Cobb, either.

"Much obliged, Marshal," he said.

"Least I can do, since I don't have Dusty Logan to send back to Texas with you."

The marshal gave Cobb directions to his house and told him where to find the best livery stable in town. Cobb wasn't quite ready to put his horse away, though. He wanted to take a ride up to Boot Hill and have a look at Logan's grave for himself. He could do that much, at least, to fulfill the mission that had brought him here.

He rode up the long, grassy hill toward the fenced-in area at the top of the slope. The gate was open. An old man was tending to one of the graves. Cobb swung down from the saddle and called to him, "Can you tell me where to find Dusty Logan's grave, old-timer?"

The caretaker snorted. "Old-timer, is it?" He pointed with the hoe he had been using to chop down weeds. "Logan's planted over there. Don't know why ever'body's so dang interested in him. He weren't nothin' but a cheap gunman, after all."

"Other folks come up here to look at his grave, do they?"

"Sometimes two or three a day. That boy Bardwell's been up here several times. 'Course, I reckon that's understandable, since it was him who put Logan where he is." The caretaker leaned on his hoe. "Still, it disturbs me a mite to see that boy standin' there by the grave with his hands on them fancy guns."

"What guns?" Cobb asked. The marshal had said that Bardwell killed Logan with an old army pistol.

"Logan's guns, o' course. Bardwell claimed 'em after he plugged that lowdown killer, and nobody wanted to argy with him. I reckon the whole town felt like a pair o' pearl-handled guns was a small price to pay for gettin' rid of a murderin' scoundrel like Logan."

Cobb's face was stonily impassive. "Thanks, old-timer."

"There you go again with that old-timer business! Why, I'll have you know—"

Cobb ignored the complaint and turned away. The caretaker snorted and went back to hoeing weeds as Cobb walked over to the grave where Dusty Logan was buried. He read the epitaph that had been burned into the cheap wooden headstone, then frowned as he thought about what the old man had told him.

Cobb hadn't really lied to the marshal, but he hadn't told the whole truth, either. The marshal had asked him if he'd ever seen Dusty Logan's guns. Cobb had said no, and that was true as far as it went. He did know something about those guns, though. Logan had taken them off one of the first men he'd killed, a notorious pistoleer named Hank Boston. Nobody had heard of Logan at the time, though the Rangers had discovered later that he'd already killed three people, including his own father, knifed in the gut when he discovered his son stealing from him. Logan and Boston had shot it out in Fort Worth, and the victorious Logan had taken that pair of pearl-handled Colts off Boston's still-bleeding body.

Boston's killing had been in a fair fight, as were Logan's numerous other killings until the day he slaughtered the homesteader and his family. He had fled from Texas then, knowing that the Rangers would come after him. He had probably thought he was safe enough in Kansas.

He'd been wrong about that, but in the end it didn't matter. The State of Texas would never take its vengeance on Dusty Logan. The kid called Bardwell had seen to that.

Cobb spat on the grave, turned around, and went to his horse. He mounted and rode back down the hill to Dodge.

The marshal's name was Seth Conway; his wife's name was Louise. And as promised, she was a good cook. She put a plate of chicken and dumplings in front of Cobb and looked on in approval as he ate. "You be sure and tell everybody back in Texas just how good that is, Mr. Cobb," she teased.

"Ma'am, you can rest assured I'll do just that," Cobb told her with a grin.

"I've heard that Texas is a mighty big place," Conway said from across the table. "Where do you hail from?"

"There's a Ranger post at a place northwest of Fort Worth called Veal Station. I work out of it most of the time. Was born not too far from there at a wide place in the road called O'Bar. But really, I go wherever the job takes me."

"Even all the way to Kansas."

Cobb nodded. "Yep."

"I'm sorry you won't have a prisoner to take back with you."

Cobb shrugged and said, "You're the one who lost the deputy, Marshal. Logan wound up getting what was coming to him, one way or the other." He looked at Mrs. Conway. "Sorry to be talkin' about such unpleasant things at the dinner table, ma'am."

"Oh, that's all right, Mr. Cobb. I'm a lawman's wife. I'm accustomed to hearing about the uglier side of life. I'm sure your wife is, too."

Cobb grinned. "Ain't got one of those. Reckon I haven't found the gal yet who'd put up with such an ugly cuss as me."

"Why, you're not the least bit ugly. You're just . . . distinctive."

"Yes, ma'am." Distinctive as all hell, Cobb thought.

After the pleasant supper, Cobb and Conway stepped out onto the front porch of the neat frame house where the lawman lived. Both men filled their pipes and puffed in silence for a few minutes. Finally, Cobb said, "I think I'll get a drink before I head back to the hotel and turn in."

"Wish I could offer you something, but Louise don't allow spirits in the house."

"That's all right, Marshal. You've done plenty." Cobb tapped the dottle from the bowl and tucked away the pipe in his shirt pocket. He put out his hand. "I'll be leavin' first thing in the morning. I'm much obliged for your hospitality."

"Be careful down there in Indian Territory," Conway said as he shook hands.

"Say good night to your missus for me, and thank her again for that fine meal."

Conway nodded. "Sure thing."

Cobb strolled the couple of blocks to Dodge City's main street. He had taken a room at one of the hotels, and he had noticed the Prairie Queen Saloon directly across the street from it. That was where Dusty Logan had met his violent end, and Cobb found himself wanting to have a look at the place. Besides, he had been telling the truth when he said he wanted a drink before he turned in.

The Prairie Queen occupied an entire block; a big, lucrative-looking enterprise. The entrance was on the corner of the building. Cobb pushed through the bat wings. The long bar was to the left, running down the side of the building. To the right were tables, and beyond them was the arched entrance to a gambling hall. Stairs in the back of the main room led up to a gallery that overlooked it. Behind that were small rooms where the women who worked here took the customers who wanted more than a drink.

Cobb wasn't interested in finding a soiled dove tonight. He just wanted a couple of shots of whiskey and then a good night's sleep before hitting the trail to Texas.

The kid at the bar, however, was looking for trouble. Cobb's instincts told him that at first sight.

The kid was slender, medium height, with light brown hair. His clothes and hat and boots looked new, and strapped around his waist was a cartridge belt with double holsters. A pair of pearl-handled Colt revolvers rode in those holsters.

Cobb knew without ever seeing them before that those were the guns of Dusty Logan, and of Hank Boston before him. That would make the kid Bardwell, who had killed Logan but probably should have died himself, if not for a stroke of pure luck.

"Yes, sir, folks just can't do enough for me now," Bardwell was saying loudly. "I walk down the street and people say there he goes, that's the fella who shot Dusty Logan. I go in the store, and the gent who owns the place says howdy do, Mr. Bardwell, what can we do for you, Mr. Bardwell, how's about you take this here new hat, Mr. Bardwell, no charge to you. Because you're the man who killed Dusty Logan."

While Bardwell was talking, one of the three drink jugglers behind the bar had refilled the empty glass in front of him. Bardwell lifted it to his mouth and tossed back the whiskey. He was already very drunk, Cobb judged, so this pattern had probably been going on for a while. Bardwell had a group of admirers clustered around him, and he was enjoying showing off for them.

Not everybody in the saloon was impressed with Bardwell, however, nor happy to listen to his drunken boasting. Cobb saw several hard, resentful glances thrown Bardwell's way. It didn't take long for a fella to wear out his notoriety. The ones who fancied themselves shootists seldom ever understood that.

Cobb went to the other end of the bar, well away from Bardwell. He ordered whiskey and added, "Not the house brand. Something better than that."

"Our house brand is just as good as any of the stuff with fancy labels on it, mister," the bartender said. "Mr. Brenham don't serve any of that panther piss in here."

Cobb shrugged. "I'll take a chance, then, but you'd better not be lyin' to me."

The bartender looked resentful. He filled a glass and shoved it across the bar. Cobb picked it up, sampled the whiskey, licked his lips, and grinned. "Damned if you weren't tellin' the truth. This is fine."

The bartender relaxed and returned the grin. "Told you so."

Cobb leaned his head toward Bardwell. "That kid sounds like he's put away quite a bit."

"He's earned the right to be loud. He's the man who shot Dusty Logan. Beat him to the draw, right there almost where you're standing."

"That so? The way I heard it, Logan's guns hung on their holsters, or something like that."

"Well . . ." The bartender spread his hands. "I was here that night and saw the whole thing. Logan had some bad luck all right, but that's just part of the game when you do pistol work. Still . . ." He leaned closer to Cobb and said in a quieter voice, "I saw the look on Bardwell's face when he grabbed iron. He figured he was about to die. No doubt of it in his mind. Nobody in the place was more shocked when he drilled Logan than Bardwell himself. Unless it was Logan. He looked mighty damned surprised, too." The bartender chuckled.

"The kid been comin' in here a lot since then?"

"Sure, nearly every night. Wearing those fancy guns, telling the story of how it happened over and over. It gets a mite tiresome, I guess, but, well, like I said, he earned the right to brag."

Cobb drank the rest of his whiskey, ordered another. The bartender drifted off down the bar after pouring it. Cobb leaned his elbows on the hardwood and tried to ignore the commotion as Bardwell kept boasting and reliving the killing of Dusty Logan.

Cobb succeeded in ignoring the racket, but one of the men who had been in the saloon longer finally couldn't stand it anymore. The man, who had the look of a rancher, slammed an empty beer mug on the table where he was sitting with friends. One of the others tried to grab his sleeve as he stood up, but the rancher shrugged him off.

"Bardwell! Don't you think you've told that story often enough tonight?"

Bardwell stiffened and turned slowly away from the bar. The men around him stepped back, giving him room as the place got quiet. Bardwell glared at the rancher and said, "Would you be talkin' to me?"

"You know damn well who I'm talking to. If I hadn't looked the other way every time you slaughtered one of my beeves last winter, you'd have starved to death on that pissant little farm of yours. I know you, Bardwell, and I'm tired of listenin' to you."

Bardwell paled under the lash of the hard words. "Are you calling me a rustler, Devers?"

"No, I never begrudged you the beef. But I don't like listening to you playing the big man just because you got lucky and Logan didn't blow a hole through you."

"Logan's the one with the hole blowed through him! I can do it again, too. If you don't believe me, just you try it, Devers. You reach for that gun on your hip. If you got the guts."

The cattleman's companions scattered. They had tried to stop him from losing his temper with Bardwell, but it was too late now. Bardwell knew it. So did Devers.

And so did Cobb.

He turned toward the confrontation, not sure if he ought to try to stop it or not. He didn't have the chance. Devers wrapped his fingers around the butt of his gun and jerked it from the holster.

Bardwell's hands were a blur as he flipped out both of the pearl-handled revolvers. Flame geysered from their barrels, and the four shots he fired in little more than a heartbeat, two from each gun, blended together in a roll of thunder. Devers rocked back as the slugs drove into his body. His gun was out of the holster but still pointing toward the floor. It slipped from his fingers and thudded to the sawdust-covered planks. Devers followed the gun a second later, pitching forward onto his face.

Cobb looked at Bardwell. The kid's mouth was stretched in an ugly grin. He holstered the guns and turned back to the bar as if nothing had happened. "My glass is empty," he said to the bartender, the words echoing a little in the stunned silence that followed the gunplay.

Cobb's glass was empty, too, but he didn't want it refilled. He just wanted to get out of the Prairie Queen Saloon, out of Kansas, and back home to Texas.

But he couldn't bring himself to go just yet, and in the morning he found himself once again in the office of Seth Conway.

"Hard to believe," Conway said with a mournful shaking of his head. "I've known Matt Devers for a long time. He had a little bit of a temper sometimes, but he was a good man. And from what I've heard, Bardwell gunned him down like he was nothing."

"That's pretty much the way it was," Cobb agreed. "I could tell the kid was hoping somebody would get proddy. Should've stepped in sooner to put a stop to it."

"It wasn't your job to do that."

"I didn't know the kid would be that fast, either. Was he like that when he pulled on Logan?"

Again Conway shook his head. "Nope. Everyone who saw it says that Bardwell was slow as molasses on the draw, that Logan was just standing there laughing at him. Hell, the kid's a farmer, not a gunman. Normally, Logan could've waited like that and still put a couple of bullets in him before Bardwell got his gun leveled. It was just bad luck that got him killed."

Bad luck, Cobb thought. He was starting to wonder.

"How'd Bardwell get so fast between then and now?" Cobb said aloud.

"I sure don't have any explanation for it, unless he's been out there on his farm practicing with those six-guns ever since he took them off Logan."

Cobb had thought of that, too. Long hours of practice could certainly improve a man's speed and accuracy with a gun, but what he had seen in the Prairie Queen the night before went beyond that. He said, "I think I'll pay a visit to Bardwell. Can you tell me how to find his place?"

Conway frowned. "Sure, but I ain't so certain that's a good idea. What are you going to do? You can't arrest him for shooting Devers, because this ain't your jurisdiction, and I can't arrest him because everybody in that saloon saw Matt reach for his gun first. Folks are pretty upset about this killing, but there's nothing anybody can do about it."

"I'm not aiming to arrest anybody. I just want to talk to him."

"No law against that, either," the marshal said with a shrug. "And if I don't tell you where to find him, blamed near anybody on the street can. So I might as well."

He gave Cobb directions to Bardwell's farm, several miles north of Dodge City. Cobb nodded his thanks, then walked down the street to the livery stable to get his horse.

Bardwell's place was a typical hardscrabble homestead, Cobb saw when he rode up to the sod shanty an hour later. There was no barn, just a lean-to shed where a mule and a scrawny milk cow stood out of the ceaseless plains wind. A few chickens scratched in the yard between the shed and the soddy. Bardwell had managed to plow up quite a bit of ground, but the crops looked like they hadn't been tended in a while. It was hard enough to make a go of a place like this without neglecting it. Cobb didn't figure Bardwell would last.

He didn't see the young man around anywhere, so he reined up in front of the soddy and called, "Hello, the house! Anybody home?"

A minute later, the door that hung on sagging leather hinges swung back, and a bleary-eyed Bardwell peered out at Cobb over the double barrels of a shotgun. "What the hell do you want?" he asked, misery in his voice.

"Just some talk," Cobb said. "Mind if I get down?"

"Talk? This early in the mornin'?"

Most farmers would have been up and working for a couple of hours by now, Cobb thought. Bardwell was suffering from a bad hangover. He'd be lucky to get any work done today.

"Name's Cobb. I saw you in town last night, in the Prairie Queen."

"You ain't one of Devers's friends, are you, lookin' to even the score? He drew first, damn it. If you want trouble, you come to the right place." Bardwell lifted the greener.

Cobb held out a hand toward him. "Take it easy. I never saw Devers before last night, or you, either, for that matter. I'm a Texas Ranger."

Bardwell blinked in surprise. "A Ranger? What're you doin' way up here?"

"I came to fetch Dusty Logan back to Texas to stand trial for his crimes there."

Understanding dawned on Bardwell's haggard face, and he began to laugh. "Well, you're just pure-dee out of luck, ain't you, mister? Logan's dead. I ought to know, because I'm the one who killed him."

"I know. I heard all about it from the marshal, and from you last night in the Prairie Queen."

"You ain't sayin' I broke any Texas law by shootin' that son of a bitch, are you?"

Cobb shook his head. "Nope. Nobody disputes that it was a fair fight. I came out here to see you about Logan's guns . . . which I notice you ain't wearin'."

Bardwell's face tightened, and once again he made a menacing gesture with the shotgun. "Them pistols is mine now," he declared. "I claimed 'em fair and square after I killed Logan."

"Wouldn't be of a mind to sell 'em, would you? Before Logan had them, they belonged to a man named Hank Boston, a pretty famous gunman down where I come from. If I could take 'em back to Ranger headquarters with me, that'd be the proof I need to close the books on Logan."

That was a bald-faced lie. The word of Marshal Conway, plus the grave Cobb had seen with his own eyes, was enough evidence of Logan's death to satisfy the authorities back in Texas. But something was gnawing on Cobb's insides, and he didn't want to leave those guns with Bardwell.

"Give up those guns?" the young farmer said. "Hell, no. They ain't for sale, and you got no right to take them from me, either. You may be a lawman in Texas, but you ain't nothin' up here in Kansas."

Cobb's jaw clenched. "I'll give you a good price for them."

Bardwell gave an ugly laugh. "You can't fool me, mister. You just want those guns for yourself. Well, you can't have 'em, you hear me? You can't!" The young man's voice rose, trembling with emotion. "Those guns are with me now! I take care of them, and they take care of me! Logan didn't know what he had, the stupid bastard. He never listened, never understood." Bardwell snapped the butt of the shotgun to his shoulder. The double barrels shook a little as he screamed at Cobb, "Get out of here! Get off my place! Leave us alone!"

Cobb started backing the paint away. Backing down from any man was like sand in his craw, but he couldn't outdraw a cocked and leveled greener. Nor could he make Bardwell listen to reason. Not now. It was too late for that.

"I'm goin'," he said. "But you best be careful, Bardwell. Sometimes the ones you think are your best friends really ain't."

Bardwell frowned over the barrels of the shotgun. "Huh? What the hell you mean by that?"

But Cobb didn't answer. He just turned his horse around and rode away.

"I told you, I can't arrest him," Marshal Conway said. "He ain't broken any laws."

"Then you're just going to have more and more trouble from him, until he finally does something bad enough."

The marshal stared across the desk at Cobb. "What makes you think that?"

Cobb started pacing back and forth in the marshal's small office, his nerves too taut to let him stay still. "Down in Texas the Rangers got a book on all the outlaws and shootists we have to deal with. Some call it the Dead Book, others the Doomsday Book. But when I got word that I was comin' up here to fetch Logan, I looked him up in the book and saw what all he'd done. He was bad enough startin' out, but he got a lot worse once he killed Hank Boston and took Boston's guns. Just out of curiosity, I checked to see what was wrote down about Boston. He was just a petty crook until he suddenly started killing folks. The first one was a badman named Joad Stillwater. I'm wonderin' if Boston took those guns off Stillwater. The records in the book didn't say anything about it, but I'm sure wonderin'."

Conway stared at him for a moment, then placed his hands flat on the desk and said, "Wait just a damned minute, Cobb. Are you saying that you think those guns are causing all the killing they've done?"

"I've seen some mighty odd things in my time as a Ranger," Cobb said slowly.

"That ain't odd, that's crazy!"

Cobb's broad shoulders rose and fell in a shrug. "Call it what you want. I saw Bardwell's draw last night. He was faster than he had any right to be."

"I just don't believe it. I can't believe it."

"Then I reckon I can't make you believe it. You'll just have to see for yourself."

"What I'll do is have a talk with Bardwell next time he comes into town and warn him not to cause any more trouble. He's got too full of himself lately, that's all, but he's not a cold-blooded killer like Logan. You're wrong about him, Cobb."

"I hope so," Cobb said.

But he didn't believe for a second that he was.

He argued with himself, thinking that he ought to just ride out like he'd intended to. Conway was a good lawman; he could deal with whatever happened. Cobb just about had himself convinced. He went into one of Dodge's numerous general stores to pick up some supplies for the trip.

When he came out a short time later, he looked down the street and saw Conway mounting up. The marshal turned his horse to the north.

Toward Bardwell's farm.

Cobb stood there staring after Conway, a muscle working in his beard-stubbled jaw. Conway had said that he would have a talk with Bardwell the next time Bardwell came to town. Could be the marshal had decided not to wait that long. Finally, Cobb took a deep breath, blew it out in a sigh, and said, "Son of a bitch." He stepped down from the boardwalk, slung the bag of supplies over his saddle, and jerked the paint's reins loose from the hitch rail. A minute later he was riding out of Dodge City in the same direction Conway had taken.

Conway was moving fast. He must be one of those fellas who gets after it once he makes up his mind, Cobb thought. A good lawman did his best to head off trouble.

He didn't just sit around waiting for it to happen.

Cobb spotted Conway up ahead of him a few minutes before the marshal reached Bardwell's homestead. Cobb's eyesight was keen and the ground was flat, so he had no trouble seeing Conway draw rein in front of the soddy. A second later, Bardwell stepped out of the door. The young man was dressed in his new clothes, obviously ready to ride into town.

And the cartridge belt with the pearl-handled Colts riding in the double holsters was strapped around his hips.

Cobb urged the paint into a run. He could tell that Conway and Bardwell were talking. Bardwell gestured angrily. Conway stayed on his horse, blocky and stubborn. Both men looked toward Cobb in surprise as they heard the hoofbeats of the Ranger's horse.

Cobb reined in about fifty feet short of Bardwell and Conway, off to the side a little so that he had a good view of both of them, especially Bardwell. Not taking any chances, as soon as the paint had stopped, Cobb reached under his right leg and shucked the Winchester from the saddle boot. He levered a cartridge into the chamber.

"Cobb, what the hell are you doing?" Marshal Conway called to him. "This ain't any of your business. You're out of your bailiwick."

"You're here because of what I told you, Marshal," Cobb replied.

"I'm here to get those guns from Bardwell until he settles down and gets it into his head that I won't tolerate any more killing."

At the mention of taking his guns, Bardwell suddenly stepped back. His hands hooked into claws over the butts of the Colts. "The hell you will!" he shouted at Conway. "Nobody takes my guns!"

"They're Logan's guns," Cobb said, edging the horse a little closer. "Before that they were Hank Boston's, and before that I figure they belonged to a man named Stillwater. No way of knowing who had them before Stillwater. But I'm sure of one thing, Bardwell: all those men are dead now."

Bardwell's face was an ugly, twisted thing. "They didn't know! They didn't understand!"

"Didn't understand what?" Cobb said.

Bardwell's voice shook. "I hear 'em talkin' to me. They call out to me, all soft and gentle like a woman. They're mine now, and they'll always be mine, as long as I give 'em what they need."

Conway was staring at the young homesteader. "Are you talkin' about killin', Bardwell?"

"Everything's got a purpose in life," Bardwell said. "Without that purpose, there's no reason. No reason for anything. Might as well be dead. Might as well not ever have been born."

Cobb's horse moved a step to the side, answering the directions of his knees pressing into its flanks. "Take the guns off now while you still can, Bardwell," he said. "You can't take both of us, not even with help. Take the guns off. You know you've got to."

Bardwell shook all over, like a leaf in a strong wind, but then suddenly he stiffened, as if all his blood had frozen in his veins. "I don't have to do anything I don't want to," he said, his lips curling into a snarl. "I'm the man who killed Dusty Logan."

105

His hands stabbed down at the pearl-inlaid handles of the Colts.

The butt of the Winchester kicked against Cobb's shoulder as he fired. The crack of the rifle blended with the involuntary cry that came from Conway's mouth. Bardwell was slammed back against the sod wall of the shanty as the Ranger's bullet smashed into him. His arms flung wide. The revolvers had leaped into his hands, but now they slid free of his fingers, tumbling unfired through the air and then bouncing along the hard ground.

Bardwell fell facedown. One hand reached out, the fingers scrabbling in the dirt as if searching desperately for something, and then the hand relaxed and lay still.

Slowly, Cobb lowered the Winchester.

Conway's face was drained of blood. He turned his head toward Cobb and said, "I saw his eyes. He was going to kill me."

"I reckon." Cobb slid the rifle back in the boot.

"You saved my life."

"Wish there had been some other way." Cobb swung down from the saddle and walked over to pick up the fallen guns. The pearl handles were warm in his hands, like he was holding something alive. A shudder went through him. As quickly as he could, he shoved them back into the holsters where they had come from. He stepped away from Bardwell's body and dragged the back of his hand across his mouth.

"See that they're buried with him," he said in a harsh voice.

"Yeah." Conway swallowed. "I'll sure do that. You can damn well count on it."

Cobb made one more visit to Boot Hill before he left Dodge City. He visited one fresh grave, and one that was older but still recent. He thought about the epitaph on Dusty Logan's headstone and figured that it ought to be changed to agree with what was written on Bardwell's:

He who lives by the guns, dies by the guns.

Then he rode away from there, hoping that during the long trip back to Texas he could forget the sound of distant voices and the song they sang.

. . . GRAVEDIGGER . . .

Ain't that somethin'? Now ya can see why I love tellin' that story. Yes, sir, them guns is buried right in there with Bardwell, and I'll tell ya a secret. When I had them guns in my hand I thought twice about actually buryin' them there. Yes, I did. I figured I could take 'em home with me and hide 'em and nobody'd be the wiser. But then I started thinkin' about what them guns did, and in the end I jest dropped 'em in there right on top of old Bardwell and buried 'em both.

'Cause guns, they done caused me enough trouble in my life without me lookin' for more . . . what's that? Well, that's right nice of ya ta ask to know some more about me, but . . . hey, there's a couple of fellas down there look like they might be comin' on up the hill. Mebbe this is the help I been waitin' for—but no. Shoot! They's a-walkin' on by, ain't they?

What's that? Oh, yeah, you asked about me. Well, I done tol' ya I come here in 'seventy-four, jest in time to bury ol' Dusty there . . . hey, I got another grave right over here I dug the very next year. If'n you think that story about Lon and Henrietta Beatty was sad this one'll really get ya ta ballin'.

It's over here—yes, ma'am, I'll get ta tellin' ya about myself, nice of ya to ask and all, but this here story, this is somethin' you—bein' a lady and all—will jest love, 'cause this here is a love story. Yes, ma'am—well, I don't know that you'd call it a happy story. Ain't many stories here on Boot Hill got happy endings, I can tell ya that. Fact is, even though I was here when it happened a lot of this story was told ta me by a little girl, so mebbe when you hear it you'll be able ta judge for yourself what kinda ending it's got.

I'm gonna be tellin' ya this story, but if'n you listen real hard you might jest hear the voice of that little girl what told parts of it ta me . . .

HARD GROUND

L. J. WASHBURN

Timothy Alexander McCabe
Beloved son
March 27, 1860–June 14, 1875
Never to be forgotten

If my brother Tim hadn't been in the saloon, he wouldn't have gotten shot. If Tim hadn't gotten shot, then none of the things that happened after that would have happened. So you could say he was to blame for all of it, in a way.

But Mama never said that. She may have thought it, but I never heard the words cross her lips.

"You stay out of that place," she told him as she brought the wagon to a stop in front of the mercantile emporium. "As soon as we load up the supplies we need, we'll be on our way back out to the farm."

Tim looked at the big building sitting catty-corner across the broad, dusty street. "Yes'm," he said, but I could tell he was thinking about all the dark and shadowy things he could find in there, like whiskey and card games and sporting women. From what I've seen of life, it's awfully hard for fifteen-year-old boys to think about anything else, though I don't know that for certain since I've never been a fifteen-year-old boy.

The three of us climbed down from the wagon and went into the store. It was one of my favorite places in the world. High-ceilinged and cool even on the hottest summer day, like a cave; it was even dim inside like a cave. Rows of wooden shelves heaped with treasures: brightly-colored yard goods, buttons, pins, needles, hammers, chisels, bags of flour and sugar, boxes of seed and boxes of nails, buckets, brushes . . . I felt I could spend a whole day in there and never see it all. Hoes and spades and picks and shovels hung from nails on the walls like holy talismans to sodbusters like us.

And in the back, next to the long counter where the owner and his clerks held court, the glass-fronted case that contained sweet little bits of heaven. I tried to stay with Mama as she talked to Mr. Harwell, the owner, but the candy case drew me to it like a lodestone draws iron.

One of the clerks came over to stand behind the case. He was young and his name was Jonas and, my gosh, to my twelve-year-old eyes he was as handsome a fella as ever came down the pike. He smiled at me and said, "Can I get you something, missy?"

Before I could answer, Mama looked over her shoulder and said, "Caroline, come away from there. You know we can't afford anything like that."

Mama went back to talking to Mr. Harwell, and Jonas leaned toward me and whispered, "Look in the box of supplies when you get home. I'll slip a candy in there for you."

Thank you, I mouthed at him, then went to stand beside Mama as she finished giving her order. Mr. Harwell jotted it all down on a scrap of butcher paper, using a stub of a pencil he kept licking between words. I glanced around for Tim.

He was gone.

Wouldn't you just know it, I thought. Mama gets on me for drifting over to the candy case, but Tim takes off for the tall and uncut and she doesn't even notice!

I knew where he was. I was willing to bet just about anything that he was standing in the door of the saloon, up on tippy-toes so's he could peek over the top of the bat wings and get himself an eyeful of all the sinful goings on in there. If he was feeling really brave, he might go inside for a minute before one of the men who worked there noticed him and made him leave because he was too young. It had happened before like that.

"Caroline, where's your brother?"

So she had noticed Tim was gone, after all. "I don't know," I said, even though I was convinced I did know.

Mama sighed. She knew, too. "Blast that boy," she muttered. "Try to raise 'em up right, and still they go astray."

Mr. Harwell nodded and said, "Yes, ma'am, children are a trial, sure enough. I know. I've got seven of my own."

Mama just had me and Tim. I think she would've liked to have a bigger family, but after Papa died, that was pretty much the end of that. Now when I look at old photographs of my mother, I can see that she was a handsome enough

111

woman, but she had her hands full with the farm and us two kids. She didn't have time for any suitors.

She looked at me and said, "Go see if you can find him while Mr. Harwell and Jonas get our order packed."

"Yes'm," I said. I stole one more quick glance at Jonas—my, he was easy on the eyes!—and then scampered out of the emporium.

Wasn't any point in looking up and down the street for Tim when I knew where he was. I started to cross toward the saloon, studying the fancy curlicue patterns painted on the big windows as I drew closer.

I was just about to step up on the boardwalk when I heard the loud, angry voices coming from inside. "I saw what you done!" one of them yelled. "You dealt that card off the bottom of the deck!"

"That's a damned lie!" the other voice shouted in reply.

I might've been just twelve years old, and female to boot, but I knew what men considered fightin' words, and if I'd ever heard any, those were it. A little tingle of fear went through me, both because violence was about to break out and because I was worried Mama might find out I'd heard the word "damned" and decide she needed to wash my mouth out with soap even though I'd only heard it, not said it. Just in case I might be tempted to say it someday, you understand.

But mostly I was worried because I was sure Tim was in there in the saloon. He wasn't on the boardwalk, sneaking a look inside, and there was nowhere else in Dodge City that had a lure so strong as to entice him to risk Mama's wrath. I figured I couldn't see well enough through the windows, since they were so gaudily painted, so while the shouts were still echoing inside the saloon, I went down on hands and knees, crawled across the boardwalk, and stuck my head under the bat wings to look for my brother.

My eyes took it all in: the men hurrying to get out of the way—cowboys, gamblers, freighters, trappers, prospectors, a couple of bartenders with slicked-down hair—and the women in their short, spangled dresses letting out little screams and diving for cover; the two men erupting out of their chairs on opposite sides of a green-covered table littered with playing cards and money, their hands reaching for the guns they wore; and a couple of steps away, backed against the wall just inside the door, my brother Tim.

He must have seen me from the corner of his eye. He half-turned and took a step toward me, saying, "Caroline, get out of—"

Then the heavens opened up in the loudest peal of thunder I'd ever heard.

Only it wasn't thunder, of course. It was gunfire. One of the men had his back to the door while the other was facing it. The man facing the door got off the first shot, but no sooner had flame burst from the muzzle of his gun than a mere flick of time later the other man fired as well, and I saw the shoulder of the first man jerk. He was already squeezing off his second shot. The bullet went past the man who had his back to the door, who was already crumpling up and falling forward across the table. That bullet sailed right on across the room and struck my brother, Timothy Alexander McCabe, in the side of the head, just behind the right temple. The impact knocked him against the bat wings, and he fell through them to sprawl on the boardwalk, landing half on top of me. A single drop of blood from the

wound fell on the back of my hand. I looked at it and started
to scream. I couldn't bring myself to look at Tim's head.

All of that happened in a lot less time than it takes to
tell it. I buried my head in my arms and kept screaming.
Heavy footsteps thumped around me. I heard men's voices.

"Good Lord, what happened?"

"Boy never had a chance. Poor son of a bitch."

"What about the little girl? Was she hit, too?"

Hands touched me and I screamed and shook and
fought. I was jerked upright.

"Seems to be all right."

"Boy never had a chance," one of the men said again.

More footsteps. Something was different about them. I
looked up and saw him towering over me. Long black coat,
broad-brimmed black hat, the left hand raised and crossed
over the body to clutch the right shoulder. Tiny lines of blood
trickled between his fingers and ran down the back of his
hand.

"What happened?" he said.

"Your second shot hit that young fella, Crofton."

"I never meant for it to. Bastard winged me just as I
pulled the trigger."

"Yeah, it weren't your fault. Just a damned shame,
that's all."

That's all? My brother was dead, his brains and blood
leaking from his head onto the boardwalk—I didn't see that
with my own eyes, you understand, but I *know* that's what
happened and I've seen it in my mind's eye so many, many
times since—and all they could say was that it was a damned
shame? I stopped screaming and wanted to hit them.

Then I heard my mother say, "Caroline? Caroline! *Tim! Oh, God, nooooo . . .*"

She pulled me away from the men gathered in the entrance of the saloon and folded me in her arms. I pushed my face against the front of her dress and sobbed.

"The little girl ain't hurt, ma'am, but the boy . . . Well, we're mighty sorry . . ."

Mama started rocking back and forth as she held me tight against her, and I felt her tears falling on top of my head like drops of rain.

"It was just a accident, that's all it was . . ."

Then the deep voice of the man called Crofton, saying, "Madam, I can't tell you how sorry I am. I deeply regret this."

"You?" she said. "You did this? You kill my son, and then you stand there and say you're sorry, it was only an accident?" Mama clutched me even tighter as she spoke.

"If there's anything I can do . . ."

"You can die and burn in hell."

I fainted then. Whether it was from the shock of seeing my brother killed, or from hearing Mama say what she said, I couldn't tell you. Even now, I couldn't tell you.

Tim was buried in the little cemetery on Boot Hill, at the top of a long grassy rise just outside town. Since the county had to pay for it because we didn't have any money, we didn't have any choice in the matter.

Mama didn't like it. She said a soul couldn't properly go to its eternal reward when the body it had inhabited was lying there surrounded by such immorality. It was true that most of the folks buried on Boot Hill had been gunmen, thieves, gamblers, murderers, and just all-around sinful people when they were alive. It seemed to me, though, that once they were dead, things like that didn't matter so much, and besides, I liked going up there to visit Tim's grave. For all the violence that had swelled the population of Boot Hill, the place itself was mighty peaceful when the sun was shining warmly and the wind swept across the prairie and stirred the grass. Going there soothed my soul more than once, let me tell you.

Only a few people came to the service, neighbors of ours mostly, and people we knew from church. When the preacher was finished saying the words, Mama's arm tightened around my shoulders and she turned me away from the grave. I could still hear the crunching sound as shovels bit into the pile of dirt beside the hole in the ground, and the rattle and thud of dirt hitting my brother's coffin.

That was when we saw him, standing beside his horse at the bottom of the slope. He had his hat in his left hand, since his right arm was supported by a sling made of black silk. His right shoulder looked bulky because of the bandages under his coat and shirt. His long brown hair moved around his head in the ceaseless breeze.

He put on his hat and climbed onto the horse, his movements awkward because of the injury. Then he rode away before we could come down the hill. That was the smart thing to do. The way Mama's fingers were digging into my arm, I knew she was ready to chew nails and spit bullets.

The man's name was Lee Crofton. He was a gambler and gunman and was reputed to have killed several men in Colorado and Wyoming, not counting Indians. He hadn't been around Dodge for very long when he killed my brother. I had heard talk that he would be moving on as soon as his shoulder healed enough. No charges had been brought against him by the law for either of the killings, since one had been in a fair fight and the other an accident, but still, as some put it, the climate in this neck of the woods wasn't all that healthy for him anymore.

Mama and I got in the wagon and drove home. The preacher and his wife offered to come with us, to "make sure we got there all right," as the preacher's wife said, but Mama told them no, we were fine. We weren't, but she would never admit otherwise. I missed Tim something fierce, like somebody had reached inside me and yanked out something that I really needed to live, but I was also practical enough to wonder how we were going to make a go of the farm without him around to help. There was only so much a woman and a little girl could do.

When we got home, Mama said for me to change out of my Sunday clothes. The vegetable patch needed to be hoed. I'd just pulled one of my flour-sack dresses over my head and Mama was still in her black church dress when we heard the horse come up outside.

Mama went to the door and opened it, then stood absolutely still for a long moment before she turned her head and said to me, "You stay in here, Caroline. Don't you come outside."

Then she reached over and picked up the old single-shot rifle that had belonged to my father. We kept it propped beside the door. She pulled back the hammer as she stepped outside. "What do you want?" she asked.

The same deep voice I'd heard that day on the boardwalk outside the saloon said, "I just thought I'd try once more to offer my condolences, Mrs. McCabe. It would be a pure relief to me if you'd accept my apology."

"I don't want your sympathy or your apology. Get off my land."

"I understand how you feel—" Lee Crofton said.

"No, you don't. You don't have the slightest idea how I feel." Mama lifted the rifle a little. "Get off my land, or I swear I'll shoot you."

I heard the long sigh that came from Mr. Crofton. "Yes, ma'am, I'm going. But if there's ever anything I can do . . ."

"I already told you what you can do."

Die and burn in hell. That was what she'd said to him in town that day. I would never forget it.

I had stood rooted to the spot while they were talking, but as I heard the horse start walking away, I hurried to the window and peered out. I saw Mr. Crofton's back as he sat stiffly in the saddle and rode away from our cabin. There was something sad about him. I could tell that even without seeing his face.

"Caroline, get away from that window," Mama said to me as she came inside and laid the rifle on the table.

I summoned up my courage and said, "Mama, it sounded to me like he's really sorry."

Her face was like stone as she looked at me and said, "Sometimes sorry just doesn't matter, Caroline. Some things can't be forgiven."

I thought about the way my brother Tim used to throw me in the air and catch me and tickle me when I was little, and about the way I felt when I laughed and heard him laugh, too, and I knew she was right.

We didn't see Mr. Crofton again for three weeks. I figured he had left Dodge City by then. But one morning as Mama and I left the cabin to get to work in the fields, she stopped short and said, "What in the world?"

He was out in the field we'd been trying to get ready for some winter wheat. He had taken off his long black coat and his vest and rolled up the sleeves of his white shirt. His broad-brimmed black hat was still on his head. He had hitched the mule to the plow and was walking along behind it, wrestling the plow through the ground. When he reached the end of the row and turned toward us, we saw that he still wore his black string tie.

Mama turned around and started back into the house. She reached for the rifle, then stopped and shook her head. I guess she figured she wouldn't need it. She stalked out toward the field instead, and since she hadn't told me to stay at the house, I went with her.

He took hold of the reins attached to the mule's harness and pulled back. The mule stopped. Mama walked to within twenty feet of him and said, "Mr. Crofton, you are not welcome on this farm. You know that. What are you doing here?"

He took off his hat and sleeved sweat from his forehead. Summer days were hot, even this early in the morning. "Just trying to lend a hand. My shoulder's better now."

Tim's wound would never heal, I thought. He would never be better.

"I don't want your help," Mama said. "I don't need your help."

Mr. Crofton waved a hand at the fields. "No offense, ma'am, but how do you intend to work this place by yourself? It's too much work for one woman."

"Caroline will help me."

He looked at me and surprised me by smiling. "She looks like a right smart worker, all right, but she's still a little girl, Mrs. McCabe."

The look he gave me made me want to smile back at him, but I didn't. I couldn't. He had killed my brother.

"We don't need any help," Mama said again. "I'll thank you to get on your horse and leave."

Mr. Crofton looked at her for a long time and didn't say anything. Then he shook his head and said, "No, ma'am. I'm afraid you'll have to shoot me to get rid of me."

"Don't think I won't! And no one will blame me, either."

"No, ma'am, I don't suppose they will."

And with that, he flapped the reins against the bony back of the mule and got it moving again. He gripped the plow handles and guided the blade through the dirt, not looking at us anymore.

"Oh!" Mama said. "Caroline, go get the gun." I hesitated, and she repeated, "Go get the gun!"

I went and fetched the rifle from the cabin. My legs wanted to run, but I made them walk instead. I had watched Tim use the rifle to hunt rabbits and prairie hens, and I remembered him telling me how you always had to be careful when you were carrying a gun.

Mr. Crofton was still plowing, still ignoring us. Mama took the rifle from me and turned toward him. She lifted the rifle but didn't really point it at him, just stared at him instead. He acted like we weren't even there, calling out softly to the mule every now and then to keep it moving. After a while, Mama blew her breath out through her tightly clenched teeth and lowered the rifle. "Stubborn fool," she muttered as she turned away from the field. She walked back to the house, carrying the rifle, and I followed her.

But I looked back over my shoulder a couple of times at Mr. Crofton as he plowed the hard ground.

He didn't come every day. I guess he had things he had to do in town. But three or four times a week, he was there when we got up in the morning, already working. He plowed the fields, he tightened the poles on the corral, he weeded the garden, he repaired the sod roof on the barn. And he always wore his hat and his string tie.

No gun, though. I realized after a couple of times he didn't have his gun belt on. I'm not sure he even brought it with him. For all I knew, he had coiled it up and left it wherever he stayed in town.

Mama didn't talk to him again for a long time. Whatever Mr. Crofton was doing, she found chores for herself and me where we wouldn't be anywhere near him, wouldn't have to see him or talk to him. During those weeks, I wrestled mightily with my own feelings, like Jacob wrestling with the angel of the Lord. Sometimes I hated Mr. Crofton with a hate that flowed through me like a deep, powerful river. He had taken my beloved brother from me, and in my darkest moments, I wished he was dead, too. It would serve him right for what he had done.

But at other times I reminded myself that Tim's death really had been an accident. Mr. Crofton had never meant to hurt him. And the other man had drawn first. Everybody in the saloon had seen that. If Mr. Crofton hadn't defended himself, he would have been shot down in cold blood.

By helping us on the farm, he was trying to make amends for what he had done. He knew he wasn't going to get Mama or me to forgive him, but at least he was trying to pay us back as best he could for what he had taken from us.

The trouble was, good intentions or not, accident or not, he couldn't bring Tim back to us. He couldn't settle the score. Not if he plowed a hundred fields or repaired a thousand corrals. He just couldn't fix what he had broken.

But as the weeks passed, I didn't hate him as much, or as often. I couldn't help it. The hate just wasn't there like it had been before.

The hottest day of the summer, he was there, plowing again, and even at a distance you could tell his shirt was soaked with sweat. Around the middle of the afternoon, after she had been glaring at him all day, Mama drew a bucket of water from the well, put a dipper in it, and handed the bucket to me. "Take this out to him," she said. "But don't you talk to him. Not a word, you hear me?"

I nodded and carried the bucket out into the field. Mr. Crofton stopped plowing when he saw me coming. When I got there, I held the bucket out to him, and he took it.

"Thank you, missy. Caroline, isn't it? Isn't that your name?"

I didn't say anything.

A smile tugged at the corners of his mouth. "Oh, I see. She told you not to talk to me. Well, that's all right, I suppose. I'm obliged for the water."

He drank several dippers of it, then took his hat off and hung it on one of the plow handles. He lifted the bucket over his head and upended it, pouring the rest of the water over his head and shoulders. A shiver went through him and he shook his head, causing drops of water to fly off his long hair. He looked like a dog shaking. I laughed. I couldn't help it. But I still didn't say anything.

He put the dipper back in the empty bucket and handed it to me. "Like I said, I'm much obliged. Feel a lot better now."

As I turned away, I saw him raise his left hand and rub his right shoulder where he'd been shot. It must have still pained him some, especially when he did too much work or moved it just the wrong way. I know hurts are sometimes like that.

I ran back to the cabin, the empty bucket banging against my leg.

Mama took the bucket from me and sniffed. "He'd better not get used to such treatment. I wouldn't see a dog suffer so in this heat, though."

More time passed, and Mr. Crofton still came to the farm, though not as much. There weren't as many chores to do. Truth be told, he had helped out so much that the place was in pretty good shape. When he was there, Mama sometimes sent me to him with the water bucket. Even though I wouldn't talk to him, he talked to me. He told me about the places he'd been and the things he'd seen—"All the way from the Rio Grande to the Milk River"—but nothing about the men he'd killed or anything else that might bring up bad memories. For him or me.

Like I said, I didn't talk to him. I didn't disobey Mama's order. But she hadn't said anything about smiling every now and then.

One of the last times he came to the farm, he was picking corn, stripping the ears off the tall plants and dropping them in a bushel basket. The crop really needed to be picked, so he started on one side and Mama and I started on the other. When we got to the center row, we were on the opposite end from Mr. Crofton and on the other side of the row to boot, so we didn't see him over the plants until suddenly he was there, reaching for the very same ear of corn that Mama was reaching for. Both of them stopped short before they touched the corn, their hands close but not together.

That moment is still with me. There in the shade of the tall, gently waving corn plants, the smell of the vegetation mingling with the rich scent of the earth, the soft, almost inaudible song of the wind, the arching blue sky overhead, Mama and Mr. Crofton staring at each other, me standing there wanting so badly to still hate him, wanting, wanting, but when I reached inside myself to grasp that hate and bring it out, it slipped away from me and was gone.

Then Mr. Crofton cleared his throat and turned away, stooping to the ground to pick up the basket full of corn. He started walking toward the house and didn't look back.

Mama plucked the last ear of corn from the stalk and gently placed it in our basket. Then we got on each side of it and lifted.

Mr. Crofton had saddled his horse and was gone by the time we got back to the cabin with the corn.

We were in Dodge City a few days later, and when we went into Mr. Harwell's store to pick up a few things, Jonas had a friendly smile for me. He looked at the glass-fronted case, letting me know that he would slip a piece of candy in with our order. I'm pretty sure Mama knew what was going on, but she never said anything, and when we got home she never seemed to find the candy before I could sneak it out of the box and hide it to enjoy later.

Mama and Mr. Harwell talked for a while as she was giving him our order, as usual, and my ears perked up when I heard him mention Mr. Crofton. "They say the fella was asking about him in all the saloons. I figure it's somebody with a grudge against him."

"A man such as that must have many enemies," Mama said.

"That's the truth. That's why all those gunfighters wind up dead sooner or later. There's always somebody after them."

My eyes widened, and my heart started to pound. Somebody wanted to kill Mr. Crofton? That was awful!

I had completely forgotten at that moment all the times I myself had thought about how I would like to point a gun at him and squeeze the trigger and do to him what he had done to my brother.

125

Die and burn in hell.

"Nobody's seen him," Mr. Harwell went on. "Maybe he got wind of this stranger and has already left town rather than face him."

"Perhaps," Mama said. "It's really no business of mine."

"No, ma'am, of course not." Mr. Harwell looked around uncomfortably. "Jonas, we'd better get this order packed."

A few minutes later, after Mama had settled up with Mr. Harwell, we started toward the door of the emporium. Jonas was carrying the box of supplies to put it in our wagon. All of us stopped as the tall, black-clad figure came in the front door.

Mr. Crofton stopped, too. The light was behind him, so I couldn't see his face very well. I could see the gun on his hip, though, the handle of it jutting up from the holster.

Slowly, he reached up and tugged on the brim of his hat. "Mrs. McCabe."

Mama took a deep, shaky breath. "Mr. Crofton." Those were the first words she had spoken to him in weeks.

"I'm afraid I won't be able to ride out to your farm and help you anymore," he said, and Mr. Harwell and Jonas both looked shocked. They hadn't known that Mr. Crofton was giving us a hand. Frankly, it surprised me they hadn't known, as gossipy a place as Dodge City was in those days.

Mr. Crofton went on, "I have a business appointment I have to keep, and then I'll be leaving, I suspect."

"Where are you going?" Mama asked.

Mr. Crofton turned his head and looked off, like he could see something none of the rest of us could. "Not far," he said.

It was only later I realized he was peering in the direction of Boot Hill.

Mama took a step toward him. "Your arm . . . ?"

"Well enough to plow and swing a hammer. But it'll never be the same as it once was."

"My God."

Again he reached up and gave a polite tug on his hat. "I really have to be going. Good luck to you and your daughter, Mrs. McCabe."

Then he stepped past her, pausing only long enough to murmur, "Goodbye, Caroline," to me before he strode to the rear of the store and said in a loud voice, "A box of .44–40 cartridges, please, Mr. Harwell."

Mama grabbed me and hustled me out of the store. "We have to get home," she said. She took the box of supplies from Jonas and practically threw it in the back of the wagon. "Get up there," she told me.

We climbed onto the seat and she took up the reins. As she flapped them and yelled, "Hyyaahh!" at the horses, I twisted and looked back. I saw a man step out of the saloon and walk into the street. He wore a high-crowned hat of a sort we didn't see many of around there. He had a short black beard and was a stranger to me.

The wagon lurched into motion so suddenly that my shoulder was thrown against the seat. I caught hold of the seat to steady myself. Mr. Crofton came out of the emporium and stopped on the boardwalk. He stood there for a second looking at the stranger who had stopped in the middle of the street.

Then he turned and looked at us. I felt his eyes on me, then they shifted to Mama. She had to feel his gaze, too, but she gave no sign of it. All she did was hurry the team on down the street.

Moving ever so slowly, Mr. Crofton came down the steps from the boardwalk and started out into the street, toward the man who was waiting for him.

The wagon turned a corner and I couldn't see them anymore, but I heard the shots plain as day, three of them ripping out so close together they sounded like one, then a fourth and finally a fifth, spaced out a little more.

Close beside me on the wagon seat, I felt Mama jerk at the sound of each shot. She never looked back.

I did, but by then, of course, there was nothing to see except the buildings of Dodge City steadily dwindling in the distance.

Mama didn't say much all afternoon. As a rule, she wasn't very talkative to start with, but on that day she was quieter than usual.

Late in the day, we heard a horse coming.

Mama said, "Lord help me," and hurried outside. I went to the window, and my heart just about jumped all the way up my throat and out my mouth when I saw Mr. Crofton sitting there on his horse, tall and solemn in his black suit.

"I'll be moving on, Mrs. McCabe," he said.

"Farther than you thought," Mama managed to say.

"This time. Who knows about the next?" He leaned forward slightly to ease himself in the saddle, and I saw he was sitting more stiffly than usual. I figure he was wearing bandages wrapped tight around his body.

Mama said, "You . . . you could stay."

Mr. Crofton smiled but still looked sad at the same time. "It does my heart good to hear you say that, Mrs. McCabe, and I have no doubt you mean it—now. But the loss that I caused you will always be there, and I don't believe it will ever go away."

"No," Mama said, her voice little more than a whisper. "I don't suppose it will."

But it might, I wanted to yell from the window. *It might. You could try.*

But they were adults, after all, and I a mere child. What did I know then of hurt and loss? Those lessons would come, as they do to all of us, but that day I was just starting to learn.

"Good-bye, Mrs. McCabe," he said.

"Good-bye, Mr. Crofton," she said.

He glanced at the window and smiled and I knew he knew I was there even though the shadows had begun to gather inside the cabin and they wrapped me in their cloak so that he could not see me. He did that as he turned his horse, and his heels dug into its flanks and urged it into a trot that carried him away from our farm.

Mama stood there just outside the door until he had vanished from sight, then she came inside and never mentioned him again. But she didn't tell me to get away from the window. She let me stay there, looking out until night fell and the prairie was dark.

...GRAVEDIGGER...

So, ya see, Timothy McCabe is the youngest person buried up here, another victim of Dodge City's violent ways. Don't really belong up here with the rest of these folks, but they wasn't really anyplace else for them ta bury him. Fact is, Boot Hill was the only cemetery in Dodge for nigh onto seven years... but that don't make no never mind. I kin tell ya about that later on. Fact is, I'm jest kinda gettin' warmed up, here. Never thought of myself as much of a storyteller but you folks is a right nice audience, and I kin see that yore findin' these tales a might interestin'.

In fact, I got me a story... come on, follow me over here... mind you don't step on that there grave, son. These folks is dead, but they still don't like bein' stepped on. Sorry, ma'am, ain't tryin' to scare the little feller, but you did bring him on up here yourself...

Here ya go. Look at that there marker. The undertaker is real proud of that one, on account of there was so many words to put on it. And ain't that a helluva name? Burial Jones Clay. My full name? Why, ma'am, most folks around here jest refers to me as the Gravedigger, and I don't mind that at all... but let me tell ya about this here fella Clay...

Ya see, most of these folks up here was killed right here in Dodge City. Like I said about poor Timothy, victims of Dodge City's violent ways. Some folks, though, believe it or not, was killed elsewhere and, for one reason or t'other, either wanted to be buried here, or ended up bein' buried here regardless.

Fact is, this here fella is sort of even buried in a special coffin. His mama—bless her soul and what a beautiful name she had, as you'll soon see—wanted him buried here and in a coffin that she supplied.

So gather 'round here 'cause this story moves kinda fast. See, Miz Utopia Jones Clay wanted her boy buried here 'cause this is where his pa, Willalee Enigma Jones Clay, is buried. He was hung by vigilantes, but that story ain't near as interestin' as this one . . .

Them folks, though, they sure had them some pretty names . . .

THE COMFORTABLE COFFIN OF MIZ UTOPIA JONES CLAY

TOM PICCIRILLI

HERE LIES BURIAL JONES CLAY
HE LIKED TO LAY FISTS ON WOMEN
EVEN HIS OWN MAMA
SHE NAMED HIM PRETTY GOOD
SEEING AS WHAT WE DONE WITH HIM

Priest had taken to building coffins.

He didn't know why but he seemed to have a gift for it, each smooth slat fitting perfectly together with the rest. Besides, he had to do something with the wagon load of Mexican pine that had been delivered four days ago. The lumber was meant to go into building more shelves for the store, but since Lamarr had gambled the goods money away in Tombstone and Chicorah had burned down the store, there didn't appear to be anything he needed to do with the pine. So he'd taken to building coffins.

The storefront Priest currently used was next door to

the millinery. All day long he'd watch the startled faces of the women peeking in, whipping their fans and spinning their parasols a little faster as they stared at Lamarr sleeping inside a box laid out on the floor. It kept Priest's mouth hiked into a grin for most of the day, and he supposed that was as good a reason as any to make coffins.

Miss Henshaw, the milliner, had been around three times complaining that business had dropped off significantly since Priest had moved in. When he heard the shop door open he figured Miss Henshaw was coming around again to yell about how the ladies of Patience weren't perusing the new summer European hat collection the way they should've been. He didn't blame her. As soon as he finished up with the rest of the pine he'd leave the Main Street boardwalk, but for the time being he had nothing else to do.

The burning breeze flung a rippling cloud of dust inside. Lamarr didn't even stir as Priest glanced up.

She walked in and set right to work appraising each box. She had to stoop and closely gape at each coffin. One eye was so puffy it had sealed shut and the other wasn't much better. Her withered dark face had been severely bruised and her bottom lip was split so bad it would probably never completely heal right.

Her name was Miz Utopia Jones Clay, and she was a granny woman. She not only took care of the black folk in the south quarter but prepared her brews, plasters and applications to anyone who needed them. She'd once tried to heal Gramps when he'd first started going Apache a couple of years back. She spent a long weekend hoping to cure the old man and get him white again, feeding him all kinds of foul-smelling stews and soups and sticking poultices on his forehead and up his nose. At the end of it, with Gramps sitting in her kitchen dressed only in a breechcloth and spouting Apache, she'd given Priest a long pitiful stare and said, "Be easier jest to get the white man out of him. Wanna try that?"

Priest didn't. He was twenty-three and already going gray, a couple of silver-tinged curls right out in front. He had enough problems. He'd brought Gramps to the edge of town and let the old man run up to White Mountain where he lived with Chicorah's people for a couple of months at a time. Gramps was up there right now. But he could only handle it so long, and then the rest of his whole white life pushed back through. When he started calling out his long-dead wife's name, Chicorah would know it was time to get him off White Mountain and send him on before he started scaring their children.

Even in the box you could tell that Lamarr topped six two and weighed in at around two hundred and thirty pounds of muscle and bone. His black skin gleamed with a sheen of sweat. His short hair was fringed with a little white, but his skin was so smooth you'd never guess he was going on fifty.

Miz Utopia glared down at Lamarr in the coffin. She bent, cocked her head, and stooped a bit lower. "He daid?"

"Not the last time I checked."

She peered more closely at Lamarr. "You looked any time in the last week or so?"

"I think he got up once yesterday around noon."

"I don't see no flies," she said, "but he gettin' a bit ripe."

"That's just his natural leaning."

She covered her nose. "Jesus is more merciful to some than others."

Priest had an empty feeling in his belly looking at Utopia Clay's beaten face, knowing that he and Lamarr were going to have to get into something. Vague distress and fear worked through him. He hadn't felt it for a few days now and, oddly enough, he'd missed it. The uneasiness and cold tension made him a little angry, and that was familiar too. For the first time in a week he felt calm and relaxed. One of these days he'd have to give this some thought.

He sighed and whispered, "Lamarr," saying it the way he had to. Lamarr instantly opened his eyes and got up.

"You shouldn't tempt the good Lord like that none, Lamarr Russell. You do and He might jest strike you daid."

"Miz Utopia," Lamarr said, easing his lips wide and showing off every white tooth in his head. "The Lord gonna strike me when He ready, no matter what's I got to say about it." Lamarr kept the smile up but Priest saw the heavy ridge of muscle suddenly bulge across his neck and shoulders.

"What you two doin' buildin' coffins now? Thought you was opening a goods store. Leastways I heard that."

"It didn't rightly take, that place," Lamarr said, trying to sound sad and doing a bad job of it. "Bad timing. Poor location. The competition in this here boomtown is fierce, ma'am, mighty ferocious."

Priest didn't argue the point and bring up Tombstone again. Chicorah had burned the shop down because he believed Gramps was possessed by *Ga'ns* mountain spirits and that Priest must have better things to do with his life than run a store. Maybe it was true.

Miz Utopia moved closer and stepped inside the coffin. "You don't make them none too comfortable."

"It was fine for me," Lamarr told her, hoping to be helpful.

"You ain't daid. The daid needs their rest. You put some pillows inside? I wouldn't want no damage. Maybe a nice soft sheet?"

"Sure," Priest said.

"How much?" she asked.

The question surprised him. Priest didn't know what to say. He hadn't sold one yet and really never thought he would. "No charge."

"Competition can't be too mighty ferocious with prices like that. I give you a dollar. You put some more pillows in here? Some cloth so nobody's head hit the sides?"

"Sure."

"I reckon I'll take it then. But I want this here coffin delivered."

Priest tried not to sigh. There was always something and wearisome lurking just around the corner. "Where?"

"The hill."

"Which hill?"

"Boot Hill." Miz Utopia sounded proud saying the name. "Dodge City. My husband Willalee Enigma Jones Clay was hung there and buried with them other fellas, and I reason if it's a good enough resting place for him then it'd be fine for the rest of the family too."

"Ma'am—" Lamarr said, but that's as far as he got.

"I know. That there Boot Hill is filled with rustlers and gunfighters nowadays, but they's a time when it was where they placed the unwanted, and I's the only one ever wanted Willalee Enigma Jones Clay. And even I's didn't wants him most of the time."

"Oh," Priest said. He couldn't help staring at her face, realizing that somebody had beaten this old woman who'd done nothing but try to help others. He could hear Chicorah telling him that he had a larger fate, the Apache sub-chief's voice as clear as if he'd just spoken in Priest's ear.

"Why you holdin' that knife that way?" Miz Utopia asked.

Priest looked down. He wasn't holding his knife. Miz Utopia blinked twice at him with her good eye and gave herself a short nod as if she was greatly pleased. She pulled a silver dollar from deep inside her skirts and said, "That there box is mine now." Opening the door, she let the wind come sweeping back in, swirls of sage leaves working over her shoes. She wet her lips gingerly so the scabs wouldn't pull too badly, turned away and whispered words that the scorching gusts brought right to Priest's ear. "He hurtin' girls."

Then she was gone, and the ladies out in front of the milliner's shop were staring in again and tittering.

Lamarr still showed his teeth, as if he couldn't shut his mouth even if he wanted to, and now there was something dangerous in that beaming smile. "She got a boy by the name'a Burial who's always been trouble. Owns a saloon. Runs with one or two other like-minded fools."

"I don't suppose Burke would be willing to roust him some."

"They fools but they smart enough to only rob other

black folk in the south quarter. Sheriff Burke don't much mind them kind of nefarious doings."

"But we, being good citizens, mind such doings greatly."

Crimson sunlight angled in through the front window, casting fat shadows across the coffins. "That boy raised a hand to his own mama. The Bible got a whole lot of vengeful, wrathful things to say about that."

"So I hear tell."

"The Lord will surely take care of him, it's true, but baby Jesus, he remarkably busy saving souls all over the land."

"Think he's ever passed through Patience?"

"Maybe he's here right now," Lamarr offered, "whispering in my left ear."

"I think I might hear him too," Priest said.

He glanced down again and saw that the knife was in his hand.

He'd have to keep ahold of himself tonight.

Coloreds weren't much welcome north of Main Street. They weren't welcome south of Main Street either, but they had to stay someplace, and the five or six square blocks behind the livery were considered the black quarter. Priest wasn't sure if it worked the other way around. He'd never stepped foot in the black quarter and kept wondering if someone might beat the hell out of him here for just being white and ignorant.

They drove the buckboard, with Miz Utopia Jones

Clay's comfortable coffin in back. Lamarr had stopped off at his shack and put in a pillow and some old blankets. He figured on what Priest was thinking and let out a low rolling chuckle that made Priest's eyebrows itch. It reminded him of how oblivious he could be to the world, on occasion. Lamarr had been a slave before he'd strangled the plantation master, and he was a Union soldier for a couple of years after that, before heading west.

"This the home of the free, or ain't you heard? You ain't gotta worry about crossing this street, or the next, or any in town or anywhere in the country."

"You think Burial Jones Clay will see it like that?"

That stopped him for a minute. Lamarr actually had to think about it, pawing his chin some. "I'd say it's doubtful."

"Then I spurn your advice."

"Hey now, no need to get choleric."

They drove around the block and across a few more streets until they came to a saloon that was already shaking sawdust into the road, with the moon hardly even in the sky yet. Burial's place was three stories high and doing heavy business. Blaring music, squealing girls, singing, and the sporadic noise of brawls drifted through the sizzling night.

"Runs with only one or two other like-minded fools, you say?"

"Come to think of it, there might jest be a few more than that." Lamarr looked up and read the sign above the bat wings. "La Forda del Reyes."

"It means 'the Inn of Kings.' "

"Ole Burial thinks a bit too highly of himself, don't he? Pretty snooty name for a whorehouse saloon."

"You sound as if you might be familiar with the place."

"Well," Lamarr admitted, "I may have stepped inside once or twice, for a glass of sarsaparilla."

The wind had shifted and the fiery breeze brought on the stink of a nearby corpse. Somebody had been killed in the past few hours and the body was still around, rotting. Priest's stomach churned wildly. He had to bite his tongue in an effort to help clear his mind, which suddenly thrashed with ugly memories. He was oblivious to the world but he'd seen a lot of death. A part of him, God damn it, actually enjoyed the smell.

Lamarr sniffed and said, "Somebody's mama's gonna have an empty plate set tonight. Good thing you got more boxes."

They walked inside the Inn of Kings and Priest felt instantly ashamed and nauseous. The action, the foul odor of the room, and the mobbing bodies all reminded him of when he was a drunk. While it was true that he'd preferred wandering naked through pigsties with a bottle in each hand and danced on rooftops daring strangers to shoot him, he'd also spent more than enough of his life crawling across the floors of places exactly like this.

The forty-foot bar was packed with drinkers, and the people kept moving up and down the wide staircase to the rooms above in a constant procession. The gaming tables were packed with well-dressed and well-heeled gamblers as well as miners and rannies just off the range. The saloon was much cleaner than he'd been expecting. He was also surprised by how many more white folks were in here. There were also a hell of a lot of guns.

Priest scanned the room and located at least four main

players right off. The bartender, a weasel-faced drunken Irishman doing a bad job of covering the back door, and two other angry-eyed Negroes who sat up front near the door, not talking or sipping their beers, just smoking cigars and keeping a watch on things. They spotted Priest and Lamarr right off, perked up in their seats a bit.

Lamarr had no interest in poker, roulette, billiards, or any other game that cities like Tombstone and San Francisco thrived on—none, except for faro. Something about it fascinated him, and a divine expression of purity would fill his face as he gave up all his cash trying to buck the tiger. Even now it was getting to him. Priest saw it in his eyes.

"Hey—" Lamarr said.

"No, we don't have any money."

"You got a wallet nearly bursting out your back pocket."

"You still owe me from your trip to Sonora." He paused. "And your trip to San Francisco, and Dallas, and in case you've forgotten Tombstone, and—"

"Now it ain't no fair you bringing up Tombstone again. I been telling you I'll get that there money back from Fatima the next time I'm in the Bird Cage. She just holdin' it for a little while for me."

"And I know where."

Lamarr pointed out Burial Jones Clay, who was seated at a poker table with five other men. He was young, much too young to be Miz Utopia's true son. This was her grandson, possibly even her great-grandson. Burial Jones Clay couldn't have topped twenty-five yet. He wore a black, high-crowned Stetson, a fancy black-and-white calfskin vest, and large-rowled, silver-plated spurs.

"Some jaspers dress for poker like they're going on a cattle drive," Lamarr said.

"If he wears spurs that size in here it means he likes using those rowels on a man when he's down."

"Sure. There's at least a half dozen of Burial's former friends wandering town with only one eye left, maybe half a nose."

"Looks like the big trouble is sitting up front."

"Shorter one is Rolle. Other is Jester. They never done a lick of good in the world. Don't worry about them none though. Burial keeps 'em too near the door to be much good. They only really there to look mean."

"They must get paid a lot to do it so well."

The place had already quieted down some, with folks angling in their seats to watch Lamarr. He had a presence nobody in the same room could avoid. "That's more like it. I'se gonna go have a chat now."

"Got anything in mind to say?"

"A whole lot. I just gonna be my irresistible, naturally charming self."

"You might want to avoid that."

Lamarr burst out laughing as he moved from the bar, letting the laugh roll on too loudly for a bit too long, until even more heads spun his way. He stood at Burial's table watching him and his men play. Without a word of introduction he sat and elbowed himself some room. Lamarr eased out the big smile again and Burial Jones Clay did the same. It was damn near almost as wide and bright.

That was quick, Priest thought. They were already into it. Lamarr cleared his throat, re-doubled his efforts, and put everything he had into his smile. It glowed so white Priest had to squint to look at it. The red sash he wore around his waist all the time was dirty and faded, and he had his two converted Navy .36s tucked in the small of his back.

Priest figured it would take them at least ten minutes before they got past each other and Lamarr finally annoyed the kid enough to start something. Burial would say, "So, you want trouble?" and Lamarr would show a little sadness in his eyes and say, "I ain't ever looked for trouble but it always do manage to find me."

Well, maybe not that corny, but it'd be close. Priest decided to get a drink.

He looked back at Rolle and Jester and noticed they were keeping their eyes on him. That was all right. The bartender was too. Priest glanced toward the end of the bar and saw the stock of a ten-gauge shotgun angled out from beneath. The guy might be a player but he hadn't had much cause to shoot anybody in here so far, otherwise he'd know to keep the weapon closer to the middle of the bar, where he could reach it from either end. Better yet, keep two or three weapons back there.

"Howdy!" Priest said.

The bartender appraised him with open bitterness. Priest ordered a beer and brought it to his lips but didn't quite take a sip. He thought he might be able to handle a drink now, but even the foam reminded him of the years he'd lost. The bartender frowned and started to gnash his back teeth, slanting his jaw. He had a tremendous belly that strained against his leather apron, making it creak and groan. His bald black crown swam with huge beats of sweat, each drop catching the lamplight and flashing it back against the polished top of the bar.

Priest checked the gunnies again and they were still watching him. He told the bartender, "Sam, give me a bottle of whiskey."

"My name ain't Sam, it's Harlan." Harlan gave him a bottle of nearly clear liquid. Priest pulled the cork and sniffed.

"Not this. Give me bourbon."

"You got enough money for that?" Harlan asked.

Priest put Miz Utopia's silver dollar down on the bar. Harlan brought back the better liquor, looking a little more upset. That was good. Priest uncorked it and got a whiff of the stuff. It wasn't bourbon but it wasn't as cut down with water. He asked, "How about shine? You got any shine back there?"

Harlan's back teeth made a staccato clicking noise and he was beginning to jitter a bit, his fat belly rolling all over. His breathing grew harsher and louder. He wanted to give Priest the full display of his annoyance, which was sort of fun to behold. Harlan took the whiskey back without comment, reached under the bar, came up with the shine, and kept the dollar. "You want anything else?"

Priest didn't have to check the liquor this time. The cork had almost completely disintegrated and the stink of the shine flooded his nose and throat. "I think that'll be it."

He brought the bottle over to the gunnies' table and put it between them. "On me, men," he said, and turned to go.

Rolle said, "A moment, please." He puffed on the cigar and carefully blew the smoke down low and away so it didn't offend Priest. Some of the worst men around were the most polite. Rolle's gaze of intense anger and hatred never let up though. Priest made him itchy. Priest made a lot of people itchy, and he wasn't exactly sure why.

"I'm Rolle," Rolle said. "And this is Jester." Jester nodded. He was the silent one who killed because he didn't like people and didn't consider them to be any different than sheep or cattle or bottles lined up on a corral fence. Still, Jester tipped his hat.

"You and your partner should leave now," Rolle continued, " 'fore we escort your dead bodies out of here."

Okay, so he wasn't so polite. "Thanks for the warning," Priest told him, and he almost meant it.

"We don't drink, and we don't want a drink from you."

"I didn't think you did," Priest said, and left them. It was time to join Lamarr. He was probably pissing Burial Jones Clay off by now.

"That old woman had no right to ask you to brace me," Burial said, folding to a pair of eights.

"She didn't ask exactly," Lamarr told him. "I sorta volunteered, you might say."

Burial let out a bark of laughter. "Well now, that was a damn stupid thing to do."

Lamarr hung his head, as if in shame. "I've been known to take a misstep or two along my rocky path."

Priest grabbed an empty chair and forced himself into the ring of men around the table. The game bothered him. He'd thought Burial had been a real gambler willing to take a major chance, but now Priest realized Burial was too cautious to be a risk taker, dropping to a pair of eights. If he was that wary, this was going to be more difficult than they'd thought.

He smiled pleasantly at the card players staring at him.

He nodded to each. "Hi. How you? Howdy."

Burial chuckled for a while, shaking his head, sort of having a good time with it before turning to Priest. "You come here to distress me and you're not even wearing a gun?"

"This looks like a friendly place. What would I need a gun for?"

"You never do know."

"I suppose I could always borrow one."

"You're as crazy as your granpappy," Burial said. His spurs jangled as he leaned forward in his chair. "I know you. I heard about you. But these are my people. Who's going to give you a pistol?"

Priest's hands flashed out under the table, reaching for the man's gun belt to the left of him and the other jasper to the right. He came up holding a .44 Colt Frontier and some tiny foreign piece he'd never seen before, pointing both barrels at Burial.

"You've got right neighborly folks, I'd say. They all appear to be the giving kind."

"Praise Jesus," Lamarr said.

Maybe all it had taken was the one breath of moonshine, but Priest suddenly felt himself loosening up, that fine rush surging through him. Maybe he liked it too much and didn't want it to end so quickly. He upended the guns and placed them on the table before the men he'd taken each one from. Both jaspers picked up the pistols and held them a few inches from Priest's head. He didn't really mind much. He still had his knife.

"You want woe and misfortune with me?" Burial asked.

Priest drew a deep breath as Lamarr answered, "Hey, that's pretty good. 'Woe and misfortune.' No, I ain't ever wanted trouble, but it always do manage to find me."

"You cotton to calamity anyway."

Lamarr's jaw muscles tightened. He'd been born and grown on a Georgia plantation owned by a man called Thompson, his mother only fifteen years older than him. Lamarr worked the fields until he was seventeen and finally strangled Thompson, and he took his time doing it, first choking the master with his left fist and then his right, making it last a good long while. Nowadays, even when he just heard the word "cotton" he wanted to kill somebody.

Burial was still having fun. He tilted his head at Priest, trying to do something charming. Possibly it worked with the ladies. "It's got to be embarrassin' to have that sickness runnin' through your family blood. You dance naked with Chicorah and his people yet? Your granpappy got hisself a little squaw up there on White Mountain? Or is he jest sittin' in them rocks planning raids on the town? You really should take that old mossy-horned codger out in the desert and shoot him."

"That what you got planned for Miz Utopia?"

Burial stiffened and finally dropped the smile. This could be it. Priest already had the knife in his hand pressed close to his leg, and he didn't worry about anybody at the table. Or the drunk Irishman who stood too far off at the moment to be of any good to Burial. That left Harlan the bartender and Rolle and Jester at the front of the room, but he was still prepared to make his move as need be.

But Burial let the prod pass, which surprised both Priest and Lamarr. Either he wasn't as eager for serious grief as he'd acted or something else was going on. Lamarr started glancing around, trying to figure it out.

It only took about a minute before they both noticed there was some extra activity going on upstairs. Burial dealt another hand and folded to a possible flush. A crying teenage Negro girl slid out of one of the upstairs rooms and stood at the top of the stairway making plaintive, bird-like sounds. Her cries were almost completely lost in the din of the saloon, but Lamarr and Priest were staring right at her. She took a few hesitant steps down the stairs and the Irishman grinned and blocked her way. She backed up, fluttering her hands uselessly, before wheeling and making a dash for it. There was some distant shouting, the Irishman cackling until he went into a coughing fit.

Lamarr still kept a good rein on himself. "Looks like that little girl wants to go home."

"Who?" Burial asked.

"That poor thing with tears in her eyes. She gone now. She went back upstairs. That where you keep 'em all?"

"Oh, that's jest Daisy. She got here with her sisters a few days back, come in from Louisiana. She needs some adjustin' still."

"So you importing young gals."

"Tha's right." Burial reached into his pile of winnings and shoved about two hundred dollars toward Lamarr. "That faro dealer over there, her name is Estrelita. She sure is a pretty tiny thing, ain't she? Those small hands and those pale fingers, I swear I have no idea how she ever got so fine at card dealing with those baby-girl hands."

This was bad, Priest thought. Lamarr didn't look any different, but everybody could tell he was shaking somewhere inside. Lamarr turned his head to stare at the faro dealer, brooding on the wonderfully fluid movements of Estrelita's thin fingers, the cards gliding along the tabletop in rapid, controlled motions. Burial drew his pistol, a .41 Colt Lightning, and started to bring it up to the back of Lamarr's head.

Priest had begun moving the moment Lamarr glanced over at the faro table. He didn't need to do much but he had to do it quickly, still worrying about the two gunnies near the front door. He reached down and grabbed hold of a chair leg on either side of him, upending the two jaspers whose guns he'd taken before. The Colt Lightning was clearing leather. Burial hadn't oiled his gun belt in a while and the barrel made a soft scratching hiss as it slid free.

Still enough time if he gave it his all. Priest spun and hurled the knife, winging it sidearm almost absently, so that the blade sort of glided straight on. The pommel struck the bartender—who was bringing up the double-barrel ten-gauge—in the mouth and knocked him backwards into the liquor shelves. A gush of blood and chips of tooth exploded from his face and he disappeared in a swell of shattering glass.

Now Priest had no knife and the freezing sweat broke along his upper lip and across his shoulders. He felt a buzz in his left ear and then another in his right. Burial was cocking the Colt Lightning, his smile completely gone, as Priest lunged forward over the card table.

Burial was fast and strong, and he managed to twist out of Priest's way even while bringing his pistol around to slam against Priest's forehead. The blow stunned him as he rolled backwards off the table and hit the floor.

A burning splash of desert brilliance flared behind Priest's eyes. At least his head was hard enough that Burial had lost his grip on the pistol and dropped it. Priest was aware enough to protect his face, knowing Burial was going to use the rowels on him. He tried to block as Burial kicked out, slashing the spurs against Priest's forearms. Priest covered his eyes. Blood spattered against his lips as he tightened up, grunting in pain. The rowels hooked closer and the agony flared up his arms. The slashes were deep and getting worse. He shouldn't have thrown the knife.

Lamarr had finally come out of it, pulling his Navy .36s from his sash and firing at Rolle and Jester, who were on their feet. Only then did Priest realize that they'd been shooting at him the whole time. The commotion grew even wilder with women screaming and folks running all over, up and down the stairway, out the doors into the street. Gunfire continued from all around. Priest grabbed for Burial's ankles, knowing he was taking a bad chance. If he missed, those spurs would chew half his face off.

Filled with glee, doing sort of a two-step stomp now, Burial shouted, "You gonna wish you was daid!"

Priest clutched Burial's left boot and undid the spur so fast that Burial was still trying to stab him with it even when it was gone. The spur chimed and rang softly. Priest reached up and jabbed the rowel into Burial's thigh. It didn't hurt him much but Burial spun awkwardly and Priest was able to kick his feet out from under him. Once they were both on the floor, Priest aimed well and dove forward. He scratched Burial directly between the eyebrows with the spur and blood ran heavily into Burial's eyes.

Lamarr was having a wonderful time, guffawing loudly

from behind an overturned table and punching any man in the jaw who got too close. They were stacked three deep around him and Lamarr was picking up guns at random and still firing at the gunnies. He'd already put the Irishman down with a bullet in the left leg, and he'd pummeled into a weeping heap of card players scrambling for cover. Estrelita appeared to be very impressed by all this, and Lamarr kept winking at her.

Priest snatched the Colt Lightning from under Burial and drew down on Rolle and Jester. Like Lamarr they hadn't dived for cover, just standing there at their table carefully aiming and blasting, still smoking their cigars and calmly returning lead from across the room. Lamarr had taken at least one bullet in his left arm, but he hadn't dropped his pistol.

Things weren't all that grave, considering. By the time Priest had his sights on the bottle of moonshine, Jester was already collapsing with his shirt on fire. Lamarr had put two shots into his chest. Priest blasted the whiskey bottle and sent the shine splashing all over. The dying gunny's shirt blazed much brighter and Rolle's cigar flared as his face was suddenly engulfed in a dazzling ball of orange flame. He howled in anguish and whirled madly around the room until Lamarr took a nice slow bead and shot him in the back of the neck.

"Well," Priest said.

Lamarr looked over. "Damn, you actually plan that?"

"I didn't think it would work."

"It shouldn't have, except we got baby Jesus on our side. The Lord surely do love a senseless man!"

Priest didn't want to think about that. He looked

around and didn't see Burial Jones Clay anywhere on the floor. He ducked behind the bar and retrieved the knife. Harlan was just lumbering to his feet, using the shotgun as a staff to prop himself up while he spit blood. Priest kicked the ten-gauge out from under him and Harlan dropped back into more shelving. He was covered in booze.

Remembering what it was like, Priest could almost feel the icy liquor drying on his chest, in his hair, the screeching nightmares flooding his throat. He took the shotgun with him and said, "Harlan, go out the back door now. You try the front and you'll be bacon by the time you hit the bat wings."

The fire continued spreading fast. Most everybody had already gotten out of the place except for a few of the rowdies that Lamarr had clubbed and the Irishman, who was dragging himself around the floor in drunken circles. Estrelita and Lamarr were talking by the faro table. Priest could see Lamarr taking the time out to play a few hands while the flames swarmed into the rafters.

He ran upstairs and pressed his way through a few of the straggler prostitutes and cowpunchers who were struggling to get their clothes on. He tried doors until he came to a locked one. Priest threw himself against it twice until the lock sprang. He found five young girls who clearly didn't belong anywhere near the Inn of Kings inside, arms around each other as they huddled together near the far wall. They were terrified of him, but he moved to Daisy and said, "Come on. We're leaving this place. There's a woman named Miz Utopia who's going to take care of you until we can get you back to Louisiana."

"Tuvi," Daisy said.

"What?"

She pointed at the window. "Tuvi wouldn't do what that man ask. She bit him. He carried her over and let her go."

Priest pulled the drapes aside and looked out the window. He saw Tuvi's body behind the saloon in the alley three floors below. Burial hadn't even cared enough to hide the corpse.

"You're all going to be fine now, girls."

They didn't believe him, as they sobbed and started coughing. Priest hoped he wasn't lying. He led the way through the clouds of thickening smoke. The heat was getting bad as the sweat slithered over him. He ushered the girls out and waved them on down the stairway. He was about to follow when Burial suddenly appeared from out of the thick haze. Burial tried an Apache war shriek as he leaped at Priest, holding the rowel out before him like a blade. It wasn't a very good likeness to an Apache scream. Gramps could do a whole hell of a lot better.

Priest watched Burial in midair, twisting as the smoke whirled, that bloody face coming closer like a death mask, and the spur catching the yellow light of flames as Burial descended. It was sort of graceful, the bizarre dance he did, coming in for the kill.

But it was too slow. Priest brought the knife up in a blur and turned aside the rowel. Burial's war cry became a confused gasp as he went tumbling past and hit the banister with his full weight. The wood cracked and Burial glanced down wide-eyed at all three flights opening into empty space below him. He waved his arms wildly trying to keep his balance. The banister splintered further as Burial reached backward for Priest.

Priest shoved him a little, and listened to the wood breaking sharply. Now Burial's scream was a lot closer to that of a real Apache. Gramps would've been proud. Just as the banister gave way and Burial began to fall, Priest grabbed him by the white calfskin vest, twirled him all the way around, and brought the stock of the shotgun up into his chin. Burial Jones Clay dropped to the carpet in a heap and Priest dragged him down the stairs.

Lamarr was still at the faro table and Estrelita was trembling where she stood, too afraid to leave. Whatever chance Lamarr had had with her was gone now. Priest motioned for the girls to go out the back door while he dragged Burial across the ruins of his saloon.

Plate glass shattered in all directions. The roof was about to come down. Lamarr had just lost another hand. Estrelita met Priest's eyes and silently begged him to let her run before they all burned to death. Sometimes it got like this. With his chest beginning to tighten, Priest took the cards from her and tossed them into the blaze that had once been the bodies of Rolle and Jester.

Relief flooded Lamarr's face to have finally been stopped. He'd been betting with the money Burial had given him and he'd lost it all. Estrelita grabbed the cash and fled.

"You ready to go?" Priest asked, coughing.

"I suppose it's time."

Lamarr picked up Burial and hauled him over his shoulder. He led the way out of the place as the smoke and flame raged around them. Priest started to stagger some and he felt the steady arm of Lamarr encircle him and pull him out of the Inn of Kings.

A couple hundred people milled in the street. Some had been inside, some had just come to see a terrible place become ashes. The Irishman wept and made baby noises. Harlan tried to comfort him but couldn't say much on account of his busted teeth. A preacher led his choir in a chorus of "Bringing in the Sheaves." Miz Utopia Jones Clay stood in the street, her arms around the five huddled girls, who were sobbing and telling her their stories. They wanted their mothers and fathers. Somebody had to bury Tuvi.

Miz Utopia hugged the teenagers tightly, a small smile on her battered face though she glared at the unconscious form of her kin lying near her feet. Priest and Lamarr sat heavily in the dirt. Miz Utopia whispered to Daisy, pointed, and sent her up the block. The girl returned shortly carrying Miz Utopia's remedy pouch.

It took the old woman only five minutes to tend to Priest's and Lamarr's wounds. She'd soaked her bandages in some kind of medicinal brew that stank and burned, but Priest immediately felt better. He climbed up his buckboard and got his hammer and nails ready.

"Miz Utopia," Lamarr said, "I don't think you'll be needin' that coffin anytime soon."

"I paid for it, and I think we needs it right now."

"But—well, ma'am, you ain't daid, and these girls here, they need someone till we can get 'em home again."

She frowned at him. "Lamarr Russell, you dang fool,

you don't think that there coffin was for me none, now do you?"

Lamarr cocked his head at Priest and went, "Hmm." He reloaded his Navy .36s and put two shots into the lid. He tossed Burial in just as he started to come around.

"What's this? Oh Lord, what's this?" Burial shouted as Priest hammered the nails in. "I ain't daid yet! I ain't daid! Where you takin' me?"

"Boot Hill," Lamarr said.

"The hell!"

"It's in Virginia City. Montana."

"Dodge City," Priest told him. "Kansas."

"Don't worry none, we find it!"

The choir had worked themselves into "Down by the River." Somebody in the choir was tone deaf and kept striking a hollow note that moved the crowd along. Priest grabbed the reins and drove the buckboard on. Lamarr still looked a little put out. Maybe they'd just ride around town for a while, or maybe they'd head out into the desert. Priest didn't know exactly how this would play out, listening to the muted cries of Burial Jones Clay lying in his comfortable coffin.

"Maybe we'll go to Tombstone first," Priest said. "I've never been there."

"Oh, you'll like it at the Bird Cage. And I'll get to see my sweet Fatima again."

"And get my money back."

"Now how many times I tole you, she jest holdin' onto it for me. You sure are a mistrustful soul."

"Born that way, I guess."

They rode until the harsh light of the burning Inn of Kings had long faded behind them. Lamarr turned to him and said, "You let me know how far you wanna go with this."

Priest really hadn't been around much. He'd never stepped foot out of Patience his entire life and thought it was about time. Tombstone sounded all right, but he had an aching to see the plains of Kansas. He recalled Miz Utopia's beaten face again. He thought of Daisy at the top of the stairs weeping, the crumpled body of Tuvi lying in a dirty alley, and all the innocent men waiting at the bottom of Boot Hill.

"We've got a long while to go yet," Priest said, snapping the reins harder.

. . . GRAVEDIGGER . . .

I wonder if when Miz Utopia Jones Clay's time comes, she'll wanna be buried here with her husband and her boy. Gonna be pretty hard for that to happen . . .

Anyway, now we're up to all the graves that I've dug since I been here. Far as you kin see, I planted 'em. And when I dig somebody's grave I always like to know the story behind their demise. Kinda makes me think that they're all my friends, ya see? Does that sound weird? Hell, even a gravedigger's gotta have some friends, don't he?

'Course, there's some folks up here died with no friends. Nobody ta bury 'em, nobody to mourn 'em. Why, here's a grave right here don't even have a name on it. Jest says "A-non-ee-muss." That how you say it? I reckon that's how. Means nobody knew his name—but see, I know different. T'weren't that nobody knew his name. Folks around here didn't wanna know his name back then, 'cause of the things he did afore he died. I mean, sometimes a fella jest does somethin' that goes against the grain, if'n ya know what I mean. I mean, he does somethin' that nobody even wants ta think about, somethin' that gets him buried without even the benefit of his name.

Most of this story was told ta me by Sam Wheeler. Sam owns the newspaper hereabouts, and he was comin' back from Wichita on the train . . .

ANONYMOUS

RANDY LEE EICKHOFF

HEAVEN HAS NO RAGE LIKE LOVE TO HATRED TURNED,
NOR HELL A FURY LIKE A WOMAN SCORNED.
— WILLIAM CONGREVE

It isn't that we do not know his name; we do. But it was taken from him by mutual assent of all on account of his actions and his death. When a man has a higher calling and betrays that calling, he betrays all and is not worthy of the immortality granted by a headstone.

I remember the beginning well. The day turned suddenly dark and cold while we waited for the train to leave Wichita for Dodge City. Huge gray clouds, their bellies swollen and dirty, rolled slowly down from the north.

"Looks like snow," Reverend Daniel McCain said, clapping his hands together. I glanced at him; dressed all in black, his face white and drawn. Quiet fires seemed to burn in the depths of his black eyes set in deep sockets. He was so thin that he made others uncomfortable when he stood next to them for he seemed too saintly for this world. He was, I discovered, a rather silent and sullen man who spoke only out of a sense of propriety. His lips were full and sensual.

His wife, Judith, stood next to him, as roly-poly as he was ascetically thin. Short, moon-faced and double-chinned, she too was dressed in black but her blue eyes sparkled cheerfully and her cheeks crinkled merrily when she smiled and she smiled often as a jester who seemed to say, Oh, do not take him too seriously for he is not as hard as he seems.

I liked Judith and visited with her. McCain always made me nervous with his talk which had somber overtones to it even when he spoke of passing things. I do not think the man had ever joked although he was pleasant enough in his own dry way.

We had been together since Chicago where we boarded the train together. Judith broke the awkward silence that follows when strangers first meet with her pleasant greeting, introducing herself and McCain, who flinched uncomfortably at his wife's openness with strangers.

"My husband is a minister of the gospel, sir," she said, beaming with affection and pride at McCain. "He has been awarded a position in Denver for his dedication and work."

"Enough, Judith," McCain said gently. "It's unseemly to take pride in one's accomplishments. It is God's work; we are merely His instruments."

Chagrined, she dropped her eyes to her hands clutching her reticule in her lap. "I'm sorry, Daniel." She looked back at him. "But you deserve to be honored for your work. The souls you've saved—"

"Are reward enough," he said, smiling at her. He held out his hand to me. "I'm the Reverend Daniel McCain," he said. "I apologize for my wife's . . . gushing." He smiled to take the sting from his words. His wife blushed, her cheeks turning rosy. But her eyes shined with pride as she looked adoringly upon her husband.

"Sam Wheeler," I said, taking his hand. His flesh felt dry, the long thin fingers brittle, but there was surprising strength in his grip. "I own the newspaper in Dodge. But," I continued, "if you are on your way to Denver, why are you going out of your way to Dodge City? You bought your tickets ahead of me," I said in explanation as he frowned at his wife.

His expression cleared. "Of course. Now I remember." He smiled. "A visit. We have friends there who we haven't seen in a long, long time."

"Oh? Perhaps I know them," I said conversationally.

"Reverend Henry Bottoms and his wife Sarah," he said. "Reverend Bottoms was my sponsor to divinity school. That was—" He frowned, trying to recall and looked at his wife for help. She responded quickly.

"Fifteen years, Daniel. That was seventeen years ago," she said, smiling. "We met in your final year and married after you graduated. We've been married fifteen years." She placed her hand gently upon his arm. "You do not think often of earthly ways."

We laughed at her teasing and spent the rest of the trip to Wichita exchanging pleasantries along the way.

"I wonder what's taking so long," McCain frowned, glancing around the platform. The engine turned over gently as the engineer puttered around the wheels with a long-spouted oil can. He kept glancing up to see if the conductor had emerged yet from the depot.

The only other passengers on the platform with us were a cowboy, looking haggard, his eyes red-rimmed, yet he was cleanly-shaven, and a drummer with two satchels. From the look of him—starched shirt front, celluloid collar, green pinstriped suit—a whiskey salesman.

Finally the conductor came out from the warmth of the depot rubbing his hands together jovially.

"Everybody ready?" A faint odor of whiskey followed his words. His eyes were bright and shiny.

"We have been ready and waiting on you for some time now," McCain said calmly, but there was an edge of admonition to his words that sobered the conductor immediately.

"Sorry," the conductor mumbled, "but it was the marshal holding things up."

McCain frowned, then a loud voice brought our attention to the end of the platform. We turned to look and saw an angry woman arguing with a red-faced marshal who was doing his best to ignore her. Behind them came six men carrying luggage and a gramophone.

"This is an outrage!" she bellowed. Her green eyes flashed angrily at the marshal. "You know it's those dried-up crones with calloused knees from praying who have made you do this, Marshal."

"The town council makes me do this, Flo," he said. "I'm just doing my job."

"By turning an innocent woman out of her home!" she snapped.

One of the men following snorted with laughter. "Been

a while since innocence been between those legs," he said coarsely.

"Aye, but a good many others have," another laughed. Judith gasped indignantly and clutched McCain's arm.

"Here, now, sir! That is no way to treat a lady!" McCain said angrily. A strange light shone from his eyes as he looked at the woman. I frowned. Judith looked up at him, her lower lip caught in her teeth. A blush crept up McCain's throat. "We are all God's children!"

Judith gave a slight nod and turned her attention back to the affair.

The marshal glanced our way, amused, noted McCain's collar, and said, "Sorry folks, but Flo Watson is gonna have to ride along with you, courtesy of the town fathers."

"Town harlots more likely," Flo said. She glanced at the man carrying the gramophone. "Here, now! Watch what you are doing with that thing! There's not another any closer than St. Louis."

"Sorry, Flo," the man said sheepishly. "I'll just put it on board for you."

"Put it by my seat," she ordered, then glanced at the rest of us. We had moved unconsciously together into a small group away from her. She winked at us.

"At least we can listen to music on our way to Dodge City. It'll help to pass the time."

She swayed up to the McCains and greeted them boisterously. She wore a bottle-green dress with a white bodice whose buttons strained over breasts to hold the fabric together and give her the suggestion of decency. But her breasts moved suggestively beneath their restraint and her generous hips twitched her dress, making it flare and dance with wickedness. Her face had a slight soft look to it, but the high cheekbones could still be seen as a reminder of the beauty she had once been. A tiny mole tucked into the left dimple of her smile.

"I'm Flo Watson," she said. "Most simply call me Curly Red. But that's up to you all. I'm not particular."

"Yes, we see that," McCain said as he gently tugged Judith toward our train car. He paused, his eyes burning on her. "I am sorry for your trouble. But if you ask God—"

Flo laughed merrily. "God forgot people like me a long, long time ago, Reverend."

"God never forgets," McCain said fervently. He started to say more, but Judith pulled on his arm and he turned away reluctantly, following her to the car. He helped his wife up the stairs, but his eyes seemed to be drawn to Flo.

She watched them, puzzled, then turned to me and the cowboy standing hat-in-hand next to me.

"Well, boys, that leaves us, I suspect," she said. The smile stayed on her face but a bitter edge had come to her words and her emerald-green eyes glittered like broken glass.

"Yes, ma'am," the cowboy stuttered quickly. "I'm . . . that is"—he blushed with youthful exuberance—"Tom Benson. That's my name, I mean."

"And I'm Harry Black," the drummer said, lifting his derby.

She smiled gently and patted the cowboy on the shoulder and I think he would have wiggled in ecstasy like a puppy if others hadn't been present.

"Well, Tom and Harry, I'm pleased to make your acquaintances," she said. She glanced at me, arching an eyebrow questioningly.

"Sam Wheeler," I said removing my hat politely. "I own the paper in Dodge City."

"The newspaper?" Her mouth took a sarcastic turn to her lips. "Then might I assume I'll find an editorial calling for my eviction soon after I arrive in your Gomorrah?"

I shook my head. "No, Miss Watson. I believe in living and let living. You cannot legislate morality."

She laughed heartily. "Well, that's a refreshing outlook upon life that I've seldom encountered."

" 'Board!" the conductor said loudly. He glanced meaningfully at his watch.

I reached for one of her bags but the cowboy beat me to it. She smiled and then laughed with glee. "You see, Marshal, there is still gallantry in the world."

"Yes, Flo," he said, stepping back so she could climb aboard the train. "Just make certain it doesn't bring you back to Wichita. Have a nice trip."

She laughed again and I followed her as she bustled into the car where the McCains had already settled themselves. They didn't turn to look as we came into the car. I thought they might have had words for McCain's face was white and tiny muscles bunched and moved at the corners of his jaws as he stared straight ahead.

We were the only passengers in that car on that trip. As we spread out to take advantage of the room in the car, I noticed McCain giving Flo curious sidelong looks with his dark eyes, but he said nothing. After many years of married life, he had learned when to call his wife to order and when to let her have a few minor battles.

"That snow's gonna get bad in a bit," the cowboy said, staring out the window with a worried look drawing his face down tightly into a frown.

The drummer nodded and lit a cigar, taking himself to the far end of the car so the smoke wouldn't bother the ladies. "Yes, I would reckon it to be a bad one," he said, settling in a seat. "But there's nothing for it but to let it come."

Judith cleared her throat and turned her head to find me. "Do you think we'll have to fear the Indians?"

I shook my head. "No, Mrs. McCain, not at all. Most have moved onto reservations. There are a few raiding parties left, but they are too small to attack a train. Especially," I added, "if that blue norther comes down as our cowboy friend here seems to think it will."

"Oh it will, ma'am," he said. "And its going to be a bad one." He shook his head and huddled deep into his sheepskin coat. "A *real* bad one," came his muffled echo.

She sighed, fixed a pair of glasses upon her nose, and opened her reticule, removing a small Bible. She settled down to read from it, her lips moving as she worked her way through the verses.

The train gave a lurch, then slowly pulled forward, moving away from the depot. At that moment, thick flakes began to fall and by the time we had cleared Wichita, the thick flakes were falling in a white curtain and a damp cold began to creep through the car. The snow fell harder and harder as we made our way toward Dodge City and seemed to lock the entire car in a cocoon of white.

"Well," Flo said brightly, "should we have some music to help pass the time? Lift our spirits? Cowboy, if you'll turn the handle on that gramophone, I'll just see what I can find in this bag."

The cowboy grinned good-naturedly and wound the spring on the gramophone.

"Aha!" she cried. "This is just the ticket, I think, to lift our spirits!"

She slid the disk onto the gramophone and carefully placed the needle. Soon the thin strains of a waltz began trickling from the huge cone-shaped speaker. I thought I recognized the music, but the sound was so scratchy that at times the music seemed to disappear entirely.

"Come on, cowboy!" she cried, holding out her arms and balancing herself awkwardly. "Let's give it a try up and down the aisle. What do you say?"

"I'm game," he grinned, and the two took to jouncing up and down the aisle, trying to time their movements to the car's bouncing and swaying when gusts of wind struck it. The drummer joined in too and the three of them laughed at their own limitations in the narrow confines.

The song came to an end and rather than try and find another, Flo simply moved the needle back to the beginning. She glanced at me, but I smiled and shook my head. She shrugged and turned back to the cowboy and the drummer and they began again their awkward promenade up and down the aisle. I noticed McCain pretending not to notice her.

The clouds seemed to come down lower and lower and the snow fell harder and harder. The train began to go slower and slower until it seemed to fairly creep along. By this time, the grimness of the day seemed to have settled over everyone and all became content to sit quietly, glancing out the windows of the car, trying to penetrate the white that seemed to surround us. Finally the silence was broken when McCain cleared his voice.

The sound caused us to flinch reflexively and he gave us an apologetic look.

"Sorry," he said. He looked at me. "Do you have any idea when we will get to Dodge City?"

I shook my head. "Sorry. In weather like this, it's anyone's guess."

"Do you think . . ." Judith began, then pressed her lips together hard to keep from voicing her thoughts. But all there knew what she had been going to say for it was on everyone's minds: Would the snow begin to drift and lock us upon the tracks in this steel coffin where we would slowly freeze to death?

And so the merriment ceased, brought on by the continued dour silence seeping from the McCains that seemed, at last, to penetrate the car, leaving us in pale gray gloom. Occasionally McCain would turn in his seat and study Flo, then shake his head slightly and turn back to sit beside his wife, quietly staring straight ahead.

At last, we made it into Dodge City as the wind began to pick up and whip the fallen snow around us like thick winding sheets.

When we stepped from the car, the cold and wind took our breath away. I peered through the snow and saw Joe Logan waiting for us with his wagon and a team of horses. Joe owned the boarding house in town where I stayed. I greeted him gratefully.

"I thought you'd need some help, Mr. Wheeler!" he shouted against the roaring of the wind. "So I brought the team down to fetch you home."

"Thanks! I appreciate it!" I shouted.

McCain appeared beside us. "Do you think you could drop Mrs. McCain and myself off at Reverend Bottoms' place?"

"I could," Joe said. "But he and his wife went up to Cheyenne yesterday. I don't think they'll be back in this weather."

"I see. A hotel then?"

"All full!" Joe shouted as a gust tried to tear his words away. "We got a couple of spare rooms at the boarding house, though."

"Enough for three more?" the cowboy said, coming up beside us. I glanced at Flo, huddled in her thin coat beside him.

Joe frowned, then nodded. "Yes. We can help you out. One of you men will have to take a pallet in the living room, but you'll be warm there."

"I've slept in worse places," the cowboy said. He turned to Flo and the drummer. "You two take the rooms."

"Thanks, cowboy," she said. "I appreciate that."

Quickly we loaded the wagon and Joe climbed upon the seat, taking the reins in his gloved hands. The horses' coats were covered with a thick blanket of snow and they leaned eagerly into their harness when Joe slapped the reins lightly across their backs.

We moved slowly through the drifting streets of Dodge City until we came to the outskirts where Joe had his boarding house. He drove straight into the corral and barn before stopping.

We unloaded our bags and forced our way through the gathering snow to the back door and entered the warmth. I sighed and stamped the snow off my boots. A sudden weariness came over me as tension slipped away. I stepped aside so the others could enter, then picked up my bag and trudged upstairs to my room.

I came downstairs a couple of hours later to find the others looking a bit recovered and relaxed from their ordeal. Flo was laughing and joking with Joe and the cowboy and the drummer while the McCains sat, stiff and quiet, in their black garb on the other side of the room, staring with disapproval at the merriment in the room.

I noticed that the drummer had opened his wares and broken out a bottle of brandy and was pouring generous measures "to chase away the cold," he said as he handed each of us our covenant glass. The McCains refused.

"Drink is the highway to hell and damnation!" Judith said loudly, sniffing disdainfully to punctuate her words.

Flo glanced at her and raised her glass. "Take a little wine for your stomach's sake. And to put off the chill," she added, shivering delicately. She had changed into a white dress with an ivory Chantilly lace shawl around her shoulders. "Isn't that what the Bible says as well?"

"But not to excess as you folks seem about to take it," McCain said. But his eyes were upon Flo and didn't seem to include everyone in the room. Bright fires seemed to glow in their centers.

I felt a moment's annoyance at his piety, but didn't say anything. Instead I sipped from my glass and visited quietly with the others until dinner was ready.

We had a hearty dinner, then Flo turned on the gramophone and encouraged each of us to dance with her "to

172

help the digestion along." The McCains excused themselves and went upstairs to their room.

It became hot in the room as the potbellied stove gave out warmth and the wind howled around the eaves and rattled the windows in their frames. The drummer broke out another bottle of brandy and we were halfway through it when a strange apparition appeared upon the stairs leading to the bedrooms above. We stared at its fury, then I recognized McCain.

"Of all the abominations that could be visited upon guests, these are surely the worst!" he said. "How dare you defile the night with your infernal music and ranting and ravings, trying to see which of you will bed the Whore of Babylon?"

"Now see here—" Joe began, but the cowboy pushed his way past to stand in front of McCain.

"And who the hell are you to preach to us?" he said. His face was red from exercise and drink and his anger threatened to boil over.

"I am the one who will pass judgment upon you," McCain said. He ignored the cowboy and glared around the room. "The decent hour for such things has long passed. Take yourselves to bed!" He looked at Joe. "And I would have expected more of you than to allow such things to happen in the sanctity of your own home. With this"—his eyes flickered to Flo—"woman. We shall speak of this in the morning!"

"In the morning," Joe said quietly, "you'll take yourself someplace else to stay."

McCain nodded silently and turned and went upstairs.

We stood looking silently, awkwardly at each other, then Flo laughed and said, "Well, we were getting pretty loud there. Maybe we'd better call it an evening."

We were all angry at McCain's sudden intrusion into our evening, but as soon as Flo spoke, it seemed as if the weary day had suddenly caught up with us and drained us. I felt a yawn coming and covered my mouth.

"I'll carry the gramophone upstairs for you, ma'am," the cowboy offered.

Flo shook her head. "It'll be all right down here unless the landlord—?"

"Why carry it up and then back down?" Joe said roughly. "Leave it where it is. It ain't hurting anything. Despite what others may think," he said angrily, glancing back up the stairs. "But we'll be rid of him tomorrow. I'll find someplace for him and that frozen biddy of his. Maybe the Bottoms left a key with someone. But"—he shook his fist at the stairs, his gray hair bristling—"they won't be under my roof tomorrow."

The music came blaring up out of the black night. I opened my eyes to a gray morning and glanced at the window. It was still snowing, but lighter now, and I lay in bed a moment, confused, listening to the harsh music rolling up from downstairs.

I rose and put on my dressing gown and slippers and went downstairs. The music grew louder as I went toward the parlor. I nearly tripped over the cowboy sprawled in the doorway. A slight trickle of blood ran from a nasty gash in his forehead. I bent and felt his pulse beating and knew he had only been knocked unconscious. A poker lay at hand. I looked into the gray light and saw Flo huddled in a robe, her feet drawn up under her, in the corner of the sofa. On the table next to the sofa stood the gramophone, music playing loudly from it. But it wasn't the music to which we had danced the evening before; this was harsh, loud, and racheting upon the ears.

"What's going on?" Judith whispered from behind me.

I turned and saw her clutching her robe at her throat, her long hair plaited in a thick braid that hung down the center of her back.

"Where's Daniel?"

Joe frowned at me, his nightcap pulled down tightly to his bushy gray eyebrows twitching angrily. The drummer looked sleepily down, bent over in half so he could peer under from his place on the stairs.

"I don't know," I said. "Joe, you'd better get a wet towel and see to our cowboy friend here."

He turned silently toward the kitchen. I heard him working the pump by the sink then soon he came back with a wet towel. He pressed it gently against the wound on the cowboy's temple. The cowboy moaned. I rose and walked slowly into the living room.

"Flo?"

She looked up at me, her eyes old and puffy, her mouth pursed tightly.

"Flo?"

She shook her head. "I think he went out to the livery stable," she said.

She rose, turned off the gramophone, then picked it up and carried it to the stairs. She stopped in front of Judith and waited until that woman stepped aside. Then she silently mounted the steps and disappeared.

"Now, what the hell do you think he was doing out in the livery stable at this hour?" the drummer asked.

Joe looked up from where he squatted beside the cowboy. "Lord alone knows," he said.

"Won't one of you help me?" Judith asked.

We turned toward her. Her face looked as gray as the light coming in through the windows. The cowboy moaned.

"He's coming around," Joe said. "Help me move him to the sofa."

We carried him gently to the sofa and stretched him out. He sighed, and his eyes fluttered. He looked around the room blankly for a moment, then closed his eyes again and let out a deep sigh.

"A concussion, I'd guess," I said. "I suppose we'd better get the doc in here."

"Where's Daniel?" Judith said again, her voice sounding like a wail.

Joe looked at me and shrugged. "I suppose we'd better check the stable," he said half-heartedly.

I nodded. Music suddenly roared down the stairs.

"Oh! Turn that off! Tell her to turn that off!" Judith screamed, covering her ears.

I went upstairs and knocked on Flo's room. She didn't answer. I opened the door and went in. She was dressed in her white dress, the shawl back over her shoulders, sitting on the bed with her back against the wall, her legs crossed in front of her.

"Would you turn the music off?" I asked.

She shook her head.

"Flo—"

She gave a loud, jeering laugh. Her face grew hard

with contempt and scorn. "You damn men! You all want something from me, don't you? Leave me alone!"

I nodded and backed from the room, closing the door softly behind me. I stood for a moment, gathering my breath, then walked down the stairs to where the others waited.

"She's still playing that music!" Judith said. Tears began to roll down her chubby cheeks. "And—and where's Daniel?"

I looked at Joe and the drummer. "I suppose," I said, "we'd better check the stable."

Joe nodded, and the three of us made our way to the back door. We had to push hard to clear the snow away from the threshold then work our way through the small drift to the stable door. Joe bent and pulled the snow away from the door. Inside, we could hear the horses moving nervously, snorting, their hooves stamping on the planking.

We opened the door and found him immediately. He had hanged himself with a rope he had looped around a rafter. He still wore his nightgown. One of his slippers had fallen to the floor. I walked over and touched his foot. It was cold. I looked up at his thin face, now a mask of terror.

"Why do you suppose he did it?" the drummer asked.

I shook my head. "I don't know," I lied.

The music came softly out to us in the stable, harsh and discordant.

"Who's going to tell her? The wife, I mean," the drummer asked. We looked at him and he backed away, holding his hands in front of him. "No, no. I don't do things like that. No, not at all." He looked at Joe. "It's your stable; your property. You do it."

Joe shook his head and sighed deeply. "I suppose," he

said half-heartedly. He looked over at me. "How do you think she's going to take it?"

"Badly," I said. "Very badly."

We looked back at the Reverend Daniel McCain swinging ever so slightly in the air coming through the stable door.

"I'll tell her," I said. "You go get the sheriff and the doctor."

Relief shone from Joe's eyes. "You're sure about this?"

I nodded. "Let's go get dressed."

"What about him?" the drummer asked.

"He ain't going nowhere," Joe said.

Judith's eyes looked bleakly through the back window as the sheriff and a couple of townsmen carried McCain out from the stable. They struggled with the drifting snow. She raised her head and looked at the ceiling. The music had not stopped. Suddenly she turned and went to the stairs.

"Judith," I began, but she ignored me and hurried up the stairs. I came up behind her, not certain what she had in mind.

She paused in front of Flo's room then quietly turned the knob and entered. Flo still sat on the bed, the gramophone within easy reach. She stared at us.

Judith cleared her throat. "Did he——" She coughed. "I need to know if he——"

Flo sighed. "The cowboy and I stayed downstairs while the rest of you went to bed. We were just talking. He has a young girl he's in love with up Cheyenne way and wanted to tell me about her. I think it was because I'm a woman and he felt he could talk to me about those things.

"We put that waltz on again and he asked me to dance with him one more time. That was when your husband came storming down the stairs. But he didn't say anything. He just stood there, looking at the two of us. The cowboy asked him what he wanted—and then they fought."

Judith stared at her for a long minute, her lips pressed tightly together. Then she shook her head. "There must have been more to it than that."

"There was," Flo said harshly. "It ended the way you see it now."

"But—"

"Go away and imagine the worst," Flo said resignedly. "That's the truth."

I took Judith's arm and tugged her gently away from the door. Tears started to fall down Flo's face. Judith shook her head.

"I'm sorry," she said in a small voice.

I closed the door behind her and took her back downstairs to the parlor. We sat there for a long time while she stared at the wide wedding band on her finger.

"You know, Mr. Wheeler, you think you know someone well after living with them for fifteen years," she said.

"Nobody ever knows everything about anyone," I said. "I don't think we even know ourselves all that well. What are you going to do?"

"Go back home," she said softly. "Back to Vermont. That's where I'm from. My parents are still alive. Old, now. They'll need someone to look after them and my sister is still with them."

"I mean your husband," I said.

She wrenched the ring off her finger and laid it on the table beside her chair. Her eyes looked coldly into mine. "I don't know that man," she said.

Then she rose and left, slowly climbing the stairs to the room she had spent with the man she thought she had known.

She left town three days later. Alone.

We put McCain down in the ice house where we put people when they died and the ground wasn't ready for them. When spring thaw came, we took a collection and had him put in Boot Hill. There wasn't enough money for a headstone and although I wrote to her back in Vermont and told her where we had buried him, she never answered.

. . . GRAVEDIGGER . . .

Real poetical, that epitaph, don't ya think? Don't know who that Congreve fella was, but I guess since the reverend didn't deserve to even have his name on his headstone they decided to give him some pretty words. If'n ya ask me, it ain't a very fair trade, a'tall.

You wanna know about me, again? Well, ta tell ya the honest truth, ma'am, my life before I came here to Dodge ain't somethin' I'm real proud of, and I'd rather not talk about it. I'd much rather tell ya some more stories about my friends, here. Now, most of these folks here ain't zackly what you'd call famous, but that don't mean that there ain't some stories with famous people in 'em. You heard of the Pinkertons? Them detectives who claim they always get their man? Well, fact is every once in a while those detectives need the help of somebody famous to get the job done.

Take these boys here. They's all buried here together, 'cause they was the Colton gang. Brothers, they was, all three of them, with Henry doin' the leadin', but Henry led his brothers straight ta hell, if'n ya ask me.

Since that last story started on a train it reminded me of this one. See, this here story takes place almost entirely on a train. Wells Fargo hired them Pinkertons to find out who was stealin' some strongboxes from the Atchison, To-peka, and Sante Fe railroad. See? Them's all famous names, ain't they? But they ain't even the one I'm talkin' about.

And wait 'til ya hear this. I heard this here story right from the detective who caught them boys—and she was a lady! A woman detective, can you beat that? But a smart one, I kin tell ya that. Smart enough ta know when she needed help, and smart enough to ask . . . well, I ain't gonna tell ya who she asked. You're jest gonna have to listen to the whole story and find out . . .

THE LAST RIDE OF
THE COLTON GANG

JOHN HELFERS
AND KERRIE HUGHES

HENRY, DAVEY AND FRED COLTON
THE COLTON GANG RIDES NO MORE.
EXECUTED FOR ROBBERY AND MURDER
ONE BY BULLET, TWO BY HANGING.
MOURN NOT THEIR DEATH, THEY DESERVED IT.

Perhaps other travelers find the rolling prairie wild and romantic, but I must confess that after a week riding the railroad from Santa Fe to Dodge City, I almost wish for something to happen on the train just to break the monotony.

Nancy Smith read the sentence she had just written in her journal and shook her head. *I don't think that will make it into the report to headquarters,* she thought. *Even if it is true.*

Shivering, she tucked a wool blanket around her legs. Although she would have been warmer in the cabin they had been staying in, she was feeling claustrophobic in the tiny space, and had taken a seat in one of the coach cars to write her report. The wood-burning stove was at the other end of the train car, surrounded by the dozen other passengers, leaving the rest of the car empty. Nancy sat on a bench at the far end of the car, writing her report in pencil, and would recopy it in ink when they reached Dodge City.

Smiling, Nancy turned to a new page. *Perhaps something a bit more professional this time.*

February 17th, 1876:
 Agent Thompson and myself have been riding the Atchison, Topeka, and Santa Fe rail line for the past seven days, taking the route from Dodge City to Santa Fe and back. Despite repeated claims of train robbers plying their illegal trade along this route and supposedly posing a great threat to the payrolls of the various mining companies in the Colorado and New Mexico territories, we have yet to see any bandit activity of note. However, Wells Fargo can rest assured that any would-be thieves will be dealt with swiftly and expeditiously. We are at the ready for any attempt on the monies carried, and will remain so until they are apprehended.

Assuming I don't faint from boredom first, she thought, looking out the window at the infinite expanse of prairie, dotted with occasional pockets of snow, like frozen whitecaps in an endless ocean of wind-whipped grass. *Still, I shouldn't complain, although when William offered me this assignment, I thought it would be a little more exciting.*

The assignment she and her partner had accepted had come to the Pinkertons by none other than the owner of

Wells Fargo, Lloyd Trevis. Having purchased the mail and banking company for a pittance in 1870, he had visited the Chicago office personally and talked to Allan and William Pinkerton for more than an hour. When their meeting was finished, William had sent for his two best agents.

Strongboxes were disappearing from trains on the Atchison, Topeka, and Santa Fe rail line. However, rather than armed robbers on horseback stopping the train and robbing it, the strongboxes were vanishing while the train was enroute through Dodge City, with the single guard overpowered, tied, and gagged.

Naturally, the first thing Lloyd had ordered was more guards on the train. On the last run that had been robbed, ten days ago, the two men that were supposed to be guarding the strongbox had simply disappeared, along with the box and its contents. Suspicion had immediately fallen on the two missing men, but the other guards on that run swore that the two men, Henry Colton and Sam Danridge, were loyal employees, and would have never stolen the money.

The mining companies that had been using Wells Fargo were now threatening to take their accounts elsewhere. Lloyd was understandably anxious to see whoever was behind the robberies caught. Carter and Nancy had accepted immediately, and within twelve hours were on their way west to Dodge City.

They had stayed in town overnight, then were up early the next morning and on the train. When they had arrived, Nancy had expected the worst, having heard stories about the lawlessness that plagued the cowtowns, Dodge City in particular. While she had been woken during the night by a bunch of mounted cowboys shouting and galloping down the street, it had otherwise been a quiet evening, with none of the wild fracases she had read about in the eastern newspapers. It seemed that the local police force, which included lawman Wyatt Earp, was taming the city's rougher element. However, looking out the back window of her hotel room, which afforded a perfect view of the city's cemetery, assuaged any doubt about whether she had reached the frontier. Although Dodge City had been founded only four years earlier, Boot Hill was already overcrowded with burial plots and rough wooden crosses.

Since then it had been nothing but the noisy clatter of the locomotive, the swaying passenger cars, hurried meals eaten during the twenty-minute stops at various stations along the way, and the fine patina of soot that her dresses and skirts had acquired during the past several days—and that she would be cleaning for the next week after this assignment was over. At least the new caballero split skirts she purchased in Kansas City had solved the last problem. They were shorter and sturdier, without the same problems as the long dresses and skirts she started the assignment with. She also needed to purchase a taller pair of leather boots and longer, thicker stockings, but at least now she could get on and off the train without tripping, and stay a bit warmer.

Ah, the exciting life of a Pinkerton agent, she thought. *Too bad I can't charge the agency for laundry expenses. Still, this is my first assignment outside the city, and I'm not going to let the Eyes down.*

The door at the end of the car slid open, and Nancy looked up to see her partner, Carter Thompson, and a very tall man she thought looked familiar but couldn't place, enter. She closed her journal, making sure the various papers and missing person's sketches, including those of Henry Colton and Sam Danridge, were secure inside.

Nancy had been working with Carter Thompson for the past year, and had learned more about being a Pinkerton agent from him than anyone else. In his dark brown business suit and bowler, he looked like a traveling banker or lawyer. But Nancy knew that his placid demeanor and gentleman's clothes concealed a razor-keen mind and an unswerving devotion to upholding the law, a trait the Pinkerton Agency strove to hone in all its operatives. An agent for more than fifteen years, he was loyal, intelligent, and honest almost to a fault. His blue eyes scanned every face in the car from long-practiced habit before falling on her. With a nod, he and the other man walked over.

"Nancy, I've been looking for you. I bumped into an old friend I want you to meet. Nancy Smith, this is Jim . . . Butler."

The pause between the first and last name was so slight that Nancy almost missed it. She saw the two men exchange a lightning-quick glance and then the taller man was stooping to take her hand.

"Madam, it is a pleasure to make your acquaintance," he said, his eyes hidden behind smoked glasses. He was immaculately dressed in pressed gray pinstriped trousers, a midnight-blue Prince Albert frock coat, dark gray vest, white linen shirt, and black string tie. Around his waist was an intricately tooled gun belt with two holsters, each containing a pistol carried butt-forward, in the style known as "cross-draw." He had long blond hair that fell in ringlets to his broad shoulders, a matching long mustache, which drooped on either side of his mouth, and a black wide-brimmed hat in his other hand.

"Thank you, Mr. Butler, the pleasure is mine," Nancy replied. "Won't you please sit down and join us?"

"Thank you very much, ma'am," he said, taking the bench seat across from Nancy and Carter, his back to the wall.

"Traveling to Dodge, are you? Will you be staying in town?" Nancy asked.

"No ma'am, I'm on my way to Cheyenne, in the Wyoming territory. I'm heading up there to meet my fiancée," the slim man replied, adjusting his glasses.

"Congratulations on your engagement. You know, Carter said you two were acquainted, yet I don't ever recall him mentioning such a handsome gentleman to me before," Nancy said with a smile.

Jim smiled and nodded, "Carter and I met during the war, when I was engaged as a scout for the Union."

"Oh, come on now, Jim, you did a lot more than that. Jim here was one of the best shots the Union had ever seen. Why, during that business at Cross Timber Hollow, in the battle of Pea Ridge, you were responsible for half a dozen Confederates killed."

"Carter, please, not so loud," Jim said, looking around. "I'm sure Miss Smith isn't interested in that old history."

"On the contrary, it's a topic that fascinates me," Nancy said. She had been a child when the War between the States had started, but had read the newspaper reports about the activity on both sides every day. In fact, it was the exploits of the Pinkertons during the war that had prompted her to join the famous detective agency as soon as she was old enough, following in the footsteps of Allan Pinkerton's first and most renowned female agent, Kate Warne. She had been with the agency for two years now, and this was her first case outside of Chicago.

"Is that so, Miss Smith? Well, here's a bit of information Carter may have neglected to tell you," Jim leaned forward, a smile on his lips. "Did you know that during the war, Carter Thompson, the man sitting next to you, saved my life?"

"Why no, Mr. Butler, he didn't tell me that story," Nancy said, glancing at Carter and trying not to smile at his flushed face.

"I hardly think what happened at Rock Creek Station qualifies as saving you, Jim," Carter said.

"Killing a man who was going to back-shoot me?" Jim said, looking over his dark glasses at Carter for a second. "Miss Smith, what would you call it?"

"I think your description of it is perfectly correct, Mr. Butler," Nancy said, still enjoying Carter's discomfort.

"Please, ma'am, call me Jim," the tall man said. "Anyway, I've never been able to repay you for that, Carter."

"And every time you bring it up, which he does every time we meet, I tell you the same thing, that it isn't necessary, Jim," Carter said, shifting to a more comfortable position on the bench.

"That's not how I see it, Carter," Jim replied, the smile slowly leaving his face.

Carter started to reply, but was interrupted by Nancy.

"Gentlemen, I'm sure this promises to be a fascinating discussion, but if you'll excuse me, I'm going to leave you two to discuss who owes who what," Nancy said, rising from her seat. The two men also stood up with her, sitting again after she had left the train car.

Nancy made her way to the water closet, passing four private compartments, each with two or more passengers. It was located at the end of the first-class car, with the car beyond that, the mail car, containing the Wells Fargo lockbox. Just beyond that car was the coal car and then the engine. Peeking out the door through its small window, she spotted a guard standing on the next platform, then ducked into the room before he could see her.

I don't know why I keep looking out there, the poor man has to go inside to get warm again when the other guard on his side goes out. I can't think of a more boring job, fifteen minutes inside, fifteen minutes outside, with one man always in and one always out. Still, this way any bandits will only catch one of them outside at a time, so the other could lock up the car and defend it.

Nancy stood inside the water closet just long enough to convince anyone who might be watching that her visit was real. She exited quietly and slowly; there was no need to rush. Two men's voices caught her attention from the next compartment.

"How much longer till Henry gets here?" said the first voice.

Henry? Are they talking about Henry Colton?

"We should be at the drop-off within the next fifteen minutes," a second man said. "I'm sure he'll be along any minute now."

Nancy heard the window of the compartment squeak as someone closed it. The voices continued, but were too muffled to make out what they were saying.

I have got to hear the rest of that conversation, she thought. Nancy pulled a lace handkerchief from her sleeve and tossed it on the floor below the window. Kneeling, she crawled underneath the closed window so she could listen unseen. Pressing her ear against the compartment wall, she also made sure to keep one eye on the hallway for anyone coming.

"Do we tie up the guards, or kill 'em like we did Sam?" Nancy barely made out the words over the noise of the train car.

"We kill them and toss off the bodies with the box," replied the other man. "Same as last time."

"I don't like the killin', Davey. Why can't we just knock em out and tie 'em up?" the first voice said.

"Cuz Henry wants the guards to be suspected, Kid, that's why," was the curt reply. "We also don't need any witnesses, all right!"

My God, they must be Henry Colton's brothers, Davey and Fred! The profile on him stated he had two younger brothers, with the youngest one known as Kid instead of by his Christian name. They killed Sam, and they'll kill the other guards if I don't get Carter and stop this now!

Nancy reached for her handkerchief just as a man came into the car from the far end and headed in her direction. He smiled at her as she rose. She was careful not to reveal her presence to the two men in the compartment. *I've heard enough,* she thought.

The man strode forward, "Do you need some assistance, little lady?" he asked.

191

"Why no," she replied, "I've got it, thank you."

"And it looks like I've got you," he replied, placing one hand on her arm while bringing his other hand out from behind his back and showing her the pistol he was holding.

"Open the door, young lady, and have a seat," he ordered.

Nancy did so and paused just inside the door. To her left was a younger man who looked startled and confused. His eyes were bloodshot and he smelled of too much whiskey and not enough soap. The man on her right seemed mean and ready for a fight. He glared at her and his hand went inside his coat, but he didn't do anything more. The man behind her nudged her in with the end of his gun; she decided to sit next to the younger one and waited for him to move over. She hoped this would give her a good view of the passageway when Carter came to check on her.

Which I hope will be very soon, she thought.

Her captor took a seat directly across from her, shoving his startled brother over and glaring at Nancy. Now that she got a good look at him, she realized this was Henry without his handlebar mustache and shoulder-length hair. She had seen his picture as a sketch only but it was close enough to reveal his identity. Looking from one man's face to the next, she saw the familial resemblance, the same wavy hair, close-set blue eyes, and pug nose, even the same ill-fitting suits, like the brothers had taken out their Sunday best and tried to pass as first-class passengers. The only thing different was the cold-blooded look in the elder Colton's eyes.

Henry growled at his two brothers, "What were you two talking about just now when I caught this little girl listening outside the door?"

"Uh, nothin'," stammered both Davey and Kid.

"Sir, I have no idea what you're talking about—" Nancy began, but was cut off by the eldest brother.

"Shut up! I know what you were doing out there, I'm not like these two," Henry said. "You both are lousy liars. At least she sounded believable," he said. "But we don't have time for this. Kid, you keep her here, I don't know who she is or what she heard, but we have work to do. We'll take care of her and the guards later."

Almost as an afterthought he added, "And no more whiskey, hand it over!" He snatched the flask that Kid pulled out of his coat pocket.

Davey rose. "I'll check to see if the change has gone," he said. He looked out the window, then stepped out and walked down the hall and stood just outside the door. "It's all clear."

With that, Henry got up and led Davey out the door between the trains. Nancy watched them leave, then heard the train door open, then close. She looked back at the Kid. He had a gun trained on her, but didn't look like he wanted to use it.

Lord, let this kid be stupid enough to fall for a fainting female, she thought.

"Oh my!" she said, raising a hand to her forehead, "Please . . . oh, please, you wouldn't . . . oh, my . . . I feel faint." And with that, she wavered and began to collapse to the side away from Kid, then rolled to the floor facedown. As she slumped to the ground, Nancy retrieved her Derringer from her skirt pocket and held it against her chest.

"Ma'am, are you okay?" she heard the Kid say.

C'mon, Kid, come over here.

The Kid leaned forward, "Ma'am?" he then reached out to touch her shoulder. "Lady?"

Nancy moaned a bit, then heard the Kid say, "Ohmigod, are you okay?" She felt him lean over her, the smell of unwashed cowboy and booze filling her nostrils. A hand fell on her shoulder and rolled her over. Nancy fell onto her back and opened her eyes, pointing the small pistol at his face. Kid's eyes grew as round as coffee cups. Nancy cocked the hammer back, the click loud in the silence.

"Now son, I don't want to have to shoot you, but I will if I have to." Nancy glanced over at the boy's pistol, which was still in his hand on the seat. "All right, before we do anything, I want you to take your hand off that gun, and do it nice and slow."

The Kid looked at his hand, then back at Nancy. He looked at his hand again, and uncurled his fingers from the butt of the pistol.

"Very good. Now, lean back and stand up, and do it slow," Nancy said. The Kid complied, his gaze back on her pistol. When he was upright, she sat up, grabbed his pistol, and scooted back to the door. "Sit down."

White-faced, the youth didn't sit as much as fall onto the compartment seat. Nancy scrambled to her feet and leaned against the door, only to start in terror as someone rapped on the glass. She tried to keep one eye on the Kid while turning to see who was at the door.

Carter stood behind the window, a short-barreled revolver in his hand. Nancy sagged in relief and opened the door.

"Came to see what was taking you so long," he said "Looks like you found what we were looking for."

"Carter, it's about time! Cuff this one. The other two Colton brothers are at the mail car. Henry and his brothers have been behind the robberies from the beginning. They're going to kill the guards if we don't stop them."

"Really?" As usual, Carter reacted to this news with his typical unflappability. "We'd best get going, then." He produced a pair of handcuffs from a jacket pocket and cuffed the unresisting Kid to a railing. Carter started to head out of the compartment, then turned back to Kid.

"I don't think they'll be able to hear any yelling, but just in case." He reversed the gun he held, but was stopped by Nancy. She extracted Carter's hip flask from his pocket and tossed it to the boy.

"Here. You might as well enjoy it, it'll be the last you'll have for a long time." The boy slumped back against the seat, and he unscrewed the cap with shaking hands. Carter watched the whole thing and shook his head.

"Let's go," he said, brushing by Nancy, who followed him out of the compartment. She joined her partner at the end of the train car, taking up a position opposite him on the side of the door.

"I didn't see anyone on the platform, they must be inside. I'll go first, you cover me, all right?" Carter said.

Nancy gripped her pistol tightly and nodded, reaching for the door with her other hand. She twisted the handle, then yanked the door open and motioned Carter to go.

Ignoring the bitter wind lashing the hallway, Carter sprang through the opening onto the platform. Not even pausing, he stepped onto the other rocking car, ending up against the wall of the mail car. Holstering his pistol, he gripped the safety rail of the car with one hand and began to reach for the door with the other. Nancy watched from the hallway, covering the door.

Carter's hand was just about to touch the handle when the door sprung open, and the figure of a man stepped forward. Davey Colton looked up in surprise when he saw the woman he thought was with his brother staring back at him through the window. His other hand was filled with a pistol, and he started to bring it up.

"Carter!" Nancy yelled, stepping back and aiming her Derringer at the man. Carter had reacted to the threat in an instant, drawing his gun, and shooting from the hip. Only a couple feet away, he couldn't miss.

Nancy and Carter's pistols barked at the same instant. Davey Colton jerked as the bullets hit him, then collapsed in the doorway. Carter didn't hesitate, but leapt through the doorway, leading with his pistol. She tried to see into the car, but couldn't make out what was happening in the darkened car.

Carter reappeared a second later. "Both guards are dead from knife wounds, I don't see the other two," he said before turning to re-enter the car.

Nancy was just about to step out onto the car platform to join him when a shot rang out. Seconds later, a man staggered out holding his side. Nancy brought her gun up, then stopped when she saw it was Carter. The agent managed to get outside to the platform, where he sagged to the floor.

"Carter!" Nancy yelled again. Before she could rush out to him, she heard bootsteps thudding on the car floor behind her. Nerves already stretched razor-thin, she whirled and brought her gun up, yelling, "Pinkerton agent, don't move!"

The man dove to the floor and she saw Jim Butler stretched out in front of her, pistols in hand. "Begging your pardon, ma'am, but I heard the shots, and thought you might be in need of assistance," he said calmly, as if he hadn't almost gotten shot just a few seconds ago.

"Jim, am I glad to see you," Nancy said. "Carter's on the platform outside, he's been shot, but I think he's still alive. We've captured one of the robbers and killed another, but the third one's still inside."

"Well, that does need taking care of, now, don't it?" Jim replied. "Let's check on Carter, and then we'll handle that last one, all right?"

"All right." Nancy stood up with Jim and they both checked the open doorway across the short space between the cars. The door slammed against the Colton boy's legs sticking out on the platform. Carter was sitting against the train car wall, unmoving save for the slight rise and fall of his chest, sending small puffs of breath into the cold Kansas air.

As if he had been doing it all his life, Jim stepped out and leapt across the gap between the cars to the other platform, landing right beside Carter. He peeked into the other car, both guns ready for any sign of movement, then motioned to Nancy to come across.

Nancy slipped her pistol into her pocket and stepped over to the other car, gratefully accepting the arm Jim offered to steady her as she came over.

"How's Carter?" Nancy asked, kneeling beside her partner.

"I'm . . . all right. Just get that . . . bastard," Carter said.

"He's not bleeding from the mouth, doesn't look like

the bullet hit anything vital," Jim said as he examined the wound.

"Yeah, except me," Carter said. "Now get going. I'm not going anywhere."

"I'll check the door," Jim said.

"Listen, I'll be back as soon as I can," Nancy said. She scooted back to take a position beside the door across from Jim.

"I, uh, didn't see anybody moving in there," he said.

"Only one way to find out," Nancy said, drawing her own Derringer. Jim nodded and used his leg to shove the body in the doorway back into the train car. When no shots were fired, he stepped inside and headed for the nearest cover, a shelf full of wooden crates. The car was silent. Nancy saw Jim wave her forward. Trying to keep low, she crossed to the rack on the other side of the car.

Nancy peeked around the side of the large box she was crouched behind, but saw nothing. Either Henry was totally hidden behind the cargo at the other end of the car, or . . .

"Think he's still in here?" she hissed at Jim.

Before he could reply, she got her answer. The car they were in lurched forward as the entire train decelerated suddenly. Nancy heard the high screech of the locomotive's brakes as the train began coming to a halt.

Nancy and Jim looked at each at the same time. "He's at the engine!" Nancy said. As one, they both ran down the length of the car and saw the open door still swinging on its hinges. Beyond the door was a ladder that led to the top of the open coal car.

Jim scrambled up the side while Nancy pocketed her pistol and followed close behind, grateful for her gloves as she climbed the freezing rungs of the coal car ladder. Jim was already on top, having scaled the ladder like a cat streaking up a tree. He offered her his hand, but she shook her head and motioned for him to watch the front of the car. Once up top, she put her lips close to his ear.

"He'll likely make a break for it, so you watch the right side and I'll take the left. First one to see anything sings out, all right?"

She felt Jim nod, and, drawing her gun again, crawled over the shifting load of coal to peek over the side, finding nothing but barren Kansas prairie and small, unmarked snowdrifts. She looked back at Jim, only to find him shaking his head.

Is he still at the engine? Nancy wondered. She nodded toward the front of the train. Jim agreed, and the two of them crawled to the front of the train, trying not to dislodge any coal pieces. Just a few steps more and they'd be at the end of the coal car. The coal had been shoveled into a steep pile as the engineer and fireman had used their supply to fuel the locomotive. They would have to slide down the pile to the bottom of the car and cover the engine quarters from there.

Nancy tensed as she drew nearer to the engineer's compartment. She looked over at Jim and saw him at the ready, both pistols out once more. He nodded, and they both stood up and jumped down to the edge of the car, pistols pointing at the open cabin.

A man in soot-blackened coveralls stood there gaping at them. Nancy motioned for him to put his hands up, and he complied.

"Don't shoot, whatever you do," the engineer said.

"What happened to the man who was just here?"

"The crazy guy with the gun? He barged in here, knocked out my fireman, stuck a pistol in my face, and made me stop the train. Then he says face the boiler and count to fifty. So I do that, turn around, and he's gone, and you two are here. What the hell is going on?"

"He's going back for the Kid!" Jim said. "Nancy, go back and see if he's there. If you can, take him by surprise. I'll come around from the other side and do the same. Hurry!" He began climbing back up the sliding coal pile toward the mail car.

Nancy jumped down from the car and ran back toward the first-class car, checking underneath the train as she went. She reached the far end of the mail car where they had left Carter and stopped. Pressing her back against the freezing metal, she listened for a moment, trying to hear any noise above the steady wind.

"You there? I say, what seems to be the problem? When is this train going to get moving again?" asked an accented voice from above her head.

Nancy looked up to see a bowler-hatted head sticking out from a first-class compartment window in the middle of the car. She put a finger to her lips and tried to wave him off.

"No, I won't be quiet. First we hear shots fired, and believe you me, I know shots when I hear them, or I'm not the twelfth earl of Huntingdon, mind you. Now the train has stopped in this Godforsaken wilderness—"

Out of patience, Nancy raised her pistol and aimed at the gentleman.

"Oh my, I seem to have caught you at a most inconvenient time. Excuse me," the man said, ducking back into his compartment so quickly he knocked his hat off his head.

Nancy leaned back and prepared to peek around the side of the car. Before she could, a voice reached her ears.

"Whoever's out there, I don't know who you are, but I've got a gun on this man's head, so you best toss out your pistol and step out here with your hands up, nice and slow, or I'll finish the job I started in the mail car, got it?"

Damn it, I hope Jim is able to do something, or Carter's and my careers are going to come to a very premature end, Nancy thought. "All right, I'm stepping out. Please don't shoot."

Nancy came around the corner and saw Carter cradled in Henry Colton's lap. The bandit had one arm around the agent's neck, and his other hand held a pistol at his temple. Nancy saw a large red stain at Carter's side, and his chest rose and fell with shallow breaths. The bandit's face was white, but his gun hand was steady. He had moved with his back to the mail car wall, so he could glance behind him from time to time.

"Well, shit, hamstrung by a woman. I can't believe it," Henry said. "Well, we're not done yet. I know you got my brother in there, and I'm sure the damn fool got himself caught alive. So here's what you're gonna do. Get in there, and free my brother. Then you bring him out here, and we'll have ourselves a little prisoner swap. Now get moving."

Have to keep him talking, she thought. *Where the hell is Jim?*

"How do I know you won't shoot us both when I bring the Kid out here? After all, you didn't let Sam live when you ambushed him."

Henry hauled back on the hammer of his pistol. "If you don't get in there in the next three seconds, I'll shoot him right now, just like I did Sam."

While Henry was blustering, a flash of movement above his head caught Nancy's eye. A hand holding a cocked pistol slowly stretched down from the roof of the rail car. Quickly Nancy focused her attention back on the outlaw.

"All right, all right, I'll go. Just hang on, I've got to get up there first," she said. Grabbing hold of the coupling between the cars, she hauled herself up onto the platform on the mail car across from Henry and Carter.

"Okay I'm ready," she said loudly, hoping Jim would get the message.

"Then what the hell are you waiting—" Henry began. The deafening roar of Jim's Navy Colt discharging, followed almost immediately by another gunshot, drowned the rest of his sentence out. A white plume of gun smoke enveloped the two men at the end of the car, but Nancy could hear Henry scream and curse loudly.

Damn, he's still alive! She rushed forward, trying to see through the haze of cordite. The first thing she saw was Henry holding his bleeding hand, with no gun in sight. Nancy didn't think, she just leapt over Carter and landed next to the bandit.

Planting her foot, she lifted her booted heel and drove it into Henry's face, mashing his nose and lips into a bloody smear, and slamming the back of his head against the mail car wall. Henry's cussing and thrashing cut off, and he slumped over.

"Carter, are you all right?" she asked, pulling him to her. His face was flecked with blood and smeared with burnt powder, and she checked to make sure he hadn't been hit again.

"Did you . . . get him?" she heard him whisper.

"Yeah, we got him, partner. We got him," she said.

A shadow fell over her, and she saw Jim slide down the overhang and swing himself onto the platform, landing on his feet with ease.

"My god, Jim, that was the most amazing thing I've ever seen," Nancy said. "I can't believe you shot his hand from up there."

Jim stepped over her and nudged the unconscious Henry's arm over, peering at the man's wounded hand and bloody face. "Heck, looks like my aim ain't what it used to be." He looked back at her and smiled. "Common sense says you don't aim for the gun hand, it might set the pistol off. Looks like you marked him pretty good yourself."

"Guess I learned from the best," she said, then paused as Jim's earlier words sank in. "Wait a minute, you mean—"

"Yep, I was aiming for his head," Jim said, shaking his own ruefully. "Best way to make sure he didn't shoot Carter. Come on, we'd better get him inside. I don't think he's going anywhere." He nodded toward Henry.

"Maybe not, but let's make sure," Nancy said. "There's a pair of handcuffs in my purse in the hallway. Could you bring them back here while I keep an eye on him?"

"It would be my pleasure, Nancy," Jim said, hoisting Carter over his shoulders and carrying him inside, leaving Nancy to sag against the wall of the train in relief. She looked down, and saw Henry's pistol in front of her. She picked it up and trained it on the fallen man, waiting for Jim to return.

The train pulled into Dodge City late that night. Jim and Nancy had taken a look at Carter's wound and dressed it as well as they could, washing it out with whiskey from a pint flask Jim produced from his pocket.

Carter had recovered enough to see Jim off when they disembarked. He was lying on a train bench, waiting for the local doctor to bring a stretcher. "Jim, on behalf of the agency, we can't thank you enough for what you did today," Carter said.

"Well, I think a lot of the credit goes to your partner there," Jim said, tipping his hat to Nancy. "Ma'am, you're about the bravest woman I've ever seen. I'll feel a lot better about Carter rushing headlong into danger next time with you backing him up."

"Thank you very much, Jim, and thank you for your assistance," Nancy said. "We couldn't have done it without you."

"Think nothing of it, Nancy. If you two ever make it up by Cheyenne, stop in and see us if you have a chance. Just ask for the Hickok place." He shook Carter's hand, tipped his hat again to Nancy, and strode out the train car and down the platform, the crowd unconsciously parting before him as the tall man walked away.

"Hickok? Carter, he didn't mean—" Nancy began.

"Yep, that's him. James Butler Hickok," Carter said.

"The 'Wild Bill' Hickok? The gunfighter?" Nancy said.

"One and the same," Carter said.

"My partner knows Wild Bill Hickok. I met—I fought alongside Wild Bill Hickok," Nancy said. "I almost don't believe it."

"You'd better, 'cause you'll have to back up my report, and I'll have to mention his part in all of this," Carter said.

Just then there was a commotion from the front of the train, and two stretcher-bearing men came toward them. Nancy stepped aside to let them pass.

"Oh, believe me, I will," Nancy said, still staring off in the direction Jim Hickok had headed.

February 17th, 1876, continued report from Nancy Smith:
We have successfully captured the men responsible for the mysterious Wells Fargo robberies on the Atchison, Topeka, and Santa Fe railroad. It turns out that one of the missing guards, Henry Colton, was behind the robberies from the beginning, and had brought in his two brothers, Davey and Fred, alias "Kid" Colton, to help when the company placed more guards on duty during the runs. Unfortunately, as told to this agent by Henry, the other missing guard, Sam Dan-ridge, was killed in the line of duty and thrown into a ravine by Henry Colton. A search party will be sent out to attempt the recovery of his body. Davey and Henry killed the two guards on duty during this incident—Jake Hansen and Daniel O'Shea—before we could save them. All three will be buried with honor, expenses paid by Wells Fargo. During our apprehension, Davey Colton was killed while resisting arrest, and Henry Colton was wounded. The youngest brother, Fred, was captured unhurt. Both of the surviving Coltons are awaiting trial in the Dodge City jail. Carter

Thompson's report details fully the events of the afternoon of February 17th, and the subsequent capture of the Colton gang.

Special mention must be made of the heroic actions of one James Butler Hickok, a citizen who was traveling on the train to Dodge City. He was instrumental in capturing Henry Colton, and acted selflessly and heroically during the arrest, including saving Agent Thompson's life. It is with great pride that I am able to report this case closed.

Authors' Note:

James Butler "Wild Bill" Hickok did indeed cross the prairie at this time to marry his fiancée Agnes. A few months after the fictional events of this story, he was killed on August 2, 1876 by Jack McCall, who shot him in the back of the head while he was playing cards. He had been married only a few months. He served the Union as a scout, sniper, and spy during the Civil War. During his last years, he suffered from what historians believed may have been glaucoma, and, seeking to avoid celebrity-seekers and reporters, often traveled under the name of James Butler.

...GRAVEDIGGER...

Wild Bill hisself! Ain't that somethin'? He was killed not long after that, but them Colton boys sure did suffer for meetin' him, didn't they? Wonder what that lady detective is doin' these days?

And speakin' of ladies, before I have to shoo you people off this hill so's I kin get back to work, lemme tell ya about the little lady who's buried over yonder ...

It's right over here. I put her in a special place so's she gets the sun most of the time. It's right here ...

This here's Sally Layton—well, I mean it was Sally. She was about the purttiest thing you'd ever wanna see, in or out of a saloon. Sure was a sad day for me the day I hadda put her in the ground, lemme tell ya. An' she had her a good heart. Yeah, I know, you heard stories about saloon girls with hearts of gold, but Sally—well, she was the real thing. I truly believe she was born with a good heart.

Poor Sally. It was her good heart that got her killed, in the end, tryin' ta keep two men from doin' what men do. This here's a real short epitaph, but a truer one you ain't gonna see up here on the hill.

So listen up, and I'll tell ya why.

THE SELLERS

Troy D. Smith

Sally Layton
1851–1878
She loved not wisely

LeRoy Reese beat his crumpled hat slowly, purposefully against the hitching post. Dust erupted from it, only to fade and merge into the dirty blanket of air which was already settled onto the street. He pulled a thin cigar from his coat pocket, struck a match and cupped his hands around it as he puffed the tobacco to life. His eyes searched the faces of the men walking along both sides of the street—quickly but without attracting attention, as was his custom.

A boy had offered to stable his horse a few minutes earlier, before Reese had even swung out of the saddle. Reese had declined. He minded his own horses, always had. He also minded his own weapons—he hoped his business would not take him north of the Dead Line, and force him to check

209

his firearms. He doubted it would. As long as he stayed south of the railroad tracks, and was careful to keep his revolver concealed, no one would ask any questions.

It was after making sure that his horse's needs were provided for that Reese had paused at the hitching post outside the Royal Flush—one of Dodge City's many saloons, one which catered more to cowboys than to their employers or to the town's many high-rolling gamblers. He drew another deep puff from the cigar, holding it and letting the smoke burn inside him, and then stepped inside.

The saloon was not very busy—it was the middle of the day, after all. The bartender stood bathed in the sunlight which poured through the front window, wiping glasses, like an actor standing in the lights at the opening of one of those Shakespeare plays.

A couple of cowboys stood leaning on the bar, beers in hand, talking quietly. Reese had no doubt that the same men would be bellowing laughter if it were night and the place were packed full of revelers. There is something about saloons on slow afternoons, when dust motes float and sparkle in the sunlight, that makes them feel like empty churches.

Reese stood a few feet down the bar from the cowboys and ordered a shot of whiskey. He slapped down his coins and threw back the shot, and held out the glass for more. The second one he only sipped at—he would make it last. LeRoy Reese never liked to dull his senses too much when he was on business.

Neither of the muttering cowboys was the man he was after. The fact that he had caught Dodge City in one of her rare quiet moments was proof that he had reached town ahead of the Lazy Crown riders. Two dozen dry, thirsty, lonesome cowhands would split the place wide open when they hit. This was what Reese had hoped for—a chance to sit quietly and let his quarry come to him, instead of having to raise questions by too much snooping around. He judged he would have to wait no more than a day or two.

"Hey," he said to the bartender.

The barman turned and glanced at Reese's glass. When he saw that it was still mostly full, his gaze turned to Reese's face.

"Something I can do for you, mister?"

"This is my first time through here," Reese answered. "You know any place a feller can get a bite to eat, that don't bite back?"

The bartender never paused in his wiping of the glasses. "Ma Garrison's is right down the street. It's on the right side when you pass out of the door, here. She serves up a pretty mean steak, it usually ain't even got no hair on it."

Reese nodded. "Obliged."

The bartender's towel stopped in mid-wipe. "She has beds upstairs, too—but by the time daylight rolls around you might be sharing that bed with three or four drunk cowboys, once they've had time to burn up most of their pay."

Reese smirked. "Expect a herd to come through today, do you?"

"This time of year there's a herd coming through every day." He jerked his head toward the door, even as he resumed his wiping with a fresh glass. "If you want to get to the whores while they're still fresh, you'd best start early."

Reese chuckled. "Thanks for the advice, friend. Sounds like you know your way around."

The bartender shrugged. "I do more in this town than wipe glasses, mister. If you're looking for a room that you don't have to share, by the way, there's a hotel around the corner. A flea-trap, and they charge a small fortune."

Reese heard heavy boots approach from behind him. The bartender set down his glass and turned his attention to his new customer. The glass did not look any cleaner, so far as Reese could see.

"Hello, Mister Thompson," the barman said. "Going hunting?"

The new arrival set a shotgun gently on the bar. Reese glanced at the man's features, and smiled—this was a pleasant surprise.

"It ain't loaded, Pete," Ben Thompson told the bartender. "Fact is, I was hoping you could hold it for me—in return for a stake, I'm tapped out."

Pete the bartender eyed the shotgun doubtfully. "I don't know, Mister Thompson. We pretty much have all the guns we need."

He was measuring his words out carefully. He clearly didn't want to be taken advantage of, but neither did he want to get on the bad side of Thompson—one of the most dangerous, and unpredictable, gunfighters to frequent Dodge City.

"You don't have none like this," Thompson said. There was only the barest trace remaining of the English accent he had brought with him to America as a child. "This is the gun my brother Billy used to kill the sheriff of Ellsworth."

Pete picked the gun up and examined it. He tried to keep a poker face, but some of his enthusiasm showed through. Everyone had heard about the incident at Ellsworth. Sheriff

Chauncey Whitney had tried to break up a fight between the Thompson brothers—his friends—and a couple of cowboys. Billy Thompson, so drunk he could barely stand, had accidentally blown the well-liked sheriff to kingdom come. Ben had barely managed to get his brother out of town ahead of a lynch mob. It was a trick Ben had been forced to pull off more than once.

Pete nodded thoughtfully. "Yeah," he said, "that does make a difference."

"It's just for a stake," Thompson said. "I'll pay you back tomorrow."

Reese turned, so that Thompson could see him.

"Ben Thompson, you sorry son of a bitch."

Thompson's cheeks flushed with anger, then recognition lit his features. Pete the bartender had tensed up—he was on the verge of dropping to his knees behind the bar, to avoid the fusillade of bullets which could begin at any moment.

Thompson grinned, then laughed. "LeRoy Reese! I'm sorry—*Captain* Reese. How long has it been, old hoss?"

Reese thrust out his hand, and Thompson pumped it. "I reckon about eight, nine years, *Major* Thompson. Since Veracruz."

"Me and Reese here fought together for Emperor Maximilian down in Mexico," Thompson explained to the bartender. "Damned if we didn't lose that war too."

"Damned if we didn't," Reese said. "Let me buy you a drink, Ben."

"Suits me."

"Hell, let me buy us a bottle."

The matter of the shotgun was forgotten, at least for

the moment. The two old comrades made their way to a table.

"It ain't like you to be broke this early in the day, Ben," Reese said.

Thompson chuckled. "When you're in a town with Doc Holliday and Luke Short, you don't always stay solvent."

"You can hold your own."

"Sure—but there's too many wolves, and not enough sheep to go around. As soon as I can build that stake into a little pot, I'm going to move to greener pastures. Maybe back to Texas."

Reese wished he had the money to make his friend a generous loan. Ben was in pretty sore straits if he was pawning guns on the cheap side of town. He considered giving Thompson a portion of what little he did have—he knew Ben would increase it in no time—but he had no doubt that his friend would refuse the offer, and likely be insulted. Reese decided to stay away from the subject.

"I've heard a lot of talk about the law they've got around here," Reese said, "but I ain't never met any of them. How much truth is in them stories?"

Thompson shrugged. "Ed Masterson is straight enough. His brother Bat is a good friend of mine. Earp is a cocky bastard—all swagger, from what I've seen. I put up with him on account of Bat." He chuckled. "Why? You aim to rob the bank or something?"

Reese chuckled as well. "No, nothing like that. I'm here on legitimate business. Some folks, though—lawmen in particular—might not look at it that way."

"Go on."

"There was this kid from Arkansas, name of Seth Barlow. He got in an argument—over a girl—in Fort Smith last year, with this other feller that happened to have a very rich daddy."

"Okay—so?"

"So, the rich boy kicked his ass. As he was walking away, though, figuring it was all over, Barlow shot him in the back and lit out of town. I got a tip he's been in Texas, and hired on with the Lazy Crown. They'll be bringing their herd in here before long, and he'll be with them. He's probably dumb enough to be using his real name, but I have a poster with his picture on it anyhow—I'll know him when I see him."

"You ain't no *lawman,* surely," Thompson said.

"Nope. Rich daddy has put up a five-hundred-dollar reward."

"You're a bounty hunter?"

"It's a living."

Thompson laughed, and shook his head. "Oh well— better than being a lawman, I reckon. I'd rather be shot than do *that.*"

They wandered on to other subjects. They talked about the war between Maximilian and Juarez, and their narrow escape from the victorious nationalists. They joked about the beating they endured at the hands of police in Matamoros. They spoke, too, of that other war—the bitter one, the one which left deeper scars. They traded stories they had both heard before—stories of Ben Thompson's days in the Texas Mounted Rifles under Rip Ford, and of Reese's days as lieutenant to the notorious Tennessee guerrilla Champ Ferguson.

When the bottle was emptied Reese bought another,

even though he had drunk little of the first. The saloon was beginning to fill up.

Reese first saw her through the bottom of his glass—a hazy, luminous figure approaching their table. He set the empty glass down and drank in the sight.

The girl had honey-blond hair which fell in curls around her shoulders, and swayed gently when she walked. She was a grown woman, not a kid—she was about twenty-five years old, maybe a little more, although her dark blue eyes seemed older. They were eyes that had seen enough of the world to recognize it.

She stopped at their table and leaned over Reese's shoulder, so that her eyes were level with Thompson's. Hunger stirred in Reese at her proximity.

"Why Ben," she said. Her voice was rich. "You came to town and didn't even stop to see me."

"The night's not started yet, my dear," Thompson said. "I hope to grow a little richer before I start getting broker." He winked.

The girl straightened and smiled. "Ain't you going to introduce me to your friend?"

"LeRoy Reese, of Tennessee—meet Sally, the sweetheart of Dodge City."

"Sally—?"

Thompson looked embarrassed.

"Sally Layton," she said. "Lots of girls don't give their last name—nor even their real first name. Not me. I am who I am. What you see is what you get." She winked. "Of course, most men are like Ben here. They only remember what they want to remember."

Thompson affected a hurt look.

Reese looked into her eyes, his own glinting, and smiled.

"Real pleased to meet you—Miss Layton."

She tilted her head playfully. "Likewise."

"I was just fixing to head down the street and get myself a bite to eat," Reese said. "Why don't you join me."

Sally stood quietly a moment, considering. She was not south of the tracks to socialize—she was working. It was not really good business to waste precious time in pleasantries with a potential customer—who would only pay once—when a new bunch of cowboys might show up at the saloons any minute. Cowboys who would stand in line to shell out their pay, and quickly.

Still, this one seemed like a nice fella. Sally liked the way he looked at her eyes and not her bosom, like he was seeing her instead of just looking at her. Like he figured there would be time to look at the rest later.

"What the hell," she said. "Let's go get us some supper then, Tennessee."

Reese stood up, and Thompson shook his head in a sadness that was only half feigned. "Damn, I got to raise me some money," Thompson said.

"I'll see you directly, Ben," Reese said. "You finish the bottle. And stay out of trouble—I might not have time to rescue you."

"Go to hell," Thompson said pleasantly. "I'll keep an eye out for your cowboy."

"Obliged."

Reese offered Sally his arm. She took it, though she did not like the gesture—it reminded her of the sort of fake charm that so many gamblers had on tap. They walked away. Thompson took another swig from the whiskey bottle, then returned to the bar to dicker with Pete over the shotgun.

Ma Garrison did in fact cook a good steak, although it was a tad pricey for a town that was hip-deep in cowflesh. Reese ate with vigor—he had forgotten how hungry he was until he smelled the food before him. Sally picked at her own meal. It had not been long since she had eaten. She tried to ignore the rude stares that Ma Garrison shot at her whenever the old woman bustled by, as she tried to ignore the stupid grins of the male customers. There would be plenty of time to humor them later when she was back to working. They would still be there. They would still be grinning.

"What brings you to Dodge City, Tennessee?" she asked after awhile.

Reese grinned, and kept chewing. "Just passing through," he said after a couple of seconds.

"You a drummer, or something?"

"Something," he answered, and grinned again. It was not the same leering grin that the other men in the room wore, and she could not help but laugh at it.

"All right, all right, I get the picture. Just trying to make conversation."

Reese shrugged. "Keep trying."

"Why should I?"

"You've got a nice voice." Reese had forgotten all about Seth Barlow.

Sally bit her lip and looked toward the ceiling as she thought. "Okay," she said. "You read much?"

"Not to speak of."

"Me neither."

It was Reese's turn to laugh. "Why'd you bring it up, then?"

"I don't know. Fellas that read are interesting, I guess. They can tell me things I don't already know."

"I seen me a couple of them Shakespeare plays, down in Austin."

"I ain't never seen one of them," Sally said. "I hear folks talk funny in them."

"They do that, sure enough. When you watch them actors, though, you can figure out what's going on."

"What was they about?"

"One of 'em was about this freed colored man that becomes an army general. He marries a white woman—then he gets real jealous, and chokes her to death."

Sally's lip curled. "Damn," she said.

"Damn is right. The other'n was about this king, that spoiled his daughters. One of them loves the old boy, but her sisters tell lies on her—he believes them instead of her, and they wind up stealing him blind."

"Them don't sound like very happy stories."

Reese shrugged. "They ain't. They show life like it is, though, in spite of the funny way they talk. Life is tough all over."

A cold shadow seemed to cross Sally's face. "I knowed this fella once that always used to read me poems. He was blue all the time. He talked about that Shakespeare stuff a lot."

"Maybe that's how come he was blue all the time."

"No, he was blue because he got his legs shot off in the war."

"Oh. I reckon that would do it, all right. Whatever become of him?"

"He shot his self one day, because I wouldn't marry him."

Reese looked up from his steak, and into her eyes. She looked away, out the window.

"I can see how a feller might do that," he said.

"I can't." After a moment, she added, "His name was Jack."

For the first time, Reese noticed the sly glances all around them. It irritated him.

"Let's go somewhere else," he said.

She turned her eyes back to his face. "I got a room in a hotel not far from here. I don't never take people there."

"The landlord wouldn't like it?"

"I wouldn't like it. It's my place."

He nodded. "I can understand that."

"We can go there."

"Are you sure? I wouldn't want to—" He searched for the right words.

"I'm sure. We can go there."

"Let's go."

They walked out, much more quietly than they had walked in.

Reese lay on the hard mattress. He felt Sally breathing beside him. He watched the smoke from his cigar as it curled toward the ceiling, and bounced off it, and faded away. He had felt empty when he first lay down here, and now he felt full—it usually worked the other way around. There was still an emptiness, though, underneath everything. It was an emptiness which seemed always to have been there, only he had never noticed it before. It was hard to move, and it hurt to lie still.

"My money is in my britches yonder," he said. The words hung in the air like the cigar smoke.

"I don't want it. I don't work in this room. This room is for me."

"I'm sorry I said that."

"No need to be. I was aiming to make money off you when I first seen you. I just don't want it now, is all."

They had fallen into each other, in a way Reese had not known in a long time. It had felt the way a dream does when it is remembered days later—after you have forgotten ever dreaming it. Reese had not wanted to take out his money, and was glad he did not have to.

"You can stay here, if you want," Sally said.

He wanted to, and he did not want to. "I better go," he said. "There's somebody I'm supposed to find."

"The cowboy Ben mentioned."

"Yeah."

"A friend of yours?"

"Never met him. His name is Seth Barlow."

"You don't seem like no lawman. Lawmen are full of themselves."

"I'm not one. This boy has a price on his head."

"You're a bounty hunter? That's worse than being a lawman."

Reese bit his tongue, but Sally knew what he had wanted to say. She said it for him.

"I'm a whore. I know. But I only sell my own body, I don't sell other people's."

221

"Everybody sells something," he said, and he began pulling on his trousers. "I'll look for you later," Reese said when he was dressed.

"All right."

He took the picture out of his pocket, unfolded it, put it before her face. "Do me a favor, darlin', keep an eye out for him."

"Good-bye," she said softly. "Tennessee."

He left. She lay there a long time.

Seth Barlow was a happy man. His pocket was weighted down with money, the dust had been scrubbed off his skin, and he was free—free in the most sinful city he had ever had the privilege of being in. He took pride in the fact that he wore his gun on the outside—some of his friends were scared to, but Seth had heard enough to know that no one cared what happened south of the Dead Line.

He felt the woman's eyes on him as soon as he walked into the saloon. She looked sad, somehow. For some reason this made her prettier than all the younger girls who were trying to get his attention. They were all too loud, and their energy was too intimidating—they were like snorting, un-broken ponies, kicking and raising dust. He edged his way toward the sad woman.

"Howdy," he said, and gave a hesitant smile. "My name is Seth."

The sad-eyed woman put a thin cigar between her lips. Seth Barlow felt a tingle—damn, this was a wild town.

"You have a match, Seth?"

"Yeah," he answered, and the hesitant smile came dangerously close to becoming the sort of stupid grin which Sally had grown to hate.

"Well—can I have it?"

"Oh, sure! Sorry." He fumbled in his pocket for the match, then fumbled to light it. He cupped his hand—even though there would likely be no errant breezes in the stuffy saloon—and let the flame lick at her cigar until it burned. The tip glowed brighter as she sucked it.

"What's your name, Miss?"

"Sally."

He took off his hat. "Charmed, Miss—um, Miss Sally."

Despite the too-familiar blend of shyness and anticipation, the boy seemed fresher and cleaner than most she had seen. His face had a trace of sadness, and it reminded her of Jack's face—wanting and needing and afraid to speak directly. Sally knew it was only a trick of her mind. She saw Jack in the boy because she had been thinking about him, had *allowed* herself to think about him for the first time in ages. Because she had opened her room to the man from Tennessee, and had not known why.

She knew that this cowboy, this Seth, was the one Reese was hunting. He had a price on his head. He was already bought and paid for, just as she was, and he did not even know it yet. Still, the face from Sally's memory coalesced and reconfigured itself onto the features of this boy, and knowing it was a fragment of the past made it no less real.

"I, um, I got money," he said. "I just got paid."

She blew smoke, a long plume, and it hung around his face. "I have a room," she said. "You should come with me."

"Yes, ma'am."

She stood and took his hand, and led him out. Seth

had visited whores before, though not often enough to have grown comfortable with them, but he had never visited one like this. She pulled him along with an urgency—not to commence the act, or to finish it—but an urgency of need which seemed to have little to do with him.

She had the same energy in her hotel room—in her bed. It was like a living thing, like a third person stuck between them and pulling them together like a magnet. Seth felt like he was caught in a tornado. It was a tornado which violently sucked the vitality from him and strewed it into the air, and raged on unsatisfied. It did not feel like any coupling Seth had known before. It was intimidating, and he did not like it—it was as if he were not really there. It was not what he had expected from the sad-eyed woman.

Sally rolled off the boy and sat up, her back against the headboard. She was hungry, and empty, and disappointed. She should never have let the boy into her room. She should never have let *anyone*—but she had been drawn to Reese, and had opened a door which would not allow itself to be shut back.

"Damn," she said, softly.

Seth sat up. "I'm sorry," he said, and there was a faint quiver in his voice. He reached to the chair beside the bed and scooped up his clothes, even the boots and the gun belt. He piled them on his lap, covering his nakedness, until he could gather the strength to put them on.

His pitiful, hurt expression softened Sally. It, too, reminded her of the young amputee Jack—of how he had always doubted his manhood, and of her efforts to convince him he was whole.

"It's not your fault, sweetie," she said. Seth shrugged.

"You're no different than other men, and it don't usually matter to someone like me. You'll learn how to take your time with a woman in a few years. If you live long enough."

This made him chuckle. "Why wouldn't I live long enough?"

She brushed the hair from his face. "There's a bounty hunter in Dodge City looking for you, Seth. You'd best gather up your gear and get out of this town, while you still can."

The blood drained from Seth Barlow's face.

Reese had no luck finding the young killer. His heart was not in it, anyhow. He felt like kicking himself. He should never have mentioned money to Sally, and he definitely should not have shown her the wanted poster. There had been a moment of life, and promise, and magic—then he had said the wrong things, and it had died away.

His feet took him back to the hotel on their own. He had not planned it. Reese sighed. To hell with Seth Barlow. He could be found tomorrow, or next week. Reese walked inside and climbed the stairs.

He opened the door without knocking. He knew there would be no one there but her. It took him a moment to comprehend, then, when he saw them sitting naked on the bed. Her eyes met his, and they saw each other's souls fall.

"I'm sorry," Reese said. "I reckon I got the wrong room."

Then he recognized Seth Barlow. The wideness of Seth's eyes proved that Reese had let it show, and the boy *knew* he was recognized.

"Don't move, son," Reese said as he reached for his pistol. Seth fumbled in his lap for his own.

"No," Sally shouted, "don't! It ain't worth it!"

She shouted this, not to the boy, but to Reese. She threw herself over Seth, covering him with her body. She was not completely sure whether she was trying to save the cowboy from Reese, or to save Reese from himself. She only knew she was trying to save someone, something—to make her bed a place of life, not of death.

"Don't sell away—" she began, but the gunshot silenced her. In his haste to pull his gun loose from its holster, pressed against him as it was by Sally's body, Seth had pulled the trigger. Even as her blood gushed onto him, warm and sticky, Seth pushed her away.

Reese put a bullet between the boy's eyes, then stood over him and emptied the revolver into his dying body. Smoke gathered around the bed. Heat radiated from Reese's gun barrel. His hand shook, wanting to shoot more, but he was empty.

He bent over Sally. Her eyes looked at him, seeing him, and then lost their focus and saw no more.

Ben Thompson stood beside Reese at the grave on Boot Hill. Thompson had also been there, at the hotel, with Ed Masterson immediately after the shooting—in case his endorsement of Reese's character would carry any weight. Masterson had let Reese go, reluctantly, and even signed the paperwork to verify that the dead cowboy was in fact Seth Barlow— but he made it clear that he wanted Reese to clear out of town.

Reese had no argument with that—but not until he had paid for Sally's burial, and seen to it that a marker was erected for her. Barlow could rot for all he cared. Barlow would be planted on Boot Hill too, of course, but Reese planned to be gone before that hole could be filled. The gravedigger was already working on it.

Thompson looked at the marker. " 'She Loved Not Wisely,' " he read.

"It's from a play I seen once. I don't remember the rest of it, not exactly."

"What's it mean?"

"It means that life is tough all over," Reese said, and then he walked away. After a moment, Thompson followed him.

. . . GRAVEDIGGER . . .

What'd I tell ya? A heart of pure gold, that gal. But like the epitaph says, too bad she couldn't be a little bit wiser . . .

Now over here we got somethin' real special. Look at how long this epitaph is. Gave us fits, it did, gettin' all them words on one stone, and then still gettin' the feller's name and all.

This story's got special meanin' to me, although I cain't rightly tell you why, right now. Mebbe another time . . .

. . . but anyway, this piano player come to town some time back and right away everybody in town fell in love with that feller's music. I tell ya, I used to sit out in front of the hotel—that's where I got a room, at the Dodge House.

Comes with the job. Anyway, I used ta sit out in front with my feet up and listen to that music just drift up the street from the saloon where he played—only sometimes the saloon was closed and he was still playin'.

'Course, I said everybody fell in love with his music, but that weren't rightly true. There was one feller didn't take to it, at all, but then he never did take to nothin' that I know of.

He walked into the saloon that day and him and the piano man—well, they just got into it right off...

THE PIANO MAN

ROBERT VAUGHAN

IF YOU DIG IN THIS CLAY
YOU'LL FIND ONLY MY BONES
I WAS KILLED ONE DAY
BY A MAN NAMED JONES
I KNEW I WAS FASTER
I WAS CALLOUS CAL COLE
BUT I MET DISASTER
NOW THE DEVIL HAS MY SOUL

The young man was wearing a black hat with a silver head-band, from which protruded a small, red feather. He was slender, with dark hair and dark eyes, and there was a grace-fulness about the way he walked and moved. He carried himself with an effortless economy of motion as he walked up to the bar, put a nickel down, and ordered a beer.

When the beer was served, he thanked the bartender with a slight nod and then slowly surveyed the interior of the saloon. It was typical of the many he had seen over the past five years. Wide, rough-hewn boards formed the plank floor, and against the wall behind the long, brown-stained bar was a shelf of whiskey bottles, their number doubled by the mirror they stood against. Half a dozen tables, occupied by a dozen or more men, filled the room and tobacco smoke hovered under the ceiling like a cloud. It was now twilight, and as daylight disappeared, flickering kerosene lanterns combined with the smoke to make the room seem even hazier.

During the past five years these kinds of surroundings had somehow become the young man's heritage. He had been redefined by the saloons, cowtowns, stables, dusty streets, and open prairies he had encountered. He could not deny them without denying his own existence, and yet, with all that was in him, he wished it was not so. He was here, in a foul-smelling saloon, in a Kansas town whose name he had not yet bothered to learn.

Seeing a scarred, upright piano in the back of the room, he asked, "Do you have a piano player?"

"We used to," the bartender said.

"What happened to him?"

"He was killed by a drunken cowboy who didn't like his music."

"That's pretty harsh criticism."

"Yeah, we thought so too, so we hung 'im," the bartender said. "We buried 'em both in Boot Hill."

"Mind if I play?"

"Suit yourself," the bartender said.

The piano player took his beer mug over to the piano, sat down, and ran through the scales once. Many a man and a few of the soiled doves had sat at the instrument since the death of the first piano player. They would run their hands across the keys, sometimes picking out a song or two in single-note melody, but most of the time just making noise. Because of that, nobody paid any attention when he first sat down.

One of the saloon patrons, looking over at him, called out in a loud voice.

"Man, don't just sit there, play."

"What would you like me to play?" the piano player asked.

"Anything you can play," the patron replied. "I wouldn't want you to tax yourself beyond your limits."

The others, hearing the stranger being needled, laughed.

The piano player nodded, then turned back to the piano. He sat at the keyboard for a moment, then he began to play. The beautiful notes of Mozart's Sonata in F major filled the room. The music spilled out, a steady, never-wavering string of melodic phrases with a single melody weaving through the piece like a thread of gold woven through the finest cloth. The playing silenced all conversation and stilled the clinking of glasses and bottles.

When he finished the piece, everyone in the saloon applauded. He acknowledged the applause with a bow that wasn't at all self-conscious, then returned to the bar for another beer.

"You want a job, piano player?" the bartender asked.

"What will it pay?"

"Free room and vittles," the bartender replied. "And whatever you can make in tips."

"I might stick around for a while."

"Only thing, don't play that kind of music anymore. When folks listen the way they was just doin', they don't buy liquor. And if they don't buy liquor, I ain't makin' no money. Can you play other songs? Drinking ditties and the like?"

"Yes," was all the piano player said.

"The name is Phillips," the bartender said. "You can have a room upstairs, it's up front, overlookin' the street."

"Thanks. I'll take my things up."

Nobody knew much about the piano player. He told them his name was Jones, but they weren't even sure of that. He was quiet, sort of mysterious most would say. But they all agreed on one thing, the man could play the piano, whether it be a snappy rendition of "Buffalo Gals" or a sentimental ballad like "Cowboy Joe."

He had a room up front on the top floor of the Bucket of Blood Saloon and he stayed there most of the time when he wasn't downstairs entertaining the customers.

Sometimes, in the middle of the night, when the saloon was closed and nobody was around, he would sneak downstairs and play the piano, not "Buffalo Gals," nor "Gandy Dancers Ball," nor any of the other ditties so often requested by the saloon patrons. On those occasions he would play real music, music that nobody knew the title to, but everyone could recognize as being the kind of great music played by the great artists.

What the piano player didn't know was that more often than not, he wasn't alone during those nocturnal concerts, for word had gotten around and people would gather on the

saloon porch, in the alley alongside, or in front of the apoth-
ecary next door, and they would listen.

"Did you hear the music last night?" they would ask
each other the next day.

"It's like an angel come down from heaven to entertain
us," another would say.

And the piano player, unaware of his growing nocturnal audience, was pleasantly surprised to see that the beer
glass in which tips were placed seemed to get fuller each day.

In a town not too far away from where Jones was practicing
his art, people were going about their business when a
stranger rode in. The stranger pulled up in front of the
saloon, dismounted, and tied his horse to the hitch rail. The
townspeople watched him with increasing curiosity as he
took off his hat and rubbed a handkerchief across his face.
His hair and eyebrows were snow-white, his skin as pale as
any skin they had ever seen. He glanced toward them with
eyes that had a light pinkish tinge, but were otherwise as
colorless as glass.

The albino was wearing a gun strapped low on his
right hip. He looked around him once, then, taking no notice
of two stable hands working at the livery across the street,
went inside.

"You know who that is?" one of the stable hands asked
after the albino was through the swinging doors and out of
hearing.

"I ain't never seen him," the other one answered. "But
I've heard him described. That's gotta be—"

"Callous Cal Cole," the first one interrupted, as though he didn't want to be cheated out of saying it.

"I was going to say that. I know'd who it was first time I seen him. I didn't need you to tell me."

"They say he's killed more'n twenty men."

"I heard it was more like thirty."

"What do you reckon he's doin' here?"

"Don't know. But if he's lookin' for anyone, I sure wouldn't want to be that person."

"Me neither."

Inside the saloon, Cole stepped up to the bar and the bartender hurried over to see what he wanted. At the opposite end of the bar a cowboy and a young woman were talking and laughing, a bottle of whiskey on the bar in front of them.

"Whiskey," Cole ordered.

"Afraid we got no blended whiskey left," the bartender said. "The cowboy over there bought our last bottle. Got some pretty good trade liquor though."

Cole pointed to the bottle in front of the cowboy. "I'll have his bottle."

"Can't. I told you, the cowboy bought the whole bottle."

"You," Cole said to the cowboy. "I'd be obliged if you'd slide that bottle down this way."

The cowboy smiled and nodded to the bartender. "Why, sure thing, I just got paid and I'm in a good mood. Pour the man a glass on me."

"I don't want a glass," Cole said. "I want the whole bottle."

"Sorry, mister, I been thinkin' for a month 'bout comin' in here and puttin' my arm around a pretty girl," he accented his remark by pulling the young woman closer to him, "and sharin' a bottle of blended whiskey with my friends. The name is Dingus McCoy. Now, if you're callin' yourself my friend, you can have a drink or two, but I'm keepin' the bottle."

Cole stepped away from the bar and turned to face Dingus. "Slide the bottle down here or pull your gun," he said.

"What?" Dingus replied, surprised by the challenge. "Mister, are you crazy?"

As quick as thought, Cole pulled his pistol and fired. His bullet shredded the cowboy's left earlobe, and sprayed blood and tissue onto the face of the bar girl. As quickly as he had drawn, Cole put the pistol back in his holster. The whole thing happened so fast that the others in the saloon wouldn't have been sure that it had happened at all, had it not been for the cloud of gun smoke that was drifting away, and the bloody piece of flesh hanging from the cowboy's left ear.

The woman screamed and ran away while everyone else in the saloon hurried to get out of any possible line of fire.

"Give me the bottle of whiskey," Cole said.

"You go to hell!" Dingus said.

Again, the albino drew, fired, and replaced his gun, doing it so quickly that some saw nothing more than a jump in his shoulder. Dingus's right ear was now as shredded as his left.

"Next time it'll be a kneecap," Cole said. "Now, give me the bottle of whiskey."

"For God's sake, Dingus, give it to him!" the bartender pleaded.

"Here! Take it!" Dingus said, sliding the bottle down the bar toward Cole.

What happened next was a miscalculation on Dingus's part. He thought that, by reaching out to pick up the bottle, Cole would be distracted just long enough to give him the advantage. But he thought wrong, for even as the cowboy was making an awkward grab for his pistol, Cole's .44 was out and booming. His bullet crashed into Dingus's heart, killing him instantly.

Cole picked up the bottle and looked at the bartender. "What do I owe you for this?" he asked, as calmly as if nothing had happened.

"Uh, nothing," the shocked bartender replied. "Dingus already paid for it."

"How much did he pay?"

"A dollar."

Cole pulled a silver dollar from his pocket, then walked over to the dead cowboy. He dropped the coin on Dingus's body. "There," he said. "We're even."

Carrying the bottle with him, Cole left the saloon, mounted his horse, and rode away.

The audience stood in tribute as their thunderous applause filled the auditorium.

"Monsieur, you have captivated all of us with your playing. You are the sensation of the year. Tomorrow we leave for Vienna, then . . ."

"I'm afraid there will be no Vienna. Tomorrow I leave for the United States."

"The United States? But I don't understand. The world is

your oyster, monsieur. Why would you go back to the United States? They are fighting a war there."

"That's why I must go. My father has called me back. I have an obligation."

"But no . . . you are beyond such petty squabbles now. You are a man of the world, a true cosmopolitan. What care you of a war between bickering neighbors? I beg of you, monsieur, do not return. Your music is a gift from God. You speak of obligation, and I agree, you do have an obligation. You have a sacred obligation to share your music with the world."

"I'm sorry, Monsieur Mouchette. I must go back."

The dream was so vivid that when Jones woke up, he could almost believe he was back in Paris. He lay in bed for a moment, listening to the sounds drift in through his window, a carpenter sawing, a freight wagon rolling down the street, Won Sing cursing, in Chinese, the employees at his laundry, and the illusion left him.

Jones opened the chifforobe then removed a cloth bag and lay it on his bed. When he opened the bag, he was overwhelmed with the smell of moth balls. From the bag, he removed the striped pants, ruffled shirt, and swallow-tailed coat he had worn when he was gracing the concert stages of Europe. He looked at them, not with an implausible longing for what he knew could never again be, but with a realistic acceptance of how things were.

He saw, too, the other instrument with which he had proven to be all too proficient . . . the employment of which had changed him forever, and had forever closed the doors to the life he once knew.

237

• • •

From the moment Jones went downstairs, he realized something was wrong. There was no conversation, no easy banter among friends and, most noticeable, no laughter. Then he saw the reason why. Callous Cal Cole was standing at the far end of the bar. There was no way to mistake him, only one man fit that description. Word of his most recent escapade, the killing of a cowboy in an adjacent town over something as trivial as a bottle of whiskey, had already reached them.

Jones walked over to the piano, sat down, and began playing a Liszt piece.

"Hey, you, piano player!" Cole called.

Jones did not respond.

"Piano player, I'm talking to you!" Cole shouted.

Jones stopped playing, then turned on his bench with a cold smile on his face. "What do you want, albino?"

Everyone in the saloon gasped in surprise and quick fear.

"What did you call me?"

"I called you an albino."

"I don't like that term."

"Would you prefer maggot?"

"What the hell, mister, do you want to die?" Cole asked, not only angry but shocked that anyone, especially a piano player, would talk to him like this.

"We all have to die sometime," Jones replied. "Now is as good a time as any, I suppose."

"You . . . you're crazy!" Cole sputtered. He was used to having people quake in fear at the very sight of him. To have this piano player show no fear of any kind, unnerved him.

"Is that why you interrupted me? To tell me that I'm crazy?"

Cole took a swallow of his drink, then wiped the back of his hand across his mouth while he tried to figure out the best way to deal with this impertinence.

"Play 'Buffalo Gals,' " Cole said.

"I'd rather not," Jones said, easily. He turned back to the piano and continued with the Liszt piece.

With a roar of anger, Cole pulled his pistol and fired. The beer glass that Jones kept on top of his piano for tips exploded into several pieces when the bullet hit it. "Piano player, if you don't start playing 'Buffalo Gals,' right now, the next one is coming right through the back of your head!" Cole shouted.

Again, Jones turned toward Cole, who was now sputtering with anger. Jones sighed. "I need a drink first," he said, getting up and walking toward the bar. "Mr. Phillips, you want to pour me a . . ." Jones started, then he sighed. "Never mind, as nervous as you look right now, you'd probably spill it all over the place. I'll get it myself."

Jones walked around behind the bar, then moved all the way down to where Cole was standing so that only the bar separated them. "Would you care to join me in a drink, Mr. Cole?" he asked.

"I've got my own drink," Cole said. "Just pour yourself a drink, then get back over there and play 'Buffalo Gals' like I told you."

Jones put both hands on the shelf just under the bar and leaned forward toward Cole. He smiled at Cole, but there was no humor in the smile. Instead, it was a cold, deadly smile, a smile that Cole recognized as being one from a man who had faced death before, and had won.

"Well it's like I told you a while ago, I'd rather not play 'Buffalo Gals.' What I'd really like is for you to leave the saloon now."

"What? You'd better get yourself a gun, piano player! And you'd better get one right now!"

"Oh, I've got a gun, Cole," Jones said. "You see, Mr. Phillips keeps a double-barreled, ten-gauge Greener back here and I'm pointing it at you right now. If you so much as flinch, I'm going to pull both triggers. What's this thing loaded with, Mr. Phillips?"

"Double-aught buck," Mr. Phillips answered nervously.

"Double-aught buck," Jones repeated. "Well, let's see, the way I figure it, that would take out about twelve inches of this bar, six inches of your backbone and most of your insides. It'll make a mess to clean up but then, that won't be your problem, will it?"

"Don't you know who I am? You're a fool to think you're fast enough to take me in a fair fight."

"Fast? Who said anything about fast? In fact, who said anything about fair? It doesn't take speed, or skill, or fair play to kill someone, Cole. All it takes is the determination to do it. And believe me, I've got the determination to do it."

Cole began blinking rapidly. For the first time in his life, he knew what it was like to be afraid. The fear that had always worked in his favor now had him paralyzed.

"Put your gun on the bar, then get out of here," Jones said.

"I'm not giving my gun to . . ."

"Now," Jones said, calmly.

So frightened that he was sweating profusely, Cole reached for his pistol.

"Use two fingers," Jones ordered.

Using two fingers, Cole pulled his pistol, then put it on the bar.

"Go."

Cole backed slowly toward the bat wing doors. Raising his hand, he pointed to Jones. "This ain't over, piano player. You hear me? This ain't over."

For a long moment after Cole left, there was dead silence in the saloon. Then one of the men breathed a long sigh of relief and said, "Jones, I would've never thought it. You've got more guts than sense. Even standing there with a double-barreled shotgun in your hands, it took guts to call down the albino."

"I'll say," another said. "Damn if this don't call for a round of drinks. Set 'em up, Phillips. I'm buyin'."

Phillips was still at the opposite end of the bar, not having moved a muscle for the last minute. He continued to stare at Jones, his eyes wide open in shock.

"Come on, Phillips, what's got into you?" the man questioned. "Didn't you hear what I said? Set 'em up for the piano player."

Still speechless, Phillips reached under the bar in front of him and pulled out the shotgun. He set the butt of it on the bar with the barrels pointing toward the ceiling.

"What the hell's that?" someone asked.

"Jones didn't have no double-barreled shotgun," Phillips said. "I was standin' back here the whole time, watchin' him. He didn't have a blasted thing in his hands."

The saloon erupted in a loud cheer as everyone realized what had happened.

"Say, Jones, I don't want no showdown with you by askin' you to play somethin' special, but I was wonderin' if you'd finish that song you'd started," someone said, and the others laughed.

"I'd be happy to," Jones said, returning to the piano. He began playing and the music was so sweet that those who listened could almost forget the drama so recently played out.

He had just completed the song, and was acknowledging the applause, when the deputy sheriff came into the saloon. The deputy was white as a sheet.

"Paul, what is it?" Phillips asked. "You look like you've seen a ghost."

"The sheriff's dead," Paul said.

"What?" Several in the saloon responded at the same time.

"Cole killed him," Paul said. "He just come into the office a few minutes ago and without so much as a by your leave, shot the sheriff in cold blood. Then he pointed the gun at me. I thought I was a goner, sure, and I started sayin' my prayers. But all he done was tell me to come get the piano player."

"Where'd he get a gun?" someone asked. "That's his'n, on the bar, there."

"He probably had another one in his saddlebags," Phillips said. "Never know'd of a gunfighter who didn't have a spare."

"If I was you, piano player, I wouldn't go nowhere near

Cole. Especially if he finds out you run a bluff on him."

"No, you've got to go," Paul said.

"Why? Why would he have to go?" Phillips asked.

" 'Cause Cole's down at the schoolhouse, right now, standin' on the front porch with his gun pointin' at the schoolmarm's head. He said if the piano player don't come down in the next five minutes, he'll kill her. Then he's goin' to start killin' the school kids, one ever' minute, he says."

Jones stepped up to the bat wing doors and looked toward the far end of the street. As the deputy had said, Cole was there, standing on the front porch of the school. His arm was around the teacher's neck, and he was holding a pistol to her head.

"Piano player!" Cole was shouting, his voice tinny from this distance, but clearly audible. "Piano player, I'm waiting for you!"

"What are you going to do, Jones?" Phillips asked.

"I'm going up to my room," Jones replied.

"No," Paul said. "Don't you understand, Jones? He's goin' to kill the teacher, then start on the kids if you don't go down there. You've got to go down there."

"Paul's right," one of the others said.

"If Jones goes down there he'll be killed," Phillips said. "Is that what you want? You want him to be killed?"

"Better him than the schoolmarm."

"Yeah," another said. "Besides, Jones brought it on himself. All he would've had to do is play 'Buffalo Gals' like Cole asked. If he'd done that, there wouldn't none of this have happened."

"Yeah, Fred has a point. When you get right down to it, Jones is sort of to blame for this whole thing. There weren't no call for him to show off like he done."

"Jones, here, was the one was talkin' and actin' so brave. It was alright when it was just him. But it ain't just him no more."

Jones looked at everyone, but he said nothing. Instead, he started upstairs.

"Where's he goin'?" someone asked.

"To get a gun, I reckon," Fred answered. "I mean, I agree with all of you, Jones is the one at fault here, so, by rights, he's the one needs to face down Cole. But I wouldn't ask him to do it without a gun."

"Yeah, I reckon you're right."

In his room, Jones opened the chifforobe again, and once more removed the bag that held his striped pants and tails. In the same bag, wrapped up in a piece of blanket over a piece of canvas, over an oiled cloth, Jones found what he was looking for, the instrument of his other profession, the disassembled components of a Whitworth .45-caliber, hexagonal bore, sniper rifle. Jones assembled the rifle, attached the long telescopic sight, then loaded it.

With the rifle loaded and ready, he opened the window and looked down toward the school. By now several people had gathered near the school, and they stood in little groups to either side of the street, out of the line of fire, but close enough to Cole and his hostage to see what was going on.

"Piano player!" Cole was shouting. "Piano player, you've only got about a minute left! If I don't see you walking down the street toward me within one minute, I'm going to blow this pretty woman's brains out!"

Jones reached down into the bundle to remove a brass plate. There was an opening in the middle of the plate, covered by a sliding bar. This was called a stadium, and by looking at his target through the opening and sliding the bar up until the figures of Cole and the schoolteacher filled the opening, he would be able to ascertain the exact range. Then, looking to the scale to the left, he read the distance, in yards, one hundred seventy-five.

Jones adjusted his telescopic sight to the proper range, and using the window ledge as a rest, sighted through the scope. With the target enlarged by the telescope, Jones could clearly see the schoolteacher's face. Cole was holding her in front of his body, using her as a shield. The woman's face reflected fear, but not panic, and Jones couldn't help but admire her for that.

In one way, Jones knew that he and Cole were alike. The most important part of any life or death confrontation between two armed men was the willingness to kill. Most men did not have that willingness, most would hesitate for a split second before making the commitment. That hesitation was all the advantage a professional killer, like Cole, needed.

What Cole, what most people didn't realize, was that Jones, himself, had once been a certified killer, and it was that experience that robbed him of his first profession. Jones had been a member of Berdan's Sharpshooters during the war, and in that capacity had killed forty-two men. These were good men, soldiers who were fighting for what they believed. They were men with wives and children, and mothers and fathers to weep over their graves. Jones knew that about them, but he had killed them nevertheless.

"You're not a good man, Cole," he said under his breath. "And while no one will weep over your grave, I'll wager the entire town will dance over it."

Because of the way Cole was holding the schoolteacher, only about three-quarters of the albino's head was visible, but that was all he needed.

Half-a-hundred people were standing in a little group near the schoolhouse, waiting anxiously to see how this drama was going to play out. Several of the men in the crowd were veterans of the recent war, and in the very next instant, it was as if they were immediately transported back to those terrible days. They heard, and recognized immediately, a sound they had prayed they would never hear again. It was the sound of a bullet hitting a man in the head. There was no mistaking the quick buzz, then the solid pop as the bullet plunged into Cole's face, just below his eye, followed by the swoosh of his brain exploding from the back of his head.

Even as the crack of the rifle shot reached them, Cole was falling backward, already dead, his gun slipping from his lifeless fingers. The schoolteacher who had been his hostage was free and unharmed.

"Where did that shot come from?"

"Who did that?"

"Look!" one man shouted, pointing to a little wisp of smoke drifting away from the upstairs, street-front window of the saloon, all the way at the far end of the street.

"It couldn't have come from there, that's too far away. No one is that good."

"Someone is."

•   •   •

The piano player didn't stay around long enough to see Callous Cal Cole buried. In fact, he didn't stay a minute longer than it took him to disassemble his rifle, put it and his striped pants, ruffled shirt, and swallow-tailed coat back in its bag. When he went downstairs a moment later, the saloon was empty. Except for Mr. Phillips.

"Everyone is down at the other end of the street, gawking at Cole," Mr. Phillips said.

"I thought they might be." Jones stepped up to the bar and Phillips poured him a drink.

"Leavin' town?"

"Seems the wisest move."

"I don't blame you none."

Jones tossed the drink down, then started toward the door.

"Jones?" Phillips called.

Jones looked back toward him.

"If you wind up anywhere near Denison, Texas, while you're wandering around, there's a fella there who would more'n likely be happy to buy you a drink."

"Oh? And who would that be?"

"The fella who is engaged to Miss Dover, the schoolmarm whose life you just saved. His name is Eisenhower. David Eisenhower. Want me to write it down for you?"

"Not necessary. Who could forget a name like Eisenhower?"

...GRAVEDIGGER...

I don't even recollect who wrote all them words that went on Callous Cole's marker. That piano man, since he was so educated an all, mebbe he did it afore he left. Who knows? He wasn't what he seemed to be after all, was he? How many of us are?

Well, that's about my favoritest story, so I think it might be time for me to be gettin' back to work. Where'd I leave my shovel? Over there? Thank you, son. Couldn't see it from here, not with the sun in my eyes. Ya know, I bet them jaspers that's supposed ta help me is waitin' for the sun ta go down—or mebbe they're jest waitin' for me ta do all the work.

Let's jest walk over yonder so's I kin get my shovel... but wait, stop here jest a minute. Lookee there, this here's the coffinmaker's grave. Can't jest go by this one without talkin' about it. What's that? No, a coffinmaker ain't the same thing as an undertaker, not by a long sight. Not the same as what I do, neither. See, the coffinmaker he actually makes the coffin that the body goes in. Some folks jest want a plain pine box, but others, for some reason, they want to be buried in the fanciest darn boxes you ever did see. Me, jest toss me in a hole and cover me up, I'll be happy as I kin be.

And we used ta have another fella hereabouts called hisself—what did he call hisself? Lemme think a minute... I got it! I think it was—yeah, he said he was a "mortician."

Now, from what I kin recollect, he done about the same thing the undertaker did, but he did it with a fancier name, and he charged a might more. So, him and the undertaker, I guess they started competin' with each other, and the coffinmaker he sort of worked for both of 'em. Doc McCarty, he jest did what docs do, I reckon. I work for the undertaker, but since I do all the hole diggin' on the Hill I guess I sorta worked for that mortician guy, too, and mebbe even the doc.

Anyway, this here fella in the ground he's the coffinmaker, you kin see that from what's writ on his stone. But what you don't know about him is that he took about as much pride in his work as anyone I ever saw around here. In fact, it was damn near an obsession with him that every box, no matter how simple or how fancy, be done jest right . . .

DEAD WEIGHT

RICHARD S. WHEELER

HERE LIES THE COFFINMAKER
BARCELONA BROWN
LAID IN HIS FINEST
SIX FEET DOWN

Dodge City does a deal of dying, which is good for business. Mostly it's a summer occupation, when the drovers push up from Texas with their longhorns and beeline for the saloons with some Yankee dollars in their jeans. They tend to perforate one another after downing a few tumblers of redeye.

We get a little help from hot weather complaints as well, such as dysentery and cholera, and sometimes the ague. There is not much business in the winter, with the Texians gone south like the geese, but sometimes a consumptive parts from us when a good Canadian blue norther cuts through, or the catarrh or lung fever swathes through town, and then Doc McCarty ends up recommending me, Phineas Agnew, to the bereaved. McCarty and I try to steal each other's business, but in the end I always win. Morticians have a monopoly. It isn't a perfect monopoly, because sometimes there is no corpus delicti. But it's good enough for a man wanting a secure living, without the vagaries of boom and bust, famine or plenty.

I always come out ahead. It's an art, you see. To maximize the profit, you have to catch them at just the right moment. The moment of deepest grief is the time to suggest the finest casket, the fanciest send-off. When those Texians come up the long trail carrying one of their own in the cavvy wagon, all swathed in canvas, killed by lightning south of town or a stampede or bad water, then's when I mint money.

Surely, I say, you would each expect the same from your comrades of the long trail? Surely your dear old mothers would want the finest money could buy? Surely you want to do better than the Bar X, or the Hashknife boys, who bought a princely box for their departed? Surely, after all that suffering on the long trail, the lonely nights, the endless rains, the dismal food, you want to provide some comfort for your friend? A fine, waterproof, spacious, oak coffin, and a dandy parade, with a coronet band playing dirges and my four-horse black lacquered equipage with cut-glass windows and black pom poms to take the departed to his last home?

That always works, and as fast as their trail boss shells out the trail wages, they're appropriating the fanciest box they can afford for old Tom or Red or Dusty, and forking over cartwheels for all the extras too.

It is a principle of my business to sell the gaudiest goods just when the widow is wiping back the first flood of tears, or when the children, bereft, orphaned, adrift, are suddenly

faced with the loss of their pa or ma, or maybe even a grand-
mother or aunt.

Now, I don't keep many coffins on the shelf because it
isn't necessary, or at least it wasn't until recently. Dodge City
was blessed with a cabinetmaker of uncommon ability, able
to do magical things with wood. I had only to call upon
Barcelona Brown for whatever I needed, and within hours
he would have a splendid box ready for me, and for a modest
price, too, which often enabled me to charge triple or qua-
druple the tariff, depending on who I was dealing with. A
new widow would sometimes count out five or six times the
price and be glad of it, certain she was doing her wifeliest
for her deceased spouse, who succumbed to a buggy wreck.

I have always been aware that my business requires a
certain political delicacy. I have been stalwart for strict enforcement of gun laws north of the Dead Line, that is, the
Santa Fe track cleaving the town, even though there are
certain popular watering holes north of the divide on Front
Street, such as the Long Branch and the Alamo.

But south of the dead line is another pasture. I have
always opposed rigorous law enforcement in that quaint
quarter because it is bad for business. If the Texians wish to
get into shooting affrays, that shines up my profits, and I
hardly see why Mayor Dog Kelley and the mucketymucks
should concern themselves with it. The cowboys are ex-
pendable Texians, not Kansans. Often I have declaimed to
assorted deaf lawmen about that very thing. For example,
I've braced Ford County Sheriff Bat Masterson several times,
and Deputy City Marshal Wyatt Earp as well, suggesting a
policy of liberality south of the dead line.

But I digress. My real vocation here is to tell about the

coffinmaker Barcelona Brown, and explain his odd fate. I called the fellow the wizard of wood. He was a skinny, dreamy bachelor with wire-rimmed spectacles and a sniffle, and if he ever thought of acquiring a spouse, I never had an inkling of it. He was wedded to wood, if you will forgive that odd perception. Brown could conjure up a box so swiftly I could not fathom how he managed it. He thought of caskets the way kings think of palaces. A proper coffin should match the character and status of the departed, and be a comfort to the bereaved. An ideal coffin should impart glory, laud and honor upon the bones within.

I shall always remember Barcelona Brown for the odd duck he was; the only man on earth so absorbed with the making of coffins that he could think of little else. It was a vocation even more sacred to him than a monk's. During those long stretches when his talents were not called upon, he sank into melancholia, and built gaudy furniture with a morose passivity that drove some customers away. He was in great demand to furnish bordellos, which wanted flame-proof nightstands and sturdy double-reinforced beds, as well as elaborate parlor appurtenances. This he would do in a detached and wooden manner, for his heart was in coffins.

Normally, on that matter he didn't deal with the public at all. I would ascertain what the bereaved desired, whether a plain rectangular box, or a diamond-shaped coffin that apexed at the chest and narrowed at the foot, or a showy affair with nickel furnishings, and lo, he would set aside all other work in his board-and-batten whitewashed shop on Chestnut Street, west of the business district, and produce the item.

Thus he acquired a reputation. Anyone in Ford County

who knew anything about send-offs wanted a Barcelona Brown box. They knew they were getting the best of the art, with the wood so keenly joined that not a particle of light burrowed through any crack, the corners so perfectly mitered that the pieces of wood seemed to become one. He plainly guarded his trade secrets, and discouraged onlookers, so that he could proceed to build his boxes all alone, under the triple-lamp work-light suspended over his bench.

He was cranky about wood, constantly haranguing Eastern suppliers to send him only the smoothest-grained oak and ash and hickory or walnut. Each of his boxes was a masterpiece of joining, but an artistic creation as well, the wood so perfectly and harmoniously blending or contrasting, depending on the style, that people laid hand to it to verify that their eyes hadn't deceived them.

Fortunately, Dodge straddled the Santa Fe Railroad, which enabled Brown to order materials from afar, even though the metropolis lay beyond the frontier, and was barely past its rude beginnings. The express cars regularly disgorged exotic wood on his account.

He began to line his coffins with various fabrics, sometimes black velvet, other times watershot white silk, or gray taffeta, all carefully sewn and glued into place. But then he decided that one's eternal rest should be comfortable, and he began buying goose down from a Slovakian farmer's widow north of town, and contracting out the manufacture of quilted liners to the various seamstresses.

"Seems to me the departed ought to be treated right, Phineas," he announced to me on one occasion, when I had hurried over to order a plain pine planter beefed up to endure a trip back to Texas. A cattleman had died in the

Dodge House of corruption of the liver, and his crew wanted to take him home to the banks of the Pedernales.

"Just a strong pine box, sealed so they won't have to endure the odors. That's what they want."

Barcelona had shaken his head. "A cattleman ought to be laid out proper," he said. "I can do what they want, but you had ought to tell them that the man deserves more respect."

Irritably, Brown had set to work, and when I called that evening, he was putting the final touches on the box. Pine it may have been under the enamel, but now it gleamed blackly in the lamplight. It boasted fine filigreed nickel handles, and a strong black lid lined with felt, and a gray silk interior.

"Now don't you go hammering the lid down," Brown had said. "You got to screw it down tight so it'll never come up or leak."

I had promised I would, and the next dawn, when the crew rode up to carry their boss home, I presented them with a pine box such as they had never before seen.

"Your late captain. He's in there, and he'll have an easy passage. Now, this here is watertighter than a brandy bottle, and you can float Mr. Roberts across the rivers in a pinch, but I don't recommend it," I said.

"That's some box," the foreman said.

"Finest made, by Dodge's own Barcelona Brown. Now, that's two hundred eighty-nine for the coffin, and a hundred twenty for my professional services."

"That's a lot for a pine box."

"That's no pine box, son, that's a Barcelona, the Tiffany of coffinmakers."

"More than we wanted."

"It's what you got. Now, do I receive the honest fruits of my labor so that I can release the departed to your tender care?"

They eyed the coffin, wonderment in their sun-blasted faces. Brown had outdone himself. This was a coffin that would promote a senator.

"Sort of fits the old man," one allowed.

They paid. Company funds, of course.

One day I happened into Brown's tidy woodworking works and discovered him in an uncommonly cheerful mood. He had, scattered about, various pieces of costly ebony, obviously from different species of the tree: some of it was jet black, the variety found in Ceylon and India; others a warmer black, found in Niger; and then there was a stack of precious Calamander of Africa, the hazel brown wood mottled or striped with black. I knew something about ebony. It comes from the heartwood of the ebony tree. The rest of the trunk is a perfectly ordinary color.

"Phineas, I'm going to make me the lord of all caskets," he whispered as he shaved a glowing black board with a draw-knife. "I have in mind parking it in your window, right there on Front Street, for all the world to witness. Guess it should bring you some business."

"I, ah, we'll wait and see," I said, not wanting to commit to anything like that.

It took him a fortnight to construct it, and when I next saw it, he was nearly done. The box glowed malevolently. It was diamond-shaped and exceptionally long. Its walls consisted of three courses of ebony: brown-black at the top and bottom, jet black in the middle, all joined so seamlessly that they seemed a single piece of wood. The interior had been lined with lead sheeting, carefully soldered at every joint to foil moisture, and somehow wedded to the wood. Royal blue watershot silk quilting lined the interior, and the north end sported a pillow, also of royal blue.

The cover, which he was still polishing, was shaped from the Calamander, and arched triumphantly over the box. A blank brass nameplate had been screwed into it.

"It's entirely watertight, once it's sealed," he said. "The lead, you know."

"It looks awfully heavy, Barcelona."

"It is. It's the heaviest coffin ever made. But look: I've added handles."

Sure enough, five ornate silverplated handles graced each side, enabling ten pallbearers to shoulder the coffin.

"It sure is a comfort. I wouldn't mind spending eternity in it myself," he said. "Fact is, I've been sleeping in it, just to try it out."

He promptly undid his apron, stepped onto a stool, slipped into the coffin and laid his hands across his breast, eyes closed. Then, after a long ticking moment, he sat upright, smiling, and eased out, being careful not to blemish his masterwork. He had the strangest, dreamiest look on his skinny face, a look such as I had never before witnessed on the face of the living, though I struggle hard to achieve just such an expression for the viewing of the departed.

That struck me as distinctly peculiar, but I said nothing.

"Done tomorrow," he said. "I'd sure like to put it in your window."

I decided it would attract business. There's nothing like

death to open the purse strings. Citizens would gape. A few would come in and inquire. The truth of it was, there was no other casket on earth that even approached this one. They buried kings of France in less. No ancient pharaoh, wrapped in his mummy windings, got to rest in a tomb like that one.

"All right, bring it over."

"I'll need some stevedores."

"I'll find them," I said. "What price shall I ask for it?"

"Oh, it's not for sale, Phineas."

"Then what is the object?"

"I have made the perfect coffin. Let the world see it."

"How about a two thousand dollar price?"

He stared sourly at me, his Adam's apple bobbing up and down. "That is obscene," he said.

"Three thousand, then."

"You don't understand. It's a work of art." He just shook his head at me as if I were a dunce.

"I will take bids," I said. "Some cattleman will want it. Either that or a madam. I imagine there are harlots hereabout who'd pay whatever you ask."

But he had turned his back to me, fondly rubbing the gleaming ebony with an oiled rag that smelled of lacquer.

I planned to force the issue: money talks. Hand him five hundred dollars in gold eagles and he would wilt fast enough. Then I would sell it for six times the investment.

I waited all the next day, but got no word from Brown that he had completed work on his masterpiece. Obviously, he was adding filigrees, or maybe inlaying some exotic wood, or parqueting the lid, or carving a lion in bas relief into the glowing ebony.

I understood. A Rembrandt of coffin-making would

not stop until he had perfected his coffin. He did not summon me that day, nor the next.

That afternoon Deputy City Marshal Wyatt Earp wandered in, as he or another of the constables often did. It was understood in Dodge that anything found in the pockets of the deceased belonged in the public till to establish city parks, and I ended up with a little pickle jar wherein I deposited silver and gold and base metal coin and bills and rings and fillings found on the late lamented. I carefully did not inquire as to the ultimate disposition of that material, but I noted that it never appeared in the town budget.

"Phineas, what's the matter with Brown?" he asked gently, supposing I would know.

I stared at him blankly.

Deputy Earp sighed. "Last night he headed for the Lady Gay and proceeded to get into a fight with three Texians, with painful results. The brawl trumped Eddie Foy for a few minutes."

"Painful?"

"Doc McCarty had to sew up his flesh here and there and splint a finger. What got into him?"

"You suppose, just because we are allied in serving the bereaved, that I know anything about him," I said. "In fact, I know very little. He's a vast mystery to me. He bachelors alone, lives and breathes woodworking, smells like varnish, has no known friends, though I call myself one, and eats solitary meals at Beatty and Kelley's restaurant, tips waitresses extravagantly, and attends the Union Church on occasion, always placing a dime in the collection plate."

"You got no idea what got into him? I'm inclined not to haul him before the JP. Let it go."

I shook my head. "Just what happened?" I asked.

"Brown was on the prod. Like he itched to start a fight. Them Texians, they took one look at the skinny fellow and just laughed it off. Lots of witnesses to that."

"Then?"

"He called one of them Texians, gent named Clay Allison, a son of a whore."

"And?"

"He took umbrage. Can't say as I blame him. But Brown should know better. Allison isn't one to call any name but mister. Anyhow, I'm gonna sort of put Brown under your care. He's not going anywhere for a few days. Hope you don't need a coffin before then."

"I can put the deceased on ice."

I concluded it was just a quirk. Barcelona Brown would soon be back at his bench, cutting and joining precious hardwoods into fine coffins, or making chairs when the body business was slack.

It took a week. Then one day Barcelona was back in his shop, sporting some purple and yellow bruises and bandaged hands, but at least he was working again. I didn't bring up the issue, thinking that whatever had planted the burr under his saddle had long since vanished.

But I was wrong.

About the time the purple and yellow began to fade from his hands and face, Barcelona decided to do some gambling. Now the man had never gambled in his life, as far as I know. But gamble he did, one memorable evening, in the Lady Gay. Naif that he was, he settled down at the green baize table that hid the south half of Ben Thompson, who was not only a ruthless gambler but also renowned for his ability to conclude arguments by perforation.

I was counting on Thompson to supply me with the major part of my trade that summer, but I guess Marshal Larry Deger or Assistant Marshal Ed Masterson or maybe even Earp warned him that he would be disinvited from Dodge if he got too fractious. And so far, he had behaved himself, much to my sorrow, as it was a slow summer and I had anticipated much more custom.

At any rate, Barcelona Brown bought into a five card stud poker game, lost steadily, fidgeted in his chair, imbibed ardent spirits, eyed the comely serving wenches, and surrendered a considerable sum. According to witnesses, Brown suddenly sat upright in his chair and called Thompson a cheat.

I've heard it from a dozen sources. They all agreed that the Lady Gay turned so silent that they could hear Dora Hand singing sweetly in the Comique at the rear, and everyone agreed that half the habitués of that spa began termiting through the cracks, including four other sports at that table.

And all agree that Thompson pushed back the rim of his bowler, his gestures catlike and dangerous, and then laughed shortly, baring yellow teeth.

"Beat it, farmer," he said softly. Farmer was the worst epithet in the sporting vocabulary.

"I called you a cheat." Brown sat there, rigid.

"Vamoose."

About then Ed Masterson got wind of it, clapped his dainty paw on Barcelona, lifted him bodily from his chair, and propelled him through the batzwing doors.

It was a wonder. Never before had dapper Ben Thompson shown forbearance under such circumstances. The town talked of nothing else for three days.

But I had begun to fathom what lay behind this sudden shift in Barcelona's conduct. Could it be? Yes, it had to be. I resolved to talk the young man out of such ghastly nonsense, and if need be, provide such company as a man adrift needs to anchor himself back in the world.

I braced him most sincerely the very next day, my black stovepipe hat in hand. He was serenely planing a walnut plank as I addressed him.

"Barcelona, my friend, how could you? Your motive is perfectly transparent. But you ignore certain realities. It is not sleep that transpires in a coffin, but eternal nothingness. You may indeed fashion a perfect bed for someone suffering lumbago, but it avails naught the person whose soul has fled.

"You may indeed wish to be buried in the finest casket ever fashioned, but do it in good time, after a life well spent. Not now. The world needs the finest cabinetmaker and coffin builder alive, and if you go, your gifts go with you.

"Plainly you are suffering the melancholia, and I intend to shepherd you until this season has passed. It is a sacrifice, of course, because I would otherwise have your custom, or that of your estate, but I am setting all that aside for the sake of friendship. Let me hear no more of these trips to the edge of the River Styx."

He smiled and nodded, and I supposed that my little lecture had its intended effect. At least I heard no more of reckless conduct on the part of my coffinmaker. He settled back into his routine, shaping and shaving wood, and yielding up masterworks of furniture, cabinets, and coffins.

All this while, that magnificent coffin lay atop two sawhorses in his shop, waiting to swallow bones. He never talked about it, and as far as I could tell, never thought to do anything more about it. I presumed that whatever had seized him had passed, and eventually it would sell just as the rest of his coffins had sold, but for a premium. Indeed, when I was making certain arrangements with Rose Dwyer, who lay in fatal decline on her four-poster surrounded by her nymphs of the prairie, I confided to her that I knew of a coffin that would surpass any other on earth, and that for a considerable sum I thought its maker might part with it.

She took the matter under advisement, but died before coming to any decision, and I buried her in a mahogany box with gold-plated handles, having supplied a bugle corps and honor guard from Fort Dodge. She said she had been in the service of her country and wanted a military burial. I knew she had at least been in the service of Fort Dodge, but didn't wish to dispute the issue. That was a particularly profitable occasion.

I did not neglect my commitment to Brown, and took him out on occasion. We went to see Fanny Garretson at the Comique, and Barcelona allowed as how her flesh resembled good birch. And we saw Eddy Foy at Ham Bell's Varieties, and Barcelona opined that the comic's flaying arms reminded him of a drop-leaf table.

"I think you should cultivate a woman," I said one night.

"That would be nice," he replied.

"You might find a proper one at the Union Church."

"I've noticed one there, shiny as an oak pew," he said.

I took that for progress.

Then one day, when the cattle shipping season was

fading, Barcelona delivered a small box while I was rouging the lips of a departed child. He stared at the small, still body and sighed.

"I've been thinking, it's time to bring that coffin over to put in your window for a public viewing," he said.

"Well, fine. I'll get my equipage harnessed up, and maybe we can empty out the Alamo Saloon to help lift it."

"You won't need the hearse. I've calculated the weight very carefully. Just bring ten men and we'll carry it. Meet me at six."

I took him at his word, and at a quarter to the hour, I entered the Alamo and announced that there would be free lagers for ten gents who would help carry an empty coffin from Brown's shop to my establishment.

That won a cadre and in due course we converged on the shop, lifted the coffin under the watchful eye of Barcelona, and carried it through the streets of Dodge to its next resting place, behind the plate glass window of my establishment, which I had prepared by draping two sawhorses in black velvet.

"That's some coffin. Heavy as sin. Who's it for?" one of the Alamo's barflies asked.

"It's not for sale," Barcelona replied loftily. "It is the culmination of my art."

"Me, all I need is a winding sheet, a wake, and a bottle in me hand," the gent said.

The remark was distasteful. I paid off the pallbearers with a silver dollar, which could be tendered for ten draft beers, thanked them, and determined to deduct the dollar from Barcelona's next invoice.

We watched the gents troop back to the Alamo. It was late and I wished to close up for the night.

"That coffin will attract attention tomorrow," I said. "It is a phenomenon."

"I brought a sign," Barcelona said.

He handed me a hand-printed placard that explained the coffin to passersby. I read it swiftly in the dying light, just to make sure its dignity was in keeping with my standards. It was. It simply announced that this coffin, made of three varieties of ebony, was the masterwork of Barcelona Brown. It had a quilted navy blue silk interior, lead lining, and was absolutely water- and airtight when the lid was screwed down. And it was not for sale.

"You really should put a price on it, Barcelona," I said. "Even a fancy price. Maybe three thousand. Who knows?"

He shook his head. "Not for sale, not ever."

"Well, what will we do with it?"

"Just display it. And keep it closed."

I agreed, and he walked off into the darkness of my meeting hall. I heard the front door click. He probably wanted his supper. I turned down the wick until the lamp blued out, returned the lamp to my workbench, and abandoned the establishment, locking the door with my skeleton key.

The next day was routine. Several people did stop by and admire the coffin, and all of them wanted to know the price.

"Ask Brown," I said. "I'd put a two thousand dollar tag on it myself."

"Two thousand? That's a fortune!"

"There'll never be another like it," I replied.

Two days later I walked over to Brown's shop, intending to order a coffin for a drover who had been decapitated falling off a wagon and under a wheel.

The place was dark and cold. "Barcelona, where are you?" I yelled, but I was just talking to myself.

I tried three more times, but the man was elsewhere. I knew he wouldn't go far, not with his prized coffin two blocks away.

I tried again the next day, and found him not at his bench. Uneasily I tried his room above the Odd Fellows Hall and found no one present. I finally realized that the constables ought to be told, so I alerted the city marshal, Larry Deger, and mentioned it to Ed Masterson too. They looked the town over, even peering into the vault of the outhouse behind his shop, and could not find Brown.

Then over oysters that night it came to me. I summoned the marshals and we headed for my establishment, where I lit a kerosene lamp and carried it to the front window.

"I think he's in there," I said.

Deger looked at Masterson, and both looked at me. None of us wanted to open that lid. But finally I did, slowly. A fetid odor smacked me at once.

Barcelona was in there, all right, still intact but a bit ripe.

Masterson sighed. "It figures," he muttered.

"I'll have the coroner look him over," Deger said. "After that, he's yours."

"I'll bill the estate," I said.

...GRAVEDIGGER...

You notice another famous name in that story? That's right, Bat Masterson. Heard about Wyatt Earp and Ben Thompson some, too. They was all here at one time or another, all them famous fellers who was good with a gun. They come, and then they go. Some was here before me, some while I was here, and there'll probably be some after I'm gone. Dodge City draws 'em, ya see. Drew Earp here twice, in fact. But that was Dodge City when it was at its peak.

Yes sir, she ain't what she once was, this town, and this here hill is proof. I mean, what I'm doin' up here now—or supposed to be doin', instead of talkin' to all of you.

I gotta get my shovel . . .

. . . gotta finish diggin' this one up . . .

What's that? Who's this one? Well, look there, his name's right on the marker. You know, this reminds me . . . a lot of them fellers came here and wore a badge, and they did well by it—did it proud, as a matter of fact. But this feller here . . . well, he got hisself killed while he was in jail and they tried to blame it on a friend of mine named Corey. See, my friend was a deputy, but had some trouble with the bottle. If it wasn't for the liquor he never woulda heard people a-callin' him . . .

A DISGRACE TO THE BADGE

ED GORMAN

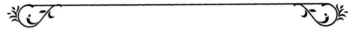

HERE LIES MICHAEL JAMES BRADY
ONLY THE LORD IS PERFECTION

Around ten o'clock, Deputy Jack Corey heard the scraping on the back of the jailhouse wall and knew he had a visitor.

Johnny Hayden was bringing provisions to his drinking partner Mike Brady. The provisions would be a pint of bourbon to get Brady through the night in his cell, the same cell Corey had tossed him into an hour ago. Happened every time Brady visited the jail, which was frequently. Brady was the town bully, a mean, reckless drunk who would, everybody knew, kill somebody someday. But his father was a powerful merchant and so about the worst punishment anybody was willing to inflict on him was a night rolling around in the vomit and piss of cell two, where the drunks stayed.

Couple things about this particular night.

One being that Jack Corey was a little old to be a night

deputy. Night deputies were usually strapping youngsters eager to break a few knuckles on the faces of such men as Mike Brady. But Corey was none of these things. He was a worn forty-one-year-old man who'd known nothing but law his entire working life. And most of his working life he'd also known, all too well, the bottle. Which accounted for him working in so many towns. Till the bottle got him fired. At his age, this was his last chance. And as of tonight, he'd failed it. Twenty-eight days dry, he'd been, on this new job in Dodge. Then tonight he stole a pint from a rummy in an alley and drank the quarter-inch or so that remained. This was around eight. Right now, he shook pretty bad. You know the way some folks wait for the cavalry to appear on the hill and come to their rescue? Well, Jack Corey was waiting for a whiskey bottle to come strutting in the door and come to *his* rescue.

The second thing was his concern that the town marshal would pay him a surprise visit. He'd done that a couple times. He knew all about Corey's bottle problem and so he kind of spot-checked him. The town marshal and his wife would be at the opera house or maybe a barn dance or maybe just out enjoying the spring weather—and then all of a sudden, there they'd be. The wife would always bring Corey a pastry or piece of bread slathered with jam, something that would make the visit seem social. But Corey knew why they popped in. They were testing him. And tonight he would fail the test. Sure as hell they'd smell the liquor on him— the marshal had a nose a hunting dog would envy—and then what would happen to forty-one-year-old Jack Corey?

He was grateful for the distraction Johnny Hayden

gave him. He raised himself from his desk chair, touched his holstered Colt .45 as if to make sure it hadn't run off and left him the way his wife had that time, and then he went out into the sweet chill spring night.

You couldn't give Hayden any points for being subtle. From somewhere he'd borrowed a ladder, which now leaned against the wall next to the open barred window three-quarters of the way up.

"Evening, Johnny."

Another man might have jerked around, scared, when he heard the deputy approaching him. Not Hayden. Hayden was secure in knowing that just about whatever kind of trouble he got in, old man Brady could and would get him out of. Hayden was young Brady's keeper and had been since they'd gone to grade school together. It was, from the outside, a curious relationship. Mike Brady humiliated Hayden every chance he got. He had knocked him out, spat on him, stolen various girlfriends, called him unforgivable names—and Hayden stuck by him. But Hayden was being paid a healthy stipend every month to keep Brady in check. Hayden always pulled Brady back from the kind of disaster not even the old man could fix. Without his watchdog Hayden, Brady would have been hanged long, long ago. Not a week went by that Brady wasn't suspected of some kind of trouble, often enough hanging kind of trouble.

"Evening, Deputy," Hayden said. He was a strong, beefy man given to dark suits and gentlemanly manners. He had a solemn face except for a certain irony in the dark gaze, a weary acceptance of all things human. "I assume you know what I'm doing, Deputy."

"He doesn't need any more tonight."

"But he's asked for it. And that means I've got to give it to him."

He started down the ladder and reached the dirt.

"In fact, I've *already* given it to him."

"Yeah, how d'ya like that, you bastard?" Brady shouted from inside.

Hayden took the stepladder down. "The livery let me borrow it. I need to get it back to them."

They started walking to the street. Hayden carried the ladder.

"You ever get tired of waiting on him?"

Hayden smiled. "You really expect me to answer that?"

"Smart man like you, you could get yourself a good job."

"Smart but lazy, I'm afraid."

"Oh?"

"My folks are shirttail kin to the Bradys. They were always nice to us. I got used to their kind of high life. On my own, I couldn't live anywhere near so well. But I've got my own little apartment in their barn out on the estate and a hell of a nice monthly wage. And I don't want to give it up."

"You don't want a wife?"

"I'm twenty-three. Plenty of time for that."

Corey looked up and down the street of false-fronts. Just about everything you wanted to find you could find in Dodge. Daytime, for the legitimate things a feller wanted. Nighttime, for the things a feller didn't necessarily want to talk about. There had been a time when Corey had loved the sounds and scents and heady alcoholic feelings of nighttime, the laughter of whores mixing with the snappy rhythms of the player piano and the bawdy fun of the banjo. But there'd always been a wife to go home to in those days, after he was done drinking and whoring. But then one day she *wasn't* there and she was never there again and something terrible had happened inside of Corey then—his heart had been cut out by his own hand—and it was still terrible and it would *always* be terrible. And he couldn't even tell you for sure what it was. Just that it changed then and the bottle problems started and he wasn't the same old Corey anymore. Not at all.

"I should take that pint from him."

"Who said anything about a pint?" Hayden said. "I brought him a fifth." He laughed. "You think a Brady would settle for a pint?"

"He'll be some fun tonight. A whole fifth."

"He can get pretty abusive."

"He sure can."

"But at least you got him locked up."

"Yeah, and his old man's gonna be all over the marshal tomorrow about how hard I hit him. But he was strangling that gambler pretty good. A minute or so more, he would've killed him."

"You're right. The marshal's going to hear about it from Frank Brady himself. But hell, he won't put up much of a stink."

"He won't?"

Hayden leaned close, as if confiding a secret. "He'll raise some hell to keep Mike off his back. But old Frank knows how Mike is. And he's sick of it. Sick of paying out money to all the people Mike beats up. And paying for all the saloons Mike smashes up. And always having people snicker about Mike behind Frank's back. Snicker and hate him. Mike's wife is sick of it, too."

Mike Brady's wife. A sullen rich girl named Debra who would be even richer when the old man died and Mike came into the entire estate.

"She's tired of him whoring," Hayden said. "Breaking up saloons and things like that, she doesn't mind. But the whoring—she sees that as a reflection on herself. That she isn't woman enough to hold him."

"Sounds like you've got a real nice groups of folks out at the mansion."

Hayden smiled again. "Like I said, Deputy, I sleep in an apartment over the barn. It's a very nice place. I don't have to be around any of them."

Then he was off, carrying his ladder down the street.

Brady, tonight's only prisoner thus far, started in as soon as Corey got back to his office.

Another half hour, Corey would make his rounds again. There might be a few drunks but mostly there'd be merchant doors to check, that would be about as eventful as the evening would likely get.

Brady gave him the full show. Sang dirty songs off-key. Called him names. Threatened to kill him. Dared him to come back there and fight like a man. He puked a couple of times. He was a skilled puker, knew how to clean himself out so he could keep going for another round. They had a Mexican wash out the four cells in the mornings. They paid him a good wage to do so.

Corey had his own concerns. He kept thinking about that fifth Hayden had brought Brady. The fountain of youth, that bottle was—or the illusion of youth anyway. When you felt better physically and didn't have the burden of your grief and remorse and when it was easy to imagine pretty gals swooning over you and fierce men running away in shamed fear.

So many things in a bottle like that. Music. And sweet memories. And hope. And dreams.

And maybe—best of all—not giving a shit. Not having any gnawing fear that you'd lose a job or that somebody had called you a name or that you'd do something foolish and embarrass yourself.

Not giving a shit. That was the ultimate blessing a bottle like that could bestow on you.

He went back there just before he made his rounds. He felt better. It was nearly midnight. The marshal and his wife wouldn't be popping in tonight. Too late. The marshal was a man of strict and stringent habit. Up at five A.M. every morning. In bed every night before eleven.

The cells smelled like a cesspool thanks to Mr. Brady here.

Brady, a scrappy tow-head, said, "You come in this cell with me, Deputy. Leave your badge and your gun out there and we'll fight like men."

"Why don't you shut up and go to sleep?"

Brady preferred light-colored suits and frilly shirts. Gambler's attire. He was handsome in a sullen way but the booze was starting to rob his face of its lines. Puffy, he was. Twenty-three and puffy as a thirty-year-old who'd been boozing since his teens.

Doubtful he'd be wearing this suit again. It'd gotten torn in his dust-up with the gambler. And blood had streamed down the back of his head and trickled in crusty ribbons down the silk rear of his vest. The crusted puke all over his shirt didn't exactly help, either.

And then Corey saw the bottle.

Must be a slow night for the kid, Corey thought. *Most nights he would've put half of it away by now.*

For there—a vision almost celestial in its splendor— there on the floor next to the cot on the right-hand side of cell two—there was the fifth that Hayden had brought Brady.

The bottle was nearly full.

"C'mon," Brady said, putting up his fists like a prize-fighter, and describing a semicircle with his clumsy feet. "C'mon in here and I'll kick the living shit right out of you!"

But Corey had eyes only for the bottle. Brady was mere unintelligible babble in the background.

"I'm gonna take that bottle from you," Corey said.

"Yeah. You just try. You think I don't know why you want it? You're a rummy and everybody knows it. *That's* why you want it!"

Corey couldn't stop himself. He was beyond the point of trying. His entire consciousness, his entire existence was focused on that bottle. He'd do what he needed to to get it.

He drew his Colt.

He put his key in the cell lock.

"I want that bottle of yours, Brady."

Drunk as he was, Brady could still understand what the deputy was all about.

He hugged the bottle protectively to his chest, the way he'd hold an infant, and grinned. "This is mine, all mine, Deputy. And you can't have it." The more he teased, the louder his voice got.

"I said I want that bottle. I'm taking it from you because you don't need any more to drink."

Brady smirked. "Sure you are, Deputy. And I'll bet you wouldn't even *think* of taking a drink of it, would you?"

"Give it to me."

He put his hand out.

Brady got even sillier, hugged it tighter and tighter, and started to rock it back and forth. "Poor little bottle. Poor little lonely bottle." Eyes watching the deputy all the time he was doing this. Knowing just how his mocking little show here was making Corey even crazier.

This time when Corey put his hand out, he saw that it was trembling. His mouth was raw with dryness. He could taste the liquor on his tongue; he could feel the mercy—*I don't give a shit anymore, you can't hurt me and I can't hurt myself anymore, and I don't give a damn if I'm a falling-down drunk or not*—the mercy the mercy the mercy—he could feel the mercy the golden bottle would bestow upon him.

And then, giggling, enjoying the holy hell out of himself, Brady took the bottle and tossed it up into the filthy air of the cell.

"No!" Corey cried, picturing drunken Brady missing the bottle as it fell back to him.

But he didn't miss.

"That was a close one, wasn't it, Deputy? That sonofabitch coulda splattered all over the floor!"

Giggling all the while.

"You give that bottle here," Corey said, moving toward the man.

"You take one more step, Deputy, and I'm gonna smash this bottle against that wall back there. And you won't be able to stop me."

"You give it here."

So dry; so desperate.

Corey started to reach for it.

Brady took it by the neck and arched the bottle so that it was only inches from the wall. He hadn't been exaggerating. He could easily smash the bottle before Corey could stop him.

"Ummmm," Brady said. "Bet you can taste that liquor in your gut now, can't you, Deputy? And this is good stuff. Not like that mule piss you drink. This here's the brand my old man drinks. And he drinks only the best, believe me."

He made the mistake of falling in love with his words, Brady did. That's what gave helpless Corey the sudden advantage. Here's Brady thespianizing like some traveling-show ham and having such a good time at it that he didn't pay attention to business—said business being, at the moment, keeping himself and his bottle out of the clutches of the deputy.

Corey actually hit him a lot harder than he intended, too. It didn't take much to knock out a man as drunk as Brady was. But Corey kind've stumbled into the punch, *pushing* it sort of like, pushing it farther and faster than he meant to.

Two things happened at once.

The bottle went flying up in the air. And Brady's head ricocheted off the wall in a way that turned Corey's stomach. The kind of glancing ricochet that could permanently cripple or even kill a man. Corey had seen it happen.

The bottle—

The bottle was just now descending. Corey pitched his

drawn .45 to the cot and lunged to position himself beneath the tumbling, falling bottle.

For now, there was no concern about Brady. The world—the universe—could be found, sum and substance, in the sweet succor of the bottle's mahogany-colored elixir.

He caught it.

And just as he caught it, Brady started his struggle to his feet.

Thank God.

The bottle safe in his hands now, he could appreciate the trouble he'd have been in if Brady had been seriously hurt.

Brady put a hand to the side of his head and said, "What the hell happened?"

Corey had seen this before, too.

A blow on the head knocking some of the drunkenness out of a man.

"You don't remember?"

Before he could answer, Brady puked again.

Corey said, "I'm gonna get you a cup of coffee."

He was back in two minutes with a cup of boiling java. He slid it through the rectangle in the cell door. "Shit's hot. Be careful."

"You sonofabitch," Brady said. An offer of coffee hadn't made him any sweeter. "You're gonna be damned sorry you roughed me up."

"I didn't rough you up. You hit your head when I slugged you. And I slugged you because you wouldn't turn over the bottle Hayden brought you."

Brady glared at the bottle in Corey's hand. "I figured

that was mine. You can bet your ass I'm gonna tell the marshal you took it from me."

Brady was on the edge of many things—still drunk but getting sober in the worst sort of way, sick to his stomach and the possessor of a large knob on the side of his head, said knob radiating pain throughout his skull. And confused of memory and barbed-wire pissed about being pushed around by a rummy deputy.

But Corey was fully sick of Brady by now.

The way Corey saw it was, he'd take the bottle up front to his desk and have himself a good strong one. One. That was all. Then he'd go make his rounds and then, if he was of a mind, he'd take another one. One. He'd wrap the bottle in his coat and take it home when his shift ended next morning and if the marshal complained about Brady's bottle being stolen, he'd just say, *He was so drunk he don't know what he was talking about, Marshal.* And the marshal would most likely believe him.

"Get some sleep."

"I just can't wait for our time to come, Deputy, you know that? Just me and you. I just can't wait."

Then he was puking again.

Corey wondered what the hell he'd had for dinner.

He did as planned. Went up front, sat the bottle down on his desk as if it were a religious icon and just stared at it for a few exquisite moments. Probably hadn't had whiskey this good but three, four times in his entire life.

And then it was time.

Open the bottle.

Pour about an inch-and-a-half into his glass.

And then sit back all comfortable in his chair and enjoy

some of the finest whiskey the good Lord had ever visited upon mankind.

Just one drink.

Voices:

(Male): He's a disgrace to that badge.

(Female): He killed poor Mike. No doubt about it.

(Male): And he'll pay for it, Debra. Don't you worry about that.

(The female began sobbing)

Corey's way was to open one eye and kind of peer about and see if this was the sort of world he wanted to have anything to do with.

Usually.

But not today. Today, he instinctively *knew* that this was a world he didn't want to have anything to do with. That "disgrace to his badge" remark for one thing. And even worse that "He killed poor Mike" line.

Mike inevitably being Mike Brady. The prisoner he was guarding—or should have been guarding—all those long and now murky hours before he began to partake not just of one drink but many, many drinks.

And then that final male comment: "And he'll pay for it, Debra. Don't you worry about that."

No, sir, he didn't need to open an eye to know that this world was an extremely hostile one.

But then hands shook him roughly. And when that didn't succeed in getting his eyes open, somebody splashed a pail of icy water across his face.

"On your feet."

281

His eyes were open now. He wished they weren't.

"On your feet."

Marshal Beck, tall, wide, white of hair and mustache, imposing in the way an angry minister is imposing, said, "You're under arrest, Corey."

Corey managed to find his voice.

"For killing Mike Brady."

Then he saw the three others: old man Brady, Debra Brady the widow, and Hayden.

"I didn't kill him."

"Oh no? Care to go back and have a look at him in the cell?"

"It'll go easier on you if you just admit it," Brady said. "You got in a fight and hit him a little too hard. He got under your skin was all. Mike—God love him—he got under a lot of people's skin. I think we can see to it that the charges are dropped to second degree. You can be out in eight years. That sure beats a rope."

At which point, the widow Debra swooned with grief and said in her ice-blonde way, "We were going to start a family next year. He was going to quit drinking and everything."

Brady took her in his long, strong arms and sheltered her from the world.

This was some alternate realm he'd awakened to. Last time he'd seen Brady, Brady had a headache and was sick to his stomach was about all. The worst thing Corey had done was come up here and get passing-out drunk. The bottle responsible was still on the desk in front of him. Drained.

He became aware of his clothes. His head and his shirt

were soaked. He said, "Let's go see Mike Brady."

All this craziness. He didn't know how long he could handle it. Beneath the water, he'd started to sweat and sweat good.

Mike Brady was sprawled on the cot. He was starting to get stiff now. The large bruise on the left side of his forehead was split down the center, like a fruit that had been halved. Blood had poured from it, streaking most of his face.

"That's the one that killed him," Hayden said.

"We'll let Dr. McGivern tell us which one killed him," the marshal said, "tomorrow at the inquest."

Hayden looked, not without sympathy, at Corey. "Mike was in an evil mood last night. Even by his standards, I mean."

"That's when he really scared me," Debra said, all finishing-school proper in her blue taffeta dress and jaunty feathered hat. Then: "God, the stench in here. Don't you ever clean this out, Marshal?"

The lawman frowned. "Do you know how ridiculous that question is?" He had his pride and not even the Bradys could intimidate him out of it. "By now, the Mexican has usually swamped out every cell. But given that your husband decided to stay longer than expected, the Mexican couldn't get in to do his work."

"She didn't mean anything by that," Brady said gently. "She's just upset."

The marshal nodded, as if he understood. But his harsh blue gaze said he didn't understand at all.

Around three o'clock that afternoon, Corey was lying in his cell, rolling himself a cigarette, listening to a couple of Negroes in the next cell talk sweetly of old St. Louis and life on the riverboats, when Marshal Beck came in with a stumpy little gal whose fierce little face scared the hell out of Corey. The Angel of Death couldn't be any more frightening.

"This is Sara Wylie and she's going to be your attorney."

"A woman?" Corey said.

"You have something against women?" she barked at him.

"No, ma'am," Corey said.

"I've won my last fourteen cases and saved three men from the gallows. I don't need to justify my existence to you, Corey. But I thought I'd tell you that for the record."

She had to know how her record would affect him. Suddenly the idea of a gal attorney was fine.

"The inquest starts in fifteen minutes," Marshal Beck said. "I'll let you two have a room in the courthouse for half an hour after it's over."

The inquest was brief and brutal.

Judge Holstein (what a monicker to get stuck with, imagine all the jokes the poor bastard had had to put up with all his life) laid out the circumstances of Mike Brady's death—between his stomach-churning bouts of hacking up sincerely green phlegm—and then called the doctor to the stand.

"Could you tell us how Michael James Brady died?"

"Yes, sir. A blow to the head. The forehead, more specifically."

Corey couldn't wait to tell his gal attorney that he'd

accidentally put a goose egg on the side of Brady's head. But he had nothing to do with the business on Brady's forehead. Of that he was positive.

"Could Michael James Brady have tripped and inflicted that wound on himself?"

"Possible. But unlikely. There's a goose egg on the side of his head, too. That makes it look like he'd been in some kind of altercation."

The judge smiled. "By altercation you mean fight?"

"Yes, sir, I mean fight."

The judge looked out at the eager, trial-happy faces of the townsfolk who'd come here. He had to be re-elected soon and he liked to show people he was just folks. "I never use those big words myself. I didn't have the opportunity you had for education, I'm afraid, Doctor. So in my court, please use the language of the common folk."

"What an asshole," Sara Wylie whispered to Corey. Right then and there he decided he not only trusted her, he liked her, too.

Twenty minutes later, the inquest was finished when the judge said, "It looks as if we're dealing with a homicide here. I'll leave it up to our good friend the county attorney to proceed with the information we've given him today."

As the others left the courtroom, Corey sat there and said, "I think I'm in trouble."

"You sure you didn't kill him?"

"Yeah. I am."

"Give me till morning."

"What happens then?"

"Well, either my plan works or it doesn't."

"And what plan would that be?"

"No sense in getting your hopes up, Mr. Corey. You just go back to your cell now and get some sleep."

Educated people are always advising you to "examine your life." Didn't somebody famous once say, "The unexamined life isn't worth living"? Well, that's well and good if you've lived a decent life. But when you've spent your years inside a bottle—model ships aren't the only thing you can slide inside an empty whiskey bottle—you find that examining your life can be a very painful experience.

All the fights he'd picked; all the whores he'd whored with; all the ways he'd cheated, bullied and lied to the various town councils he'd worked for; all the jobs he'd gotten fired from. And most especially, the fine and lovely woman all his drinking and whoring and cheating and bullying and lying to had driven away.

That last one always made him feel cold and empty. And tonight in his jail cell, he'd never felt colder or emptier.

It was funny. About the only thing he *hadn't* done in his life was what he was now accused of—killing Mike Brady.

To everything else, he had to plead guilty as charged.

At seven o'clock in the morning, Corey woke up to find the marshal and young Sara Wylie standing in front of his cell door.

The marshal slid the key in and Sara, obviously happy to be saying it, said, "You're free to go. The doctor decided that Mike Brady's death was an accident after all."

"But he said there was no way—" Corey started to say.

"Well, that isn't what he's saying now," the marshal said. "Now do you want out of that cell or not?"

Corey grabbed his boots. Stomped them on and stood up. The marshal handed Corey his jacket, his gun. And then presented him with some paper money and a ticket.

"What's this?"

"Traveling money. And a train ticket. You'll be leaving town at noon. Which isn't very long from now."

"You're running me out of town?"

The marshal frowned and looked at Sara Wylie. "Miss Wylie, would you take this ingrate down to the café and try to explain to him how lucky he is not to be charged with murder?"

She led him quickly away, like an angry mother dragging a very, very bad child off for punishment.

"Why'd he change his mind?"

"He being who exactly?"

"He being the doctor who said it couldn't have been an accident."

"Because I talked to Mr. Brady late last night."

"Brady ain't no doctor."

"True, but Brady runs this town. And this town includes the doctor."

The breakfast business was still strong in the smoke-infested café. Corey had to keep rolling cigarettes in self-defense. The young lawyer lady looked hog-happy.

"You mean he told the doctor to change his mind?"

"That's right."

"Why'd he do that?"

"Because I told him if he didn't, I'd drag every man, woman and child that his son had ever abused onto the witness stand and we would destroy the Brady family name forevermore, to quote Mr. Poe's raven."

"And he went for it?"

"Of course, he went for it. What choice did he have? He's a businessman. He has to worry about his reputation. You get a couple rape victims up there—one of them I'm told was only fourteen when Mike Brady attacked her—and Brady's got himself some real trouble. So he decided that he'd just have to live with the fact that you killed his son. But he does want you on that train."

"Wait a minute. I didn't kill his son."

She made a funny face. "You didn't? Really?"

"You think I did?"

"Well, he was locked in his cell and you were the only one with the key—so who else could've killed him?"

"Anybody who came in there and saw me passed out and decided to settle a score with Brady."

"Gee, I thought for sure you killed him."

"I'm sorry to disappoint you."

"I wouldn't've held it against you. He deserved to be killed."

He patted his pockets. "I don't know how I'm gonna pay your bill."

"It's been taken care of."

"It has? By who?"

"By Mr. Brady. He says as long as you're on that noon train and never come back to town, he'll consider it money well spent. He said seeing you would just remind him of his son."

She stood up. "I've got to go meet a client."

Corey was still unhappy she'd marked him as the killer. "You think he killed somebody, too?"

She laughed. "No, but I do know for a fact that he burned down two barns and had some kind of carryings-on with one of Mel Fenwick's sheep."

A number of pretty ladies got on the coach in which Corey rode. They also wore summer-weight dresses and picture hats. Most of them carried carpetbags.

He tried to lose himself in their presence. Usually the sight of a pretty lady took him to a realm of ecstatic fantasies. He wanted romance as much as sex. He wanted that feeling of blind stupid glee he'd felt all those early years with his former wife.

But all he could concentrate on were the facts that a) Brady had ordered the doctor to change his autopsy report, b) Brady had ordered charges dropped and c) Brady had given him money and a ticket out of town, on the stipulation that he never return again.

Now that didn't sound right, did it?

All Corey could think of was what Hayden had told him that time, that Hayden, old man Brady and wife Debra had all turned against Mike. Could no longer tolerate him.

What if one of them had killed him?

He could think of no other reason for the charges being dropped and himself being pushed out of town.

A drunk remembers things sometimes, even after the worst of blackouts. What if Brady was afraid that Corey's memory would come back? What if Hayden had snuck in and killed Mike? Or even the old man? Or even Debra?

The train pulled out.

Corey was present in body only.

His mind was still back in town somewhere.

Four-and-a-half hours later, he left the train and went into the depot there and bought himself a ticket back to town. He had been many things in his life but he'd never been a killer. And by leaving town that was the impression he'd created.

His first stop was the general store where he bought writing supplies. He sat in the café and wrote out his letters. A lot of people stared at him. They assumed, just as that young lawyer had, that he'd killed Mike Brady. By now, the whole town knew that old man Brady had seen to it that Corey wouldn't be charged for it, not if he left town. So what the hell was he doing sitting in the café?

There was an old drunkard who did errands for folks during his few sober hours of the day. Corey gave him a dollar and told him where the letters were to be delivered. Hayden, Debra or old man Brady killed Mike Brady. The letter was designed to force the killer to reveal himself or herself.

He'd just sent the drunkard on his way when he saw the marshal walking toward him.

"You musn't recognize a gift from God when He puts one in your hand, Corey. Old man Brady doesn't want you here."

"I won't be here tomorrow morning. I just want everybody to know I didn't kill Mike Brady."

The marshal snorted. "You think anybody gives a damn if you did or not? They're just glad somebody did."

"Yeah but I don't want nobody thinkin' it was me. I don't kill people, Marshal. Never have, never will, not unless it's to save my own life."

The marshal glanced around the busy street. "You'd better keep out of sight, Corey. Old man Brady sees you, Lord knows what he'll do."

"Somebody's bound to tell him, anyway. I haven't exactly been hiding since I got back."

The marshal shook his head. "It's your life, Corey. All I know is I would never have come back here."

Corey shrugged. "I guess I just ain't as afraid of the Bradys as you folks that've lived around him for a long time."

"You get on his bad side, Corey," the marshal said, "and you'll be afraid of him soon enough. You mark my words."

He walked off down the street.

Corey got sick of people staring at him. There wasn't any particular ill-will in their stares, they were just curious about him. But as a drunkard, and a man who'd done some terrible and foolish things while trapped inside the bottle, he was tired of being a curiosity, of being sniggered at, whispered about, pointed to. A lot of elbows had been nudged into a lot of ribs when Corey walked by.

The saloon called, of course. Shot her silk skirt to reveal a good three inches of creamy white thigh, with the implied promise of showing even more as soon as he *answered* her call.

But he knew better. Knew that this was a lady who, for all her considerable and undeniable charms, had brought him only grief, sorrow and shame. Not her fault, really. His. For being so weak.

He found a good, lonely, grassy section of riverbank and sat there all afternoon, rolling cigarettes and napping a little and listening to the rush and roar of the downstream dam. He idly played loves me, loves me not with a number of flowers. He lost six times in a row. But on the seventh time he won so he gave up the game. He wasn't even sure who he had in mind, loving me and loving me not, maybe his former wife or maybe some dream girl, but it was fun to play. No matter how old and used-up a man got, loves me, loves me not was always fun to play.

The killer came at eight that night, right up on the ridge that sat above the dam.

Corey sat on a boulder, waiting to see which of the three he'd sent his letter to would show up.

> I SEEN YOU GO INTO THE MARSHAL'S
> OFFICE THE OTHER NIGHT AND KILL MIKE BRADY.
> I WILL TELL THE JUDGE IF YOU DON'T MEET
> ME AT THE DAM AT EIGHT O'CLOCK TONIGHT.

The moon was high, the breeze was so sweet-scented with spring it half drove a man crazy, he was so happy with the flowers and the river and the blooming trees and the smell of grass, he just didn't know what to do with himself.

Hayden saw him and came over.

"You're not very smart, Corey, you know that?"

"I guess that's about the only thing nobody's ever accused me of being. Smart."

"Old man Brady gave you a train ticket and money. You should've kept going."

"You killed him."

"What makes you say that?"

"I sent you the letter. You showed up, didn't you?"

Behind him, another voice said, "I showed up, too, Corey. Does that mean *I* killed him?"

A new scent, a lovely, elegant and somehow elegiac scent, was on the breeze now. A rich woman's perfume. Debra Brady came from the shadows into the moonlight.

"What're you doing here?" Corey said.

"Hayden's right," she said. She wore a white blouse and vest and black riding pants. Knee-length riding boots lent her a rich-girl air. Poor girls couldn't afford boots like that. But her voice, her manner was gentler than he remembered it. "I wish you would've just kept on going."

They stood together now. He wondered what he'd wondered when he'd talked to Hayden the other day. Wondered if there was some romantic connection between Hayden and Debra.

"Did you kill him?" Corey asked.

"What's so important about knowing?" Hayden said. "Hell, man, just walk away from it."

"I don't want people to think I'm a killer."

Hayden smirked. "They think you're everything else."

"Maybe so. But not a killer."

"Oh, what the hell," said a third voice. "We may as well tell him. There isn't a damned thing he can do about it, anyway."

And from the same shadows where Debra had stepped, now stepped old man Brady.

"What're *you* doing here?" Corey said.

"Your letter. Now why the hell'd you go and write that stupid damned letter?"

"Because I want to know."

Old man Brady, who was built like a New York professional wrestler, low to the ground, wagon-wide, and possessed of a face that could intimidate Satan, came closer to Corey and said, "You already know all you need to know. He's dead and you didn't kill him."

"People don't believe that."

"People here. But you don't live here, Mr. Corey. Or you won't soon as you get on that train and stay on it. California's nice."

"I was actually thinking some about California."

"Good. Think a lot more about it. There's a train leaving here in an hour. There's still time to get yourself a ticket."

"Did you kill him, Mr. Brady?"

Brady sighed, pawed at the front of his business suit. He didn't look comfortable in a suit. Too confining in both the physical and spiritual sense.

Brady looked at Debra and Hayden. Then back at Corey.

"He raped a girl."

"I know about that," Corey said.

"This one you don't. He raped my niece's daughter.

Thirteen years old. She's pregnant. My own son did that."

"He doesn't need to know all this, Mr. Brady," Hayden said.

"Hayden couldn't deal with it," Brady went on. "And neither could Debra. And neither could I. I don't know what was wrong with him. Some folks said I spoiled him and I guess I have to admit I did. But that don't mean spoiled kids go out and do the things he did. There was somethin' else wrong with him. That's why I had to have Hayden with him all the time. With my niece's daughter—"

"He knocked me out," Hayden said, "and then went into their house. She was in there alone, sleeping."

"You want to know how he died, Corey?" Brady said. "We had a meeting—Debra, Hayden and myself—and we drew straws. The one with the longest straw killed him. It didn't happen right away. We had to wait until the right time. We didn't mean to get you involved. We figured on hitting him when he was in his cell. Figured it'd look just like an accident. But then the doctor and the marshall got all hot and bothered and blamed you for it. I'm sorry it happened to you, Corey. I really am. But that's why I made the doctor change his mind and call it an accident."

Corey said, "So which of you killed him? Who drew the longest straw?"

Three passive faces stared at him. And then every one of them smiled.

Brady said, "You ever tell anybody about our little talk, Corey, and we'll just deny it."

"You ain't gonna tell me which one of you killed him?"

"No," Brady said, "we sure ain't."

•   •   •

All the way to California, Corey kept changing his mind. One minute he'd think it had to be Hayden. Then he'd think that it had to be old man Brady. And then he'd wonder— could a woman have done it? Why not? A ball bat or a small length of iron. Either one could do the job. Just lay it swift and hard up against a man's forehead and—

But then he'd get tired of his guessing game for a while and he'd roll himself a smoke and look out the window at the rivers and mountains and endless plains of the frontier.

California would mean a new start for him and he wasn't going to mess it up, the way he'd messed up so many other new starts. He was sure of it.

...GRAVEDIGGER...

Corey told me that story hisself, just afore he left for Californey. Could be it wasn't all true, but I think it was. Might be he was a disgrace to the badge, after all, but he weren't no killer. I sure hope he managed to make a new life for himself after he left here. It's hard givin' up that bottle, though, real hard...

Well, here I am, back where I started when you got here, a leanin' on this shovel and wonderin' where the hell the rest of them jaspers are! I tell you, this here Brady feller is the last one I'm a-diggin' up by myself. Them fellers better show up here with a shovel each or there's gonna be some kinda hell to pay.

Hey, watch it there, boy! You take a step back and you jest might go rollin' down the hill. See, we got to use every foot of space we got here on the Hill, and that means that we bury 'em not only on top of the hill, but on the slopes, too. That there grave you was about to step on ... well, lemme see, is that ... yep, that's who I thought it was— Lizzie Palmer.

Well, I done tol' you a tale of a saloon girl with a good heart, didn't I? Guess I oughtta tell ya about Lizzie, then. See, Lizzie was a kinda sweet gal when she came to Dodge City but Dodge—well, she's got a way of squeezin' all the sweet outta a gal, sometimes. I mean, the ones who got some mean in 'em, this town has a way of bringin' it out.

But mebbe I'm not bein' fair to Lizzie. She was a purty gal, that's for sure, and after what happened to her mebbe she had to turn mean to survive.

Well, mebbe I'll tell ya this one last story and then you kin decide for yourself ...

PLANTING
LIZZIE PALMER

MARTHAYN PELEGRIMAS

HERE LIES POOR LIZZIE PALMER
WE LOVED HER OH SO WELL
WE HOPE SHE WENT TO HEAVEN
BUT WE FEAR SHE WENT TO HELL

Lizzie Palmer was the kind of gal that a man would kill for. Not to be in her company, mind you. Hell, for one silver dollar she'd lay down with anyone. Lizzie was certainly not what you'd call particular—not by any stretch. No, when I say Lizzie Palmer could make a man kill for her I'm not referring to any of that special kind of persuasion ladies of her sort are able to use to influence men. That girl could get pretty near anything her heart desired by intimidation. That and threats. Why, I seen her threaten a man twice her size until he had tears running down his sorry face. She was mean—in a way you had to admire. It takes people with strong natures and staunch bodies to survive out here in

Kansas. The land and people are unforgiving. I don't think you'll find one person—man or woman—who would fault Lizzie for being the way she was. Mean in a way that demanded respect.

But Lizzie wasn't always like that. Naw, she was sweet and shy when I first met her. I remember it was back in the summer of 'seventy-six. It was a memorable day of sorts 'cause Brick Bond had killed hisself three hundred buffalo. He'd come into Dodge to celebrate and yanked Lizzie along with him—right into that saloon. No place a respectable woman would be seen.

"Hi," was all she said when we was introduced. She just kept staring down into her lap, holding onto Brick's arm like she was going to faint if she let go. It wasn't till months later that I got a good look at those brown eyes of hers. Dark and rich, like the color of tobacco.

"Bring that whiskey bottle over here!" Brick shouted to the bartender. "And three glasses!" Then he slapped me on the shoulder. "Can't go forgetting my good friend Jake, here."

"Brick, you know I don't drink," she said coyly. "Papa always told us girls that . . ."

Brick laughed loudly. He did everything loud. During all those years hunting, shooting that Big 50 Sharps rifle, Brick had deafened hisself with his own gun. "Yeah, well, you preacher's daughters all turn wild sooner or later."

"Why would you say something like that?" she asked.

"Because ya'll know from the very start that you're forgiven."

"That ain't so," she protested. "I'm good because it calms my soul."

"Well," Brick said, grabbing her into his arms. "You better think about calming my soul tonight." Then he kissed her on the mouth for a full minute. Everyone stopped to look.

Ole Brick was a suspicious sort. Suspected his skinners had been stealing from him and started keeping a tally of his kills. Was known for the figures he scribbled on scraps of paper stashed all over the place. Soon accusations started getting thrown in Lizzie's direction. Brick said he had proof that she had been with other men and no matter how much she tried, Lizzie could offer nothing that would convince him otherwise.

'Course, nothing was ever proven about his men's thievery nor Lizzie's faithlessness. But Brick's prediction about her future was right on the money.

After four months of bad temper and good times, Brick took off. I heard tell he was spotted down in Wichita. Lizzie was left to fend for herself and I remember thinking at the time that the poor girl was ill-prepared to make it on her own in a place like Dodge City.

Boy, was I wrong!

"I ain't no whore," Lizzie told me while we sat drinking in the Long Horn.

"No proper lady would be sitting here with the likes of an old codger like me."

"You're not so old." She looked me up and down. "Younger than my paw I bet, and he's only forty."

I thanked her for the compliment but silently cursed her for comparing me to her father. It was the first time in the few months I'd known her that she'd given me any inkling as to her feelings toward me. She was pretty enough to get quite a few unfatherly thoughts running through my head but I never did anything about none of them. First out of respect for Brick and then the fact that she looked so sweet and innocent. But after that conversation any plans I had about being with Lizzie was dashed just as sure as if she'd doused my insides with cold water.

Now that our relationship was decided, I offered some friendly advice. "The point I am trying to make here is that with Brick gone, you've got to hightail it back to your family and you want to do that with some of your reputation still intact."

"I ain't going back to Missouri. And I ain't concerned at all about what the busybodies in this town or any other town care to say about me." She picked up the glass of beer in front of her and drank it all down. Defiant as hell.

"Besides," she continued, "you're a fine one to talk, Mister Eat 'Em Up Jake."

I could feel my cheeks burning. "You don't know what you're talking about."

"Is that so?" She sat back, slowly crossing her arms across her chest, enjoying herself. "Way I heard it was that you had a king up your sleeve. Cheating at cards. Damn near got caught, 'cept you were quick enough to order a sandwich, slip the card inside and gobble it down."

What could I say? The girl had her facts straight.

"So don't go lecturing me about no reputation. There ain't nothing wrong at all doin' whatever it takes to survive. And if I happen to have a quick mind, seems to me there are plenty of opportunities to make a life for myself right here."

I wondered if it had been the months she'd lived in our fair town or knowing Brick Bond that had toughened up Lizzie. "Opportunities are certainly abundant ... more so for someone with a good head, that's for sure. But there is one big difference between the two of us that I'm afraid you're overlooking here."

"And what would that be?"

"Besides our ages, are you forgetting, my dear, that you are a woman and as such accountable for your conduct?"

"Now you even *sound* like my daddy," she grumbled. "But let me ask you this ... who do you suppose made up your precious rules of accountability?"

I opened my mouth to answer but she kept right on going.

"I'll tell you who makes up these rules—men like you. Brick came and went. I sat and waited. Brick yelled. I listened. Now he's left me, and according to you, I'm suppose to fall apart. Sit in my room, crying all day, brokenhearted. Is that it? I'm supposed to run back home and beg my daddy's forgiveness all the while hoping that a good man, if there is such a thing, will have me? I ain't never done anything I'm ashamed of, Jake. And I never will. Just because I'm staying true to my nature, like you and every other man in this town is doin', don't mean that I'm not a respectable woman."

I took a good long look at the gal sitting across from

me. She got my attention all right along with a big chunk of my respect. I shook my head, trying not to let on that she also amused the hell outta me. "You're right, Lizzie. But being right don't change nothin'. That's the way it's been and that's the way it's always gonna be."

She blew a frustrated sigh across the table at me. "Does that mean you ain't gonna help me or what?"

"If you're determined to stay here . . ."

"I am!"

". . . then I'll see if I can get you on at the Lady Gay. At least you'll be safe there. The owner and me have known each other a long time."

"And you'll ask him to look after me? Treat me different from the other girls? Is that what you're thinking?"

"Well, yes," I said sheepishly at first. Then after a moment I got bolder. "What's wrong with that? Wanting you to be safe?"

She just smiled at me. "Nothing, Jake. Thanks."

By week's end, Lizzie was dealing faro at the Lady Gay Saloon and Dance Hall. She kept the room at the boardinghouse off of Bridge Street that she'd shared with Brick. Said it was easier than moving all her things. But I knew she was the owner of very few possessions. Maybe she was still hoping Brick would come back for her.

Even though there had recently been a city ordinance against gambling passed, everyone knew it was just for show. The *Ford County Globe* wrote that "square games are among the necessary belongings of any town that has the cattle trade." They knew it, everyone knew it. Dodge City would never be free of gamblers. Them laws were put on the books just to rid the town of deadbeats, thieves and eyesores. But you cain't keep the bad apples outta the barrel. They keep falling down in there.

Lizzie started off fair and honest. The men loved her smart comments and her table was always crowded with admirers. 'Course her tight dress and shiny hair didn't hurt none either. But I couldn't help noticing the longer Lizzie worked there, the meaner she got. Guess it was bound to happen. People in that place, back in them days, was different. Most required special handling. Guns was going off, fights broke out so often we just stepped aside and waited for the commotion to end.

Until the night Brick came back to town.

Lizzie was sitting cross-legged, on the corner of a billiard table. I remember she was wearing a fancy white dress. When I come in, she smiled at me.

"Well, how's it goin', Eat 'Em Up?" she asked, dangling her feet like she was sitting on the edge of a river, cooling herself off. "Ain't seen you in how long?"

"Two months, maybe three," I told her. "You're looking fine, Lizzie."

"Surprised to see me still here. I can tell," she said laughing.

"Kinda."

I remember thinking that we was the only folks at that end of the saloon—Lizzie, me and the bartender. At the other end a wheel of fortune was running and maybe thirty people stood around it, shouting out numbers and throwing down their money.

"Slow night?" I asked.

"Things'll pick up. It's still early." She grinned at me. "But I guess it is past your bedtime. You being such an old codger and all."

Even while she kidded me, I could tell she was harder than the last time I'd seen her. It showed mostly around the eyes. These little wrinkles fanned out toward her cheeks, making her skin look brittle. Her words were playful, all right, but her spirit was dead serious. Before I had a chance to reply, Brick walked in the door.

Lizzie glanced over. I couldn't figure out if she was surprised or not.

He had a friend with him. A big fella, dressed in dirty buckskins. I could smell both of them as they walked down to our end of the saloon.

"Lizzie!" Brick shouted. "Where's my hug?" He held out his arms but she didn't move.

"You'd have better luck getting a hug outta that ugly friend of yours." She nodded toward the bar where the big guy had stopped.

I couldn't believe my ears, hearing her talk to Brick that way. And I got my second surprise when ole Brick took her abuse. Never raised a finger to her.

"We only got whiskey and beer," I heard the bartender tell Brick's friend. That was all he said to the man. Nothing malicious in his tone.

The big man beat his fist on the bar and said something

I couldn't make out from where I stood. Then all of a sudden he rushed behind the bar.

Before we knew what was happening, the two of them started hollerin'.

Lizzie looked over, bored, then turned to Brick. "Why is it that all you ever bring in here is trouble? Can you tell me that?"

"Are you forgettin' that I brung you in here one time?"

"Oh gracious no, Brick," she said sarcastically. "How could I ever forget all the nice things you done for me?"

"Christ Almighty, woman, I'm just standing here. How can you blame me for what's going on all the way over there?"

"All's I know is you're no good, Brick. I hate . . ."

Before Lizzie could finish her insult, I noticed the gun in the bartender's right hand. Quicker than a flash, he brought it up to the other man's ear. "Now go sit down!" he yelled at the big guy.

But the other man drew his gun and poked it into the bartender's belly. "No one tells me what to do. Hear me?"

The two of them stood there for a while. Trying to decide what to do while the three of us stood there watching. The folks at the other end of the saloon was too excited with their game to even notice what was going on.

Lizzie started to get off the billiard table. "Between the two of them they ain't got a single brain," she said.

"What you think you're doin'?" Brick asked, holding her back. "Sit tight and shut up, girl. It's between the two of them; it don't concern you."

"Is that how you figure it? Or are you just covering up

the fact that you're too cowardly to control your friend? This here's my place of work, Brick. People come here for a good time, not to see two morons fight over a lousy drink!"

Brick looked back toward the bar, then at me. "Go ahead Jake, tell her this here's got nothin' to do with bein' brave." Before I could say something, Brick looked back at Lizzie. "I'd a thought you been workin' here long enough to know when to shut up and wait for the fightin' to stop."

Lizzie looked Brick straight in the eye. "Well, look who's givin' advice over here." Then she started making noises at him like a chicken.

I couldn't help myself. It was funny . . . so I laughed.

Brick's friend turned to look at what the hell was so funny, I suppose. Then things started happening pretty fast.

The bartender, who by this time was getting tired of being threatened, saw his chance and pulled on his trigger.

The big guy's head got blown to bits. Poor fella still had the gun clenched in his hand. Alls I could figure was that the shock of being shot must have made his Colt go off. Even without his faculties, that man managed to squeeze off a shot in our direction.

Lizzie was still clucking at Brick when he sorta exploded all over her pretty white dress and dropped down like a sack of flour, right at her feet.

We all just stood there, not knowing what to do next. You woulda thought you was in church, that's how quiet it got. The bartender was covered with blood and I could see a dark puddle running across the floor in the corner.

That's when Lizzie jumped off the table and what she done next will stay with me forever.

Bending down, she dipped both her hands into Brick's blood. Rubbed her palms together like she was trying to keep away the cold. Then she hollered, "Cluck, cluck, cluck! Cluck, cluck, cluck!"

Holding both hands high above her head, she clapped them together. They made a wet slap. Slowly she brung them down in front of her. Then she clapped and clapped until Brick's blood was spattered all over her.

Now you might think that people turned away from Lizzie after that frightening display. But truth be told, they rallied around her. For there weren't one man or woman in that place who hadn't had something bad happen to them. Big strong men were gunning each other down or keeling over from the hard work. The women were all the time dying out on that prairie. Children were being buried either from the fever or something or other if they did happen to make it from their mamma's womb into this cruel world at all.

And beneath it all was that infernal human emotion—love. Love of the land, love for money, whiskey, women. Love always taints everything, even back then. Even in Dodge City. And there weren't nothing—then or now—that garners more sympathy like a jilted lover.

Some said Lizzie just got so overcome by Brick's death that she broke down, her being such a gentle woman. But none of them heard the last conversation she was having with Brick before he got killed. Not like I did.

While I didn't agree with most folks, I did feel from the start that poor Lizzie Palmer had gotten a bad shake from Brick. That's why I escorted her home that night and saw to it that Lily, one of the dance hall girls, got her cleaned up and tucked into her safe bed.

It was close to two weeks before I seen Lizzie again.

She walked into the Lady Gay in a pretty dress, much like that white one I'd seen her in last time, only this one was red. Maybe she figured that should she be so unfortunate as to be in the line of fire again, the blood wouldn't show up so bad.

I walked over to the door, hoping maybe to keep her from coming too far inside. "Why, Lizzie, don't you look fine today," I told her.

"Thank you, Jake."

"How're you feelin'?"

"Much better." She never looked me in the eyes but past me, like she was searching for someone more important.

"What brings you here?" I asked.

"Cain't lay around no more. Need some money to live—have to go to work."

I was surprised. "But I thought . . ."

"I know what you and the rest of them thought. That *now* I'd be going back home. Gee, Jake," she looked at me like I was a bug, "all the time you keep going on about what a good friend you are and all the time you want me to go away. Why is that do you suppose?"

"I just want you safe, Lizzie, that's all."

"Well don't I look safe to you?" She held her arms out and twirled around. Still our eyes never met.

"Finer than ever, Lizzie. I didn't mean nothin'. Just that Brick woulda wanted . . ."

"Don't matter what Brick wants. He's dead."

And with that, Lizzie pushed past me and made her way to the back room where some of the other girls was gathered. After talking to one of the dealers I found out that Lizzie didn't deal faro no more. She was now a dance hall girl, getting paid to dance with the men that come in for drink and a little fun.

Money was easy to get back then if a man was willing to do any job. When I got tired of the buffaloes, I scouted for a wagon master and then there was the cattle moving in and out of towns from Texas. The business of staying alive just sorta chewed up the time and before I knew it six months had passed.

The piano man was having hisself a time, playing a lively tune and all the girls was paired off with some dirty, grinning character. They all looked like they was trying so hard to have a good time—the girls, that is. Men are happy anytime a pretty gal smiles their way, don't matter if they have to pay for that grin or not.

Lizzie didn't see me as I walked back to the bar. Or at least that's the impression she gave me then. It was coming on midnight and the place was lit up and noisy as hell. I ordered my beer and was getting ready to take it over to a table in the corner when I seen this fierce-looking gal in a green dress get all fired up about something Lizzie was saying.

The guy Lizzie was with tried getting away from her but that girl hung on tight. Then I could hear her shout, "You stay right where you are!"

I couldn't make out if she was yelling at the ugly ole gal in the dirty green dress or the poor guy who had his arms around Lizzie.

Then the other woman pushed her partner away from her. She had so much weight behind her and pushed so hard that the startled bastard went flying across the room. After he got back on his feet he scampered out the door like a dog with a butt full of buckshot.

The piano man stopped playing once he seen what was happening. Looking bored, like this kinda thing happened every night, he slammed the lid over the keys and got up to go stand by the bar.

"You know damn well and good, Lizzie Palmer, that Ed there is my sister's fiancé."

"I don't give a damn who the hell he is! And you, Tilly, are nothin' but a smelly ole whore that no one wants to be seen with. So go back to your pen, eat some more slop and shut up!" Then she grabbed onto the guy she was dancing with and started moving him across the floor like the piano was still hammering out a tune that only she could hear.

Well that Tilly girl started for Lizzie but Lizzie kept Ed between her and the whore.

"I'm just dancing, Tilly. Look," Ed shouted to her. "I don't even have my arms around her." And again he tried pushing Lizzie away but she wouldn't let go.

Tilly got so frustrated she picked up a glass off a table and hurled it at Lizzie's head. Her aim was pretty good.

The blood come pouring outta that cut, down Lizzie's forehead and I could see it traveling alongside her ear.

"You bitch!" Lizzie screeched, and shoved Ed away from her as she ran for Tilly.

I was starting to think that every time I was to meet up with Lizzie Palmer it would be my misfortune to see that pretty gal covered in blood.

Lizzie had to run by me to get to fat Tilly and I reached out and grabbed onto her. "You're hurt, girl, cain't you see that? Stop it now. I'll take you on home."

"Leave me alone, Jake. I can take care of this myself."

I shouldn't have, but I tossed her over my shoulder like a sack of dirty laundry. She weren't all that heavy. And then I aimed both of us right out the front door.

A few of the other guys was holding back Tilly but she never stopped shouting at us. As I walked, I had to hold Lizzie's ankles together to keep her from kicking me in the face. She put up a real fight.

I walked out of the Lady Gay, down Front Street and right to Lizzie's place without once stoppin'.

"I hate you, Jake! Let me down! You have no right to do this!" She never shut up. Not even to take a breath.

I didn't say a word. Couldn't think of nothin' to say.

Her door was unlocked. I walked into her room and threw her down onto the unmade bed. She must have tired herself out from all the kicking and screaming 'cause she laid back kinda relieved.

I soaked a rag in the basin of water she had on the dresser. Then I took it to her and tried cleaning her wound but she grabbed it away from me. "I can do it!"

"Lizzie, darlin' . . ."

"Don't start any of your darlin' bullshit with me, Jake.
Just leave me alone. I want you to go. You're never around
when I need you, so just git outta here. Leave me alone."

"I ain't going nowhere. Not now. I'm staying with you
till I'm sure you're all right."

Everything musta caught up with her then. She started
to sit up and the next thing I knew, she was out cold. Fainted
away.

I may not be good for much, but I am good as my
word. I said I'd stay with her and I planned to do just that.
While Lizzie slept and fidgeted, I sat beside her bed, watching her, rocking in that white chair she ordered from the
catalogue. She loved that chair. It creaked with each push I
made backward but after a while it got to be kinda soothing.

Lizzie laid like that for several hours and while I
watched her I had time to notice all them boxes stacked in
the corner. They looked to be Brick's things. I knew Brick
didn't have no family of his own. But I'd never spent one
minute's worth of thought wondering where his earthly possessions ended up. As the night got longer and that ole
rocker started causing my back to get stiff, I started poking
around in them boxes.

Lizzie got better after two days. I fed her some barley soup
I got down at the hotel and she was talking about going
back to work when the fever started up.

I brung the doc down to look at her and he said the
wound on her scalp had gotten itself infected. We tried our

best but nothing we done could cut the fever.
After five days... poor Lizzie died.

I went back to the Lady Gay to deliver the sad news. The men felt mighty bad, said Lizzie was an honest woman, worked hard for what she got. But none of the gals there had much decent to say.

After talking to my friend, the fella that hired Lizzie on in the first place, I convinced him we should take up a collection. Send Lizzie off in the style she never knew in her miserable life. A casket was special ordered. I chipped in extra to have the lining made with white satin imported from France that they had down at the tailor shop. A little pillow stitched with violets was made for under her head.

There was this tubercular minister in town. He'd come late last year from New York City, trying to get his health back. But he weren't getting no better and hated Dodge so much that we was able to convince him to perform the service for Lizzie. None of the regular men of God would help us out, seeing as how Lizzie was a whore and all. We even had enough money left from our collection to pay for that minister's train fare back home. He done a real nice job. Spoke almost like he knew Lizzie.

A bunch of us planted Lizzie Palmer that day. Careful, like she was a flower. Not any of the men had any stories to tell about her that you would think of as heartwarming. I doubt if any of them even liked Lizzie that much. Naw, I think they was there on account of feeling so guilty. Guilty that one of their sisters or mothers could end up like Lizzie and no one done nothing to change her life for the better. Just took advantage of the service she offered.

And if none of them came because of their guilt I guess that was their own business. I can only tell you for certain why I helped carry Lizzie's casket up to the top of that hill. It was my way of making things right. After all, it was the least I could do considering all I stole from her.

Well, I guess you could say I stole from Brick, not Lizzie. 'Cause while Lizzie laid there in her bed, suffering from that infection of hers, I had plenty of time to go through all them boxes Brick left behind. And inside was all kinds of notes Brick Bond had writ hisself. Names of places where he'd left money in banks. Towns where he had connections trading his hides for top dollar. He even kept track of what people done. Things people who managed to make something of themselves didn't want known. All them numbers and names on all them pieces of paper.

One bank in Hays believed me when I said I was his brother. Gettin' the money outta that account was easy. I figured the rest of the collecting I had to do would go fine. I've always had a way about me that makes folks believe what I say.

Oh, I suppose I coulda taken that money and got Lizzie a proper doctor. Maybe even got her to Wichita. There was time, and she did suffer so. But she had a proper funeral and burial on account of me. And after a few years, all that folks'll remember is the grandeur of the spectacle. They'll figure that she musta been truly loved—had to be if so many cared that she have a fancy ending.

Memories are like that. Most times only the good ones

come to the top. They'll forget the truth—that Lizzie Palmer was a whore who never had no friends an' never done much of anything for no one else.

Besides, a man's gotta plan for his old age. Cain't keep hoping some pretty young thing will love him and tend to him when he cain't fend for hisself.

Lizzie woulda understood . . . she was mean like me.

. . . GRAVEDIGGER . . .

See what I mean? First Brick just up and leaves her and a gal's got to survive, ain't she? All that mean, that mighta just been in self defense. But then ol' Jake, can't say he treated Lizzie all that good—'specially after she was dead. Jake left town soon after that, but I can still hear him a-tellin' me that story. Fact is, I kinda sound like ol' Jake when I tell it . . . or mebbe that's jest in my head.

And mebbe the sun's a-gettin' to me from these past five years or so that I been a-plantin' folks up here on the Hill. Well, now, I'm unplantin' 'em, ain't I? What? I didn't tell ya that? Well, shoot, folks, ya see all these holes up here, don't ya? We planted 'em one at a time, but now we're diggin' 'em all up an'—

Well, lookee here. I gotta stop and tell ya somethin' about this feller right here. He come a long way to end up buried here, and believe me, he was as surprised as a man could be when he bought the farm. After all, he thought he was makin' a killin'—if you excuse my use of irony—but when he showed up here all he did was get in my way.

Why, I was about to fill in that hole over there—jest 'bout two feet away from here—and before I could get that feller over there covered, this feller showed up and he t'weren't nothin' but . . .

A DAMNED NUISANCE

MARCUS GALLOWAY

A killer, a thief and a damned nuisance
besides . . .

                Shakespeare, NM — 1878

Owen Lindsey had a lot of plans for the winter of 1878.

Killing a man was definitely not one of them.

Christmas had passed, leaving everyone in town feeling in good spirits and ready to get on with the new year. But after all the turkeys had been cooked and every gift had been handed out, life had to go back to normal.

Normal life for Owen meant walking back into Shakespeare's General Store and opening up for another day of figuring tabs and wrapping parcels. It wasn't a very exciting life, but it had worked just fine for well over forty years. In that time, Owen had raised a family and watched a beautiful daughter become a wife and mother. He'd set aside enough money to become a partner in the store and even put a little in the bank.

That, he'd always believed, had been his first mistake.

Apart from doctors, Owen distrusted banks the most. In fact, his wife Isabelle had always told him that when it came to those two institutions, he became downright suspicious.

"I trust 'em," he'd always reply. "In fact, I trust that they'll never fail in making a mess out of things every damn time."

He never felt sick until after Doc Wilson had put his hands on him. And he never felt so far removed from his hard-earned money as when he'd handed it over to a bank. That had been back in the spring, at Isabelle's insistence. Banks got robbed either by crooks in fancy suits or those that wore masks and Owen didn't have much use for either one of them. Now that the holidays were over and Owen's faith in others had gone back down to its normal level, he waited for the slowest time of day before heading to the hat rack.

After living his whole life in the Southwest, Owen's bony frame looked as though it had been covered by tightly-stretched leather. His hair had thinned out to a gray ring above his ears and his stomach had expanded to a slight paunch over his belt. Isabelle teased him about the weight he'd taken on, saying he looked like a piece of old rope with a knot in the middle. Ever since then, Owen had started wearing vests buttoned over that knot. By way of an apology, Isabelle had given him a pocket watch on a chain for Christmas which now dangled over his belly and swung back and forth as he walked.

Snatching an old brown hat from the rack, Owen checked the time and got ready to leave.

"Where you headed?" asked his partner and good friend, George Mysner. George wasn't the most ambitious of men, but was a solid partner and was too lazy to go through the hassle of cheating on any of the figures. He looked a bit younger than Owen, thanks mostly to a more padded frame and a full head of light brown hair.

Setting the hat on top of his head, Owen turned before opening the door. "I'm goin' to the bank. Gonna take my money out."

"Isabelle won't care for that too much, you know."

"I know. But she won't have'ta know I did it. Not for a while anyways."

George shook his head. "You can't keep nothing from that woman of yours. Besides, what are you fixin' to do with your money? Sock it away beneath the floorboards?"

"Whatever I do, it'll be better than letting some strangers keep it. Just watch the store for a few minutes while I'm gone. This won't take long."

Ignoring George's disapproving stare, Owen opened the door and stepped outside. A crisp breeze whipped down the streets of Shakespeare like an invisible rake that sliced right through skin and scraped its prongs over human bones, freezing them down to the marrow. He clapped his hands together and rubbed them vigorously, wishing for the welcome feel of the sun's heat on his face and the warm brush of summer across his cheeks.

Shakespeare wasn't as big a town as some, but it had been growing steadily for as long as Owen could remember. They were sometimes visited by cattle drivers and railroad scouts, both of which brought plenty of business to the Double Decker Saloon, which was right down the street.

There was supposed to be a herd coming through any day now, which was just another thing to quicken Owen's steps as he made his way down Main Street and headed toward the bank. Cowboys were nothing but trouble. Just like all the types that sat around in the saloon with nothing better to do all day than drink and gamble.

Owen grumped to himself all the way to the bank and once he emerged from the small wooden building with his savings tucked safely away in his pockets, he finally started to feel better about things. The whole world could do what it wanted with itself, but that didn't mean he had to be a part of it. Let everyone else deal with cheats and thieves. Owen Lindsey was done with them.

He hadn't made it more than twenty feet from the bank's front door when he heard the thunder of approaching horses coming from the other end of the street. It didn't take long for Owen to realize that the horses were coming directly toward him, and in a few seconds they charged around the corner amid a cloud of swirling dust.

The stampeding animals showed no signs of slowing. In fact, the closer they got, the easier it was to hear the whooping and hollering of the men riding on their backs, pushing the beasts to even greater heights of frenzy.

Owen took another step back onto the boardwalk until he was all but pressed up against the front of a restaurant. Even after his extra precaution, the horses still managed to thunder by and spray a fine layer of dirt and filth all across Owen's suit as they passed.

Bits of grime and worse clung to his favorite hat. When he reached down to check his pocket watch, Owen found it dripping wet. Since the horses had torn through a drainage ditch, he only hoped it was water clinging to his shiny new timepiece. Otherwise, he might as well just throw the thing away. When Owen grit his teeth together, his teeth crunched on bits of dust.

Suddenly, Owen felt anger boiling up inside of him. He couldn't see much of their diminishing backs, but one of them wore a red bandanna tied around his head, probably to make sure that he didn't swallow too much of the trail dirt he'd kicked up.

The horses disappeared around a corner and folks walked back into the street as though nothing had happened.

"Did they get ya, Owen?" came a voice from the restaurant.

Owen threw himself around in a tight half-circle, ready to give hell to whoever had just spoken to him. It was Jack Hart, owner of the Double Decker.

"Looks like they did, but good," Jack said as he walked over and started brushing off Owen's jacket. "Sometimes them cowboys are in an awful rush."

Owen choked down his anger and took a breath. After all, it hadn't been Jack who'd done the damage. "Sure. An awful hurry. They might'a ruined my watch and I got a mouthful of . . . lord only knows what."

"Take it easy, now. How about you come on down to my bar and I'll buy you a drink? That should help clear your throat."

Nodding, Owen couldn't help the smile from creeping onto his face. "A drink? Sure. That sounds pretty good."

•   •   •

The whiskey went down as good as ever. In fact, it did a fine job of getting rid of the grit that had coated Owen's mouth. By the time he knocked back his second glass, he was ready to forget about the stains on his clothes, polish off his watch and just get on with the rest of his day.

Then, someone walked into the Double Decker who brought a quick stop to all the shopkeeper's contentment.

He was a tall cowboy with a mop of unruly black hair sprouting up at odd angles from every part of his face and scalp. Staring down each man in the saloon, he bared a mouthful of crooked yellow teeth and spat a wad of brown juice onto the floor. Every inch of his clothing was covered in dirt, from the tips of his battered leather boots to the ends of the red bandanna tied around his neck.

"What the hell kind of shit hole town is this?" the stranger blustered in a voice that had been coughed up from the depths of a swamp.

Jack did his best to retain his composure as he put on the toughest face he could manage. "I beg your pardon?"

"My friend and I just pulled into town and so far we ain't even seen anything worth robbing. This must be the sorriest excuse for a wide spot I seen in any road I ever been on."

Rolling his eyes, Owen turned his back on the man and looked back to his drink. "That didn't even make any sense."

If the stranger had any faults, bad hearing wasn't one of them. As soon as those words came out of Owen's mouth, the man with the red bandanna stormed over the loose boards covering the saloon's floor until he was standing directly behind the older man.

"What the hell did you just say?"

Owen felt a knot cinch tight in his stomach and his innards run cold. "I didn't say anything."

"Yeah, well that's funny, because I swore I heard you open that mouth of yours just a few seconds ago."

When Owen didn't speak up right away, Jack broke the silence by slapping a clean shot glass onto the bar. While filling it up with whiskey, he said amiably, "Nobody said nothing, mister. Since you're new in town, the first round's on the house."

"Better make it two," the stranger said. "One for me and one for my friend."

Once again, the front door swung open and a set of heavy footsteps thumped into the saloon. When Owen turned to look over his shoulder, he immediately recognized the ugly face of a local outlaw named Russian Bill.

Owen had never met the outlaw before, but he'd seen his face on the wall of the sheriff's office every time he'd been in to visit with the local peacekeepers. Thanks to his fiery temper, Bill was worth a nice piece of change. Since Owen was no lawman, he turned slowly back around and kept his head low. That was when he felt the stranger's large, pawlike hand slap him across his shoulder blades almost hard enough to bring his whiskey up from his gut and onto the bar.

"Hey Bill," the stranger screamed. "I don't think this old-timer likes us much."

The floor rumbled slightly beneath Russian Bill's weight. The stool next to Owen groaned like a living thing in pain and the hairs on the back of Owen's neck stood on end.

"Shut yer hole, Sandy," Bill grunted. "This codger

wouldn't be so rude to us. Not when it could be so bad fer his health."

The words slid into the air like a greasy snake's tongue. They dripped with menace and didn't carry even the slightest hint of a Russian accent.

Owen, who liked to think he knew what was going on inside the heads of such brutal characters, straightened up so as not to show any signs of weakness and turned to face Russian Bill. "Sorry about that," he said. "Can I buy you a drink?"

Russian Bill's face looked as though it had been chiseled out of sun-baked rock. Hard and gritty, his skin was cracked in several places and scarred in several more. His eyes smoldered like coals dying at the bottom of a fire and the lines in his forehead were deep enough to plant crops in. "We already got free drinks, old man. What else you got to offer?"

The hand on Owen's back tightened until Sandy's fingers dug in deep enough to press against a nerve. Jolts of pain shot through Owen's neck and torso, causing him to squirm uncomfortably in his seat.

"Yeah," Sandy said. "What else you got?"

Owen couldn't help but notice the ignorant slur in the stranger's voice. Bill might have been a killer, but at least he had character. This other one was nothing more than a dullard trying to gain a personality by association.

"I . . . I don't have much of anything," Owen stammered. "I'm just a—"

The stench of stale cigar smoke and jerked beef permeated Owen's senses as Sandy leaned over his shoulder and spoke directly into his face. "What about the watch? That looks like something we might like."

Owen thought about plenty of good things to say in response to Sandy's request. He thought of plenty of threats that would have made the other men shake in their boots and curse the day they'd ever even considered walking into the Double Decker Saloon to start trouble.

Unfortunately, he didn't have the sand to say a single one of them.

Instead, he slowly drug the watch from his pocket and set it on the bar.

"God dammit!" Owen shouted when he finally made it back to his store.

The place was empty. George had either run home for some reason or was sleeping in the back room. Either way, Owen didn't much care. All he could think about was what he would like to do if he ever saw those two cowboys again.

His eyes skipped toward the shotgun he kept under the counter as he stuffed his life savings into a strongbox. Visions of glorious, bloody retribution danced in his head.

"I swear to God almighty, if I see them again I'll—"

The rest of his divine promise stuck in his throat like a fly that had been sucked in by mistake as the front door swung open to reveal a pair of familiar figures. Although they were swaying unsteadily thanks to the whiskey they'd slammed down only minutes ago, they still managed to fill the entire frame. Their boots rattled the bell over the door as well as several empty cans and jars lining nearby shelves.

Dangling from Russian Bill's hand was Owen's pocket watch. He held it by the chain in front of his wide, ugly face and said, "This has got shit all over it. We need somethin' else."

Owen could feel the shakes coming. All he wanted was to get away from these foul-smelling drunkards.

Sandy reeked of alcohol and staggered toward the counter on bowed legs. After fidgeting with the bandanna around his neck, he stepped up so he could stare directly down into Owen's face and snarl viciously when he said, "You didn't go to no law, did you?"

"No . . . sir."

Holding his stare right where it was, Sandy took in the sight of Owen Lindsey as though he was looking at his worst enemy. His eyes slowly crawled over Owen's features until they landed on the counter. From there, they drifted to the cash register and toward the back room where George kept his office.

At that moment, Sandy's hand flashed to his side and drew an old Army-issue Colt. "How much you got in the till, old man?"

Owen's stomach flopped inside his body and cold beads of sweat poked through every pore in his body. Putting on the best poker face he could manage under the circumstances, he tried not to think about the wad of bills he'd stored under the counter for safekeeping. "N . . . not much. Just a f . . . few dollars."

"Well, hand it over."

Russian Bill looked at his partner with mild amusement. "Leave the man be, Sandy. Can't you see he's about to piss himself?"

"Yeah, I can see that." When he thumbed back the hammer of his pistol, the gun made a well-oiled *click*.

The next thing Owen felt was the touch of steel against his temple.

Like a coyote circling its prey, Sandy leaned in close and took a quick inhale. His nostrils flared as they took in the scent of Owen's fear, which oozed from him like slime from a frog's back. "You ain't movin' fast enough for my taste. If you value your life, I'd suggest you move a little quicker."

Owen's hands trembled furiously. The more he tried to get them to work, the less they wanted to cooperate. He turned toward the register, putting some distance between himself and the gunman. Even though he had a hard time poking the right buttons to get the drawer open, his mind was still racing with plans on how he could get to the shotgun stored beneath the counter. The weapon sat right above his strongbox, waiting for just such an emergency. Now that he needed it, Owen could not stop shaking long enough to use the damn thing.

Finally, the register drawer popped open, rattling on rusted tracks accompanied by the weak tinkle of a bell that was in dire need of replacing.

"Aww, shit," Russian Bill grumbled. "Would ya look at that? Looks like we went through all this trouble for less than five dollars." The big man started laughing, but not hard enough to keep from drawing a pistol to cover his partner.

Sandy's head lowered and wobbled slightly back and forth, making him look like a poorly made doll that couldn't keep its chin up. He started to say something, but all that came out was a frustrated huff of air that smelled like the Double Decker's outhouse after a bunch of cowboys had been drinking away their pay for an entire weekend. He clenched his dirty teeth together and started walking away. Finally, he wheeled around and pointed the gun at Owen's face.

"Hand it over anyway, you stupid son of a bitch!"

After Russian Bill got ahold of himself, he leveled his eyes at Owen as well and said. "That's right. And put yer hands up over yer head."

This was it.

Everything in Owen's gut told him that he'd feel the bite of a bullet chewing through his head at any second and he would never get the chance to fight back. "You can have the money just don't—"

"I said reach for the rafters!" This time, Bill punctuated his command by cocking his own gun. Unlike Sandy, Bill's hand was steady as a rock. As he started walking around the counter, his steps were quick and confident. "I'm just gonna take a look at what else you got behind there. Sometimes places like this have a stash of extra cash or even a . . ."

His words stopped and his eyes grew wide.

Owen felt all the air drain out of his lungs. The room started to spin.

Bill looked at Sandy with wide eyes as he bent down, snatched something up off the floor and held it up like a trophy. ". . . or even a strongbox."

Dropping to a low crouch, Owen brought his hands down to his double-barreled salvation when he saw Sandy's face turn his way. Before he could react, Owen felt the impact of steel against his face as the ground seemed to tilt crazily beneath his feet.

His ears rang with the sound of the impact Sandy's gun made against his skull and a flow of blood trickled from the newly created split in his lip. Still, somehow, he managed to keep from falling backward . . . at least, until Russian Bill knocked him down with as much force as he might have used to swat a fly.

When Owen hit the floor, he felt a sharp stab of pain come up from his tailbone and spike through his entire body. His butt hit the floorboards and his back slammed against the door to the back room, slamming it shut just as George was on his way out to see what was causing all the commotion.

Owen swore he could hear the crunch of breaking cartilage as George hollered in pain behind him. By the time he peeled his eyes open to see where the next blow was coming from, Owen was just barely able to make out Bill's back as he darted around the counter and headed for the door. Owen's arms were a jumble above his head and as he tried making a final grab for the shotgun, he saw someone poke their head into his field of vision and smile a crooked, filthy smile.

"Uh-uh," Sandy drawled. "You ain't gonna tell a soul about this." His hand came up, pointed the pistol and then pulled the trigger.

Owen's vision was clouded over by the smoke belched out from the outlaw's barrel and his senses screamed out for him to do something before that bullet found its mark.

But it was too late.

Hot lead ripped through flesh and bone that disintegrated into red paste as the bullet tore a path through it. Blood sprayed onto the wall and across Owen's face as he slumped against the wall like a puppet whose strings had been cut.

Doc Wilson had been trained during the War between the States. He worked fast and efficiently and once he saw that his patient wasn't going to need a limb hacked off or a chunk of metal dug out of his flesh, he moved on to the next one. All the complaints that came after that were the nurse's problem.

"Stop your bellyaching, already," the grizzled veteran said to George after he'd finished stuffing cotton into both of the man's nostrils and tying a bandage loosely around his head. "It's only a broken nose."

"Christ, it hurts!"

Doc Wilson wiped his hands on the apron he'd tied around himself when working with patients and pointed to the back of his office. "Yeah, well, count yer blessings. You could've gotten something a lot worse."

Sitting there, propped up in one of the four beds, Owen stared back at the world with blank, expressionless eyes. His skin was pasty and dry, stretched over slack muscles like so much old newspaper. And written all across that parchment was a tale of defeat, pain and humiliation.

Doc Wilson walked back to Owen's bed and wrapped his hand around his patient's left wrist. He then lifted the limp arm up high so he could inspect the bandages that had been woven around Owen's hand like a thick tangle of cobwebs. Already, the tips of the bandages were soaking through with blood.

"How you feelin'?"

Owen shifted grudgingly, blinked once and then looked at the doctor. "I'm less one finger. How the hell am I supposed to feel?"

"It could'a been worse," Doc Wilson said as he peered intently at Owen's left hand. "The bullet did a nice clean job. All I had to do was stitch up the wound."

"I know," Owen grunted. "I was there. I felt every damn time you stuck that blasted needle into me like I was nothin' but some kind of—"

"All right," Doc Wilson interrupted as he set Owen's hand down across his lap. "You'll be fine. Anything else bothers you, talk to Betty. She can tend to you and your friend for the next few days just as well as I can."

Before Owen had a chance to unleash the next stream of complaints he'd prepared, Doc Wilson turned and walked back to his desk and busied himself with some paperwork. Owen knew it would be useless to pester the doctor any further, since that would only drive the man to escape through the front door. Besides, Owen had better things to do than complain.

Looking over to where George was sitting, he felt bad about breaking his partner's nose, but then again, he figured the old fool had it coming. After all, where the hell was he when those two killers were about to put a bullet through his skull? Where the hell was he when that one with the bandanna was shooting him out of sheer spite?

Owen turned away from George, not wanting to watch another second of the other man whining about a broken nose when he'd lost . . .

It was painful just thinking about what had happened. Idly running his fingers over the bandages, Owen pinched the wrapping together in the spot where his left index finger used to be. Sure, it could've been worse. If that thief hadn't been so damn drunk, he surely would've put his bullet straight through Owen's head.

Owen felt the tingling echoes of his missing finger and grit his teeth against the pain. All he wanted was a chance to get back what he'd lost.

His money.

His pride.

An explosion rocked through Owen's ears, reminding him of the blast that had relieved him of one of his ten favorite fingers. Another followed soon after, but it only took a second for him to realize that the sound had not come from a gun. Instead, it had come from the front door being opened so hard that it nearly punched a hole through Doc Wilson's wall.

Owen almost hated to look, but he forced himself to turn toward the ruckus. Rather than finding those two thieves standing in the doorway, he saw the excited young face of George's youngest boy, Arnold.

The eighteen-year-old kid was struggling for his next breath and was barely able to catch the door before its momentum slammed it shut right in his face. Catching the door with his arm, Arnold scanned the room and eventually spotted where his dad was sitting. "The sheriff caught 'em," he said excitedly.

"What?" George shot to his feet and wobbled a bit as the pain from his nose shot between his eyes and up through his brain. "Who did he catch?"

"Them two outlaws that robbed your store. He caught 'em both! They're in jail right now!"

Before anyone could ask another question, the young man turned and ran off to spread the news to anyone else who would listen. Doc Wilson and George sat discussing the turn of events as though the two robbers had already been dealt with. George especially seemed pleased that Sandy and Russian Bill were cooling their heels in a jail cell, but that wasn't enough for Owen.

Not by a long shot.

Owen got to his feet, biting back the pain that coursed from his mutilated hand and ran though his arm and leaked into his chest as though his veins had been filled with strands of molten steel. Already, he could feel the stump that used to be his finger beginning to swell.

Rather than fuss with that, Owen walked up to the hat rack next to Doc Wilson's desk, plucked his from amid the others hanging there, and set it on top of his head.

"You probably shouldn't leave just yet," Doc Wilson said when he noticed Owen was up and about. "You still need some rest. If you do too much, you might pull them stitches free."

Owen kept walking. "I still got a job to do," was all he said before opening the front door and stepping outside.

He kept right on walking until he got to his house where he stopped in just long enough to grab a rumpled burlap sack that had been stored beneath his bed. Isabelle bombarded him with questions, but Owen kept on walking past her and back outside. From there, he went to the store and walked around the counter.

Looking down to the spot where he'd cowered against the door during the robbery, Owen saw the holes in the wall from the bullet and the black-and-red stain where his blood had mixed in with the dirty smoke belched out from Sandy's weapon. On the floor at his feet, right where he'd left it, was the shotgun that he'd been trying so desperately to grab earlier that day.

He reached down and took hold of it. Although the weapon felt strange in his left hand, Owen couldn't help but smile a little at the delayed gratification of finally being able to wrap his fist around that handle and slide his finger over that trigger.

His next stop was the old barn which sat behind the livery stable. With George's boy acting as messenger, Owen knew the news would have spread to all the right people by now. Even without the use of a messenger, the group had met inside that barn for the last ten years every time the jail was filled with someone besides the occasional drunk or rowdy from the saloon.

That barn had acted as the headquarters for Shakespeare's Vigilance Committee ever since the members had taken up arms against some filthy murderer whose name was forgotten even to the committee's founding members. Normally, Owen had been the one to try and talk some sense into the members, but this time, he hoped they were ready for some quick, bloody justice. When he stepped into the barn and looked around, he knew he wouldn't be disappointed.

Six pairs of eyes stared back at him from behind

crudely fashioned hoods. Owen took the burlap sack he'd been carrying and fit it over his head, moving it around until the two holes he'd cut in the material lined up with his eyes. Next came the long piece of twine which he tied around his neck to cinch the sack closed.

"Heard about what happened to yer store," said one of the men behind his hood. "We was just about to send someone for ya when we heard that them two was in jail."

"No need," Owen said through the dirty shroud. His finger pulsed with pain that lanced all the way up to his shoulder. Thinking about what the committee had been gathered to do was the only thing that helped him fight back some of the discomfort. "If you're all ready, we've got a job to do."

Each of the members nodded solemnly, picked up their guns and marched out the door.

"You got no right keepin' us in here!" Sandy shouted as he pressed his ugly face up against the bars and glared at the sheriff who sat with his feet propped up on the edge of his desk. "We wasn't doing nothin' but walking down the street. Is there a law against that, you ignorant piece of shit?"

In the last several hours, Sheriff Isaacson had grown accustomed to the rantings of his newest prisoner. Until now, he'd chosen to ignore them. But when he looked out the window for the fiftieth time, he finally saw what he'd been waiting for. The lawman got to his feet and put his hand on the handle to the front door. As soon as he heard the thumping of footsteps on the walk outside his office, he pulled it open and stepped aside.

"I asked you a question, you goddamn mule in a badge! What gives you the right to—"

Sandy choked on the rest of his sentence the moment he saw the group of men step inside. They walked like a funeral procession, carrying torches that crackled in their hands, occasionally sending a wisp of flame to lick the ceiling. There were seven of them in all, every one of them carrying a gun and staring at the prisoners through square-shaped holes cut in burlap hoods.

Sheriff Isaacson nodded to the men and stepped in front of them. "It is my duty as an officer of the law," he recited dryly, "to order you men to hand over your weapons and leave these premises."

Without even bothering to look and see if any of the eyes behind those shrouds were turned his way, the lawman held up his hands and pressed his back against the wall. "Since you armed men insist on using force, it looks like I'm in no position to stop you."

The grim parade moved past the sheriff and stood in front of the cell. They parted to let one of their own step forward and jab the barrel of his shotgun between the bars. One of the others held out a gloved hand, which the sheriff immediately filled with the keys to the cell.

"We're the members of the Vigilance Committee of Shakespeare, New Mexico," said the masked man with the shotgun. "You two are in our custody now." Turning to the sheriff, he asked, "What are they charged with?"

The lawman shrugged and took his seat behind his desk. "Russian Bill was caught stealing a horse outside the hotel. Looked to me like they were about to hightail it out of town."

Fidgeting with his right hand, the lead member of the committee glared at Sandy through the ragged squares in his cowl. "Anything else?"

"No, but that's enough to make sure Bill hangs."

After shifting his shotgun over to the crook of his right arm, the committee leader took the keys that were handed to him and unlocked the cell. "Actually," he said as the door swung open on rusted hinges. "They're both gonna hang."

Sandy's eyes grew into bloodshot saucers. His mouth hung open and he scooted back away from the door as though an invisible hand was pulling him to the wall. "What? You can't hang nobody! You're not the law. We ain't even had a trial yet. Tell 'em, Bill."

Russian Bill shook his head slowly. "I stole the horse. Hell, half the town saw it."

"Then just hang *him*," Sandy pleaded. "I didn't do nothing to die for. This is all a big mistake! You gotta see that this don't make no sense!"

As Sandy begged in a voice that got higher and higher in pitch, the hooded men reached into the cell and dragged both prisoners out by the fronts of their shirts. Bill didn't even try to fight as he was shoved roughly from the jail and toward the front door. In stark contrast, Sandy planted his feet and grabbed hold of anything he could as no less than four committee members hauled him away from the office.

Sandy kicked and screamed. He pleaded with the masked men, but found not one bit of pity in all those cold, emotionless eyes peering at him like so many scarecrows that had been given just enough life to perform their grisly task.

Sandy begged and pleaded and begged some more as he and Bill were led down the streets of Shakespeare and shoved into the very hotel where they'd been arrested in the first place. Once there, one of the committee members tossed a pair of ropes over the rafters and tied one end to a hitching post just outside the door. The other ends dangled about eight feet from the floor, nooses swinging slowly back and forth.

Owen watched from behind his mask, savoring every last plea that came sliding out of Sandy's mouth. Even though his hand still ached like a bastard, it was worth the pain to be present at this makeshift courtroom as the leader of the Vigilance Committee stepped forward.

"Russian Bill," said the masked man who stood before all the rest. "You've been found guilty of stealing horses and robbing a general store here in town. How do you plead?"

Bill spat on the floor and stood beneath his noose. "I ain't never pleaded before and I ain't about to start now. Fuck all of ya. I stole them horses and all the rest. Let's get this over with."

Owen couldn't help but admire the outlaw just a little bit. Most of the men he'd seen hung faced their final moments with tears in their eyes and piss running down their legs. As for Bill's partner . . .

"You can't hang me!" Sandy moaned. "People done a helluva lot worse than me and they're still in jail. What about . . ." He floundered for his next words, squirming like a worm on a hook while two committee members held him by the elbows. Suddenly, his eyes lit up with fleeting, desperate hope. "What about Bean-Belly Smith? Just a few weeks ago, he shot a man in a hotel dining room for taking the last egg in the house. He didn't get drug out and strung up like this! And he killed a man!"

Owen turned to his fellow vigilantes and could see them looking back and forth at one another. Whispered exchanges passed between the masked men, followed by a couple of subtle nods. Knowing these men after having lived in the same small town with them for several years, Owen could tell that Sandy's pathetic groveling was actually having an impact.

That, quite simply, would not do.

Jabbing his shotgun into Sandy's gut, Owen could feel another spike of pain shoot through his arm from the place his finger used to be. The sensation was dry kindling on top of a fire that burned inside of the shopkeeper, giving his voice a hard, cutting edge. "Shut your damn mouth and get your head inside that rope." Turning to the committee, he said, "This one's hanging too . . . for being too much of a damned nuisance to live."

Shrugging, the committee members nodded and raised their guns to back Owen's play.

"Sandy King," said the leader. "You've been charged with being a damned nuisance. How do you plead?"

At that moment, Sandy got a look in his eyes that reminded Owen of something he'd once seen on the face of a pig just seconds before the slaughter. The animal caught sight of the ax as it was falling toward his neck and looked blankly up at the blade. There was no fear. No terror. Just resignation. All choices had been made and there was nothing left to do but wait.

A pig was smart enough to know when that time came. But as for Sandy . . .

"Jesus, no! You can't do this! I'll—"

The next day, Owen counted the money in his strongbox and came up fifty dollars short. The money wouldn't be missed too horribly, but it still bit into his craw that Sandy King had managed to get away with something else that belonged to him even after he was dead and gone.

Dead and gone.

That had a nice sound to it.

Owen opened up his shop and waited for George to come through the front door a couple hours late as usual. When the bell over the entrance rang, Owen had his back turned.

"When are you going to get up early enough to—" he said as he turned around. The words jammed up in the back of his throat when he saw who had walked into his shop.

It wasn't George. In fact, it wasn't anyone else he'd ever seen in town before. Well, not in person anyway.

The man who stood in front of him, glaring at Owen with eyes that cut through all the way to the back of the shopkeeper's skull, was another one of the faces hanging on the sheriff's wall. It was one of those faces connected to local legend and in the flesh, that face caused Owen's blood to run instantly cold.

His name was William "Curly Bill" Brocius. A known thief and killer who ran with the likes of the Clantons and MacLowerys over in Tombstone. A man who, despite the healthy price on his head, wasn't worth the risk of collecting it. "You the man who killed Sandy King?"

Owen's eyes darted around the store, searching for anyone who could help. The shotgun lay at his feet, but might as well have been in the next county for all the good it would do him. "N . . . no. I'm just—"

Curly Bill lunged over the counter and grabbed a handful of Owen's shirt. He pulled the smaller man almost out of his boots until their faces were close enough to smell what the other had had for breakfast. "I know who you are, you cowardly little prick. You and your kind hide behind masks and think you've got the right to hang whoever the hell you choose."

Owen tried to protest, but was too scared to breathe, let alone form a coherent sentence.

"You don't even have the guts to let a man see your face before you string him up. And you don't even have the balls to stick together when the shit really starts to fly," Bill said. He paused for a few seconds to let Owen stew as a wicked grin slipped onto his face. "I was just stopping in to see your doctor about a bullet that clipped me on the way through these parts and he said something about a shopkeeper who got his finger blown off by Sandy King. You know what else he said?"

Owen shook his head meekly, knowing why he'd been right all these years to never trust a damn doctor.

"He said the town's Vigilance Committee took care of Sandy and Russian Bill real good. All it took was a few right questions to the right people, a little friendly persuasion, and your so-called friends saw their way clear to letting me know which member of that committee was yelling for Sandy to swing."

Owen could feel the color draining out of his face as a veil of cold sweat formed on his skin.

"Me and Sandy rode together. We go way back. And the only reason I don't kill you right here and now is because I need you to do something for me."

"What? Anything . . . I'll do it . . ."

"Sandy's family lives up in Dodge City. You'll take his body up there and give him a proper burial. I'll be checking in on him real soon, so you'd best be quick about it. And if there ain't no grave with his name on it when I get there . . . I'll track you down and blow off the rest of yer fingers before you die." Grabbing Owen's hand roughly and slamming it down onto the counter, he added, "Along with yer toes . . . and ears . . . and nose . . . and—"

"I'll do it," Owen spat out.

Curly Bill threw the shopkeeper back against the wall and nailed him there with a hard, lingering stare. "You're damn right you will," he said, his lips barely moving enough to shift the dirty mustache above his lip.

Owen watched Curly Bill leave. Part of him was strangely impressed that he'd seen such a famous man up close. The rest of him, however, was sorry that he'd ever opened his general store.

If not for his business, he never would have been in possession of his money. He never would have had a strongbox. He never would have been behind this counter. And he never would have met up with Sandy King: the man who took his money, his finger, his peace of mind, and now quite possibly his life.

344

Owen didn't even wait for George to show up before closing up the store and heading over to the undertaker's parlor.

Getting from Shakespeare, New Mexico, to Dodge City, Kansas, wasn't very hard. He was forced to ride on a loud, dirty train across the country even though Owen would have most certainly preferred the leisurely pace of a stagecoach. And that was after dragging Sandy's body all the way to the station as the robber's flesh started to fester and stink inside his poorly made wooden box.

The hardest part for Owen to swallow was the fact that he'd had to pay for all of this using the money he'd fought so long and hard to get. First, it had taken the better part of a year to earn it, then came dealing with the banks, having it stolen from him and then taking it back from Sandy King's effects once he'd been cut down from the hotel ceiling.

Next, Owen had to deal with transporting the ripe carcass halfway across the country and riding to the lonely stretch of planted souls called Boot Hill.

The gravedigger had been easy enough to deal with, since all he'd asked for was the body and a small fee. By this time, a sizeable chunk of Owen's money had been spent in travel fees and countless other expenses connected to putting this miserable son of a bitch into the ground. Finally, after a week that had dragged on like a month, Owen stood in the cemetery looking down at the pinched, waxy face of Sandy King.

"Any last words?" the gravedigger asked.

Sandy's coffin lay open at the bottom of a six-foot hole, displaying its contents for the audience of one. Owen had put an announcement in the local paper telling Sandy's family when they could see their dearly departed. But after waiting for no less than an hour after the posted time without meeting a single one of them, Owen decided not to wait any more.

"Last words?" Owen grunted. "How about these . . . go to hell, Sandy King. And don't ever come ba—"

Owen stopped himself when he spotted something sticking out of Sandy's shirt pocket. Kneeling down, he examined the body a little closer. "I'll be damned," he said after reaching down toward the dead man's chest. Doing his best to ignore the cold, waxy feel of dead skin, Owen pulled a fifty dollar bill from Sandy's pocket and held it up for the world to see.

"At least I got something for my trouble," Owen said to the gravedigger. "He . . . uhh . . . owed me this and forgot to pay it back."

The gravedigger shrugged and bent down to drop the lid onto the coffin when a deep, scratchy voice thundered through the air.

"Just what the hell do you think yer doing?"

Owen spun around with the fifty hanging between his fingers. Walking toward the open grave was an old, stooped-over woman flanked by no fewer than two hulking figures on either side. Every one of them stared at Owen as though they were about to rip him limb from limb.

"I asked you a question," the old woman said. "What in blazes are you doing to my boy?"

"Oh . . . uh," Owen stammered. "Mrs. King?"

She nodded. Pointing to Owen's hand, she asked, "Did you steal that from my son?"

"No . . . not exactly. My name's Owen Lindsey. He robbed my st—"

"Shut yer mouth." Tears began welling up in her eyes, which made the boys beside her even madder. "You killed my boy and then you rob his grave!?"

Owen's eyes became wide as twin moons set into his face. His stomach dropped all the way down to the soles of his shoes. "Here . . . you can take it. I don't—"

The smaller of the boys, who was still big enough to look down at the top of Owen's head, jabbed a blistered finger at the shopkeeper's chest. "Bill told us you was comin'. He said he'd let us be the ones to pay you back for what you done."

"Pay me back? Oh no, that's not necessary. Here," Owen said while reaching for what was left of his savings. "Take this . . . all of it . . . as my donation along with my sincere . . ."

The King boys drew their pistols as their ma plugged her ears.

Owen's pleas were lost amid the noise that followed.

. . . GRAVEDIGGER . . .

. . . and lookie here. I was gonna dig him up next, which is why you can't reads nothin' on his marker but the first line. Here, let me hold it up so's ya can read it proper:

A KILLER, A THIEF AND A DAMNED NUISANCE BESIDES
HERE RESTS OWEN LINDSEY
TWO FEET FROM WHERE HE DIED.

There ya go. I'll jest drop that over on its face, this time, seein' as Owen's comin' up next.

Why am I diggin' them up? Well, like I said, Dodge City has changed some. Ain't the wild place it used ta be, no sir. We got a marshal's real good at keepin' the peace and we got a right and proper schoolmarm comin' to live and work here. And guess where they decided ta put the school-house? That's right. The town council decided that all these bodies have got to be moved to a new cemetery, and they're gonna build a schoolhouse up here. Don't that beat all?

So, here I am, diggin' up bones, ya might say, an' I'm supposed ta have men and horses and buckboards up here ta help me dig, and then move 'em all, stacked in the back of a buckboard like cordwood, probably. Town fathers said they wanted us to be quick about it, and not so careful . . .

Well, wait a second. Here's a feller comin' up the hill now. Mebbe he's got some news for me. I'm gonna have to ask you folks to find your way back down the hill. What's that? Well, don't mention it, ma'am. I was happy ta tell all of ya the sad stories of these poor folks buried up here. Hope I didn't scare your yung'ns too much. There ya go. You folks make your way down the hill that way, and I'll jest go down this way and see what kinda news this feller's got for me . . .

. . . damn fool place to built a schoolhouse, if ya ask me . . .

EPILOGUE

Story in the *Ford County Globe,* dated February 4, 1878:

THE DEATH OF BOOT HILL

The skeletons removed from Boot Hill were found to be in a high state of preservation and even the rude boxcoffins were as sound as when they were placed in the ground. The coroner said they were as fine a collection of the extinct human race as he ever handled. They are now resting side-by-side, like one big happy family, in Prairie Grove Cemetery, northeast of the city.

...and further down was another story...

Epilogue

Famous Gunman Masquerades as Gravedigger

It was discovered yesterday that well-known Missouri Gunman John Russell has been masquerading as the gravedigger here in Dodge City for the past five years. Nobody here in Dodge ever knew him by any name other than Gravedigger, including this reporter. It is clear, now, that this was by design, as Russell was attempting to leave his killin' ways and reputation behind. And for a while, he had succeeded.

Yesterday another Missouri gunman, Emmett Gates, came to town, recognized Russell and called him out. Although Russell had not handled a gun in five years he accommodated Gates and gunned him down on a slope of Boot Hill. Gates now has the distinction of being the last man killed on Boot Hill.

As for John Russell, he has vanished to parts unknown . . .

And a few pages further in, this ad appeared in the same issue:

WANTED: Gravedigger, no experience required. Reply to the Dodge City Undertaker.

Printed in the United States
80475LV00003B/57

9 780765 300829